The Cedar Tree

The Cedar Tree

Ross Glover

To order additional copies of this book, contact:
Xlibris Corporation
1-888-795-4274
www.Xlibris.com
Orders@Xlibris.com
29726

1

THE CEDAR TREE

Max Mendeaux is a snot. No, he's more than a snot, he's a turd. And he's the biggest one in Laceola, Georgia. He walks around, his long keen nose stuck up in the air, with an expression on his face as if someone had tied one of my baby brother's soiled diapers around his neck. He never pays attention to anything around him, and that's why he'll never see me up in this old cedar tree.

I don't like Max, and truly I never have. But after what he said to Jack Copeland, my best friend, I hated him. Max has always been a know-it-all. He thinks he's smarter than us just because he's thirteen and in the ninth grade, and we're twelve and in the seventh. He thinks he knows everything about the War Between the States. He doesn't. He thinks he knows more about Christmas tree lights than anybody.

Last Christmas, Mama bought these new bubbling lights for our tree. After we decorated—okay, trimmed—the tree, me and Jack Copeland were out in the front yard looking at the lights through the window when Max came along.

"Know how they made those lights bubble?" he asked, just like that, with no *how do you do* or nothing.

"We're not interested," Jack said. "We like them because they're unusual and pretty."

Max started talking about some kind of special liquid or something that doesn't boil away and how he put a switch on his Christmas lights so he can turn them off without unplugging them. He sounded like Mr. Pritchard, our seventh-grade teacher.

I wanted to ignore him, but I couldn't help but ask, "Can't you just watch the lights bubble without thinking about how they're made?"

"It's simple, really. Basic electricity. We've had those bubble lights in 1947, two years ago. My family is always first in Laceola to get new stuff."

"Do you like them?" Jack asked.

"They're decorative but rather plebeian. But I understand why you think they're so attractive. You're a plebeian yourself, Jack Copeland."

You've got to remember Jack is mild mannered and not easy to rile. He always goes by "Sticks and stones may break my bones, but words will never hurt me." So Jack didn't say nothing. His face turned red, starting from both cheeks and moving up to his hairline and disappeared under the clump of brown hair that permanently flops down just above his right eye. His brown eyes narrowed into slits, but he didn't utter a word.

"Max Mendeaux, that's the last straw. You tell Jack you're sorry for calling him a plebeian."

"I will not. Jack knows he and his whole family are plebeian. So are you."

Max is like that. And what gives us, me and my friends, the raw tail is that our parents think he's a super kid or something. They're always saying, "Why can't you be like Max? He's on the honor roll, he plays in the band, and he's on his way to being an Eagle Scout. How nice of him to be a substitute Sunday school teacher for the little kids."

They can't see that Max is a turd of the first order or even worse. He's a real b-a-s-t-a-r-d. My mother would kill me if she found out I said that. Anyway, I'm laying for Max. I finally figured out a good plan to avenge my friend and me for all the insults that Max has heaped upon us. I'm fixin' to puncture his behind with a match stem dart I made. I got this joint of bamboo cane and made it into a blowgun. So I took this match stem, actually it's a whole kitchen match, and drove a needle into one end. Then I put a paper stabilizer, like what goes on the tail of a rocket, on the other end. I've gotten pretty accurate in blowing the dart out of the cane joint. I wish I had some kind of poison. Maybe I should put turpentine on the end of it. I plan to plant my needle dart right into Max's butt. It'll be sweet revenge. And I'll do it or my name's not Sport Kirk.

That's why I'm up in this cedar tree. Max comes by here every afternoon from band practice. And this cedar is a perfect cover. I can see everything that goes on up and down the sidewalk on both sides of Walnut Street all the way to Main Street. And I can spot anyone taking a shortcut on the footbridge across Little Snake Creek.

My cedar tree grows close enough to the sidewalk that people have to walk underneath some of its high limbs. I'm like the Phantom, the Ghost Who Walks. I may not have a Skull Cave, but this is my secret hideout. No one can see me through the thick branches and green needles. I don't mind the sticky tree resin although my mother complains about it when she washes my clothes. I love the smell of cedar needles. It makes me feel, well, you know, close to nature and protected. I can sit up here and think without anybody bothering me. Of course, the birds will raise sand if I'm in here when they come to roost.

I wonder if birds can see good in the dark. They always come to roost just before dark, so I guess they can't. Birds don't roost in trees without leaves. The redbud and oak trees are just beginning to bud, so the birds won't be building nests for another three or four weeks.

Old snot Max will be surprised. I can hear him screaming now. It'll serve him right for what he called me and Jack. He'll find out just how mean this plebeian can get. Damn, I mean, dang Max anyway. As you can see, I'm trying to quit cussing after Mama overheard me three days ago. She doesn't understand that every now and then a man can slip and say something he shouldn't say around ladies. I know my daddy does, and President Truman cusses too. But to be on the safe side, I'll make a real effort not to cuss.

I'll bet Max don't use bad language. He's such a goody-goody. He's probably been saved three or four times at the First Baptist Church, but I don't know if he gets baptized every time he gets saved.

One time a bunch of us were talking about ghosts when Max walked up and looked down his nose at us.

"There are no ghosts," Max said. "It's an old wives' tale about spirits. The Bible says that ghosts don't exist."

Letting that sink in, he asked, "Have any of you ever seen a ghost?"

We shook our heads. "No."

"So I rest my case."

"Max," I said, "you never had a case 'cause this ain't no supreme court. Let me ask you this. Do you believe in God?"

"Yes," Max said.

"Have you ever seen God?"

"No."

"Well, I rest my case."

My friends laughed so much that Max just walked away. It's not often we can get Max's goat, and we really enjoy it when we do.

Oops! Here comes Old Man Howard. He'll never see me because he's always looking down. Last summer he came by when I was hiding up here in my cedar tree. Just as he got past the tree, I said hello real soft. Old Man Howard stopped and looked around, but he couldn't see nobody. Satisfied no one was around, he started on down the sidewalk. I let him walk a few more yards, and I said hello again. He stopped and stuck a finger in one ear and then the other to dig out earwax. He stood there for a couple of minutes listening before walking as fast as he could. I didn't say anything else 'cause I thought I would bust a gut trying to keep from laughing out loud. Jack Copeland said this trick was the best he ever heard of.

Today, I'm not playing any tricks on Old Man Howard. "Business comes before pleasure" is what my granddaddy says. I'll wait for Max, the turd, and bury this dart in his butt.

Old Man Howard walks past my hideout and stops to listen. I guess he remembers the voice out of the sky, and it's hard to resist saying something. He moves on down the sidewalk and disappears from my view.

It's about time for Max to come by. It feels like I've been up here for hours. What if his mama picked him up from band practice? I guess I can wait for another day. I know. I'll give him a little more time before I go home and do my homework or listen to the radio. He'd better not make me miss *The Lone Ranger*. That's one of my favorite radio shows. I also listen to Henry Aldridge.

Jack and I like the same things. Both of us have our own collection of model airplanes. He doesn't have any brothers or sisters, and his daddy was killed in Germany in a B-17. His mama works at the bank. My mama said that Jack and his mama have had a hard time since the war.

My granddaddy served over twenty years in the U.S. Cavalry. He fought together with Black Jack Pershing in World War I, but he wasn't hurt or nothing. Not like Mr. Hubert. My granddaddy told me Mr. Hubert is shell-shocked. That's why he walks around dressed in his brown 1919 suit and shirt with stiff high-neck collar and never says anything to anybody. My daddy has a punctured eardrum and was turned down when he tried to enlist. He worked in a defense plant during World War II. Uncle Earl enlisted on his eighteenth birthday and served in the Pacific. He spent a year and a half in some kind of special hospital before the army sent him back to Georgia. My family never talks about what happened to him, and Uncle Earl never talks to me. He goes to McIntosh College under the GI Bill and lives with Granddaddy.

Me and Jack like Western movies and war movies. Our favorite star is Gilbert Roland as the Cisco Kid. We really liked *Red River*, and it was the best picture made in 1948. John Wayne always has to beat up somebody, so he beats up his own son, who is played by this new actor, Montgomery Cliff. Last week Mama and Daddy took me to see *Twelve O'clock High* with Gregory Peck. Jack wasn't allowed to go with me. It was a lot better than *Command Decision* with Clark Gable. Jack didn't see *Command Decision* either.

I think I see Max coming. Oh no. That's Dink Roberts. Dink may be slow, but he's a friend. We fish and catch frogs on Little Snake Creek. He helps us find things we've lost or left behind somewhere but have forgotten where we left them. He saved my bacon when he found the new coat I left in the vacant lot.

He works in people's yards, raking leaves, cutting shrubs, and doing things like that. It's about all he can do 'cause his mind just doesn't work too good. My mama says Dink has the body of a twenty-year-old, but he has the mind of an eight-year-old. He'll never get any better.

Dink is strong. One time he was helping us dam up a stream before it ran into Little Snake Creek, and we needed a big boulder. Dink found a two-hundred-pound monster and brought it to us. Nobody teases him not because he's so strong but because we like him. And if we did tease him, our parents would beat the stuffing (notice I said *stuffing* instead of the other s word) out of us.

His parents live in Chicago and work at Sears and Roebuck. Dink's daddy left home a long time ago and got a degree from college. My granddaddy said he was too smart to stay around Laceola and deserved the opportunity to better himself.

Dink moved to Laceola when he was five or six years old to live with Miss Sally, his grandma, and Aunt Nicey, his great-great-grandma. Aunt Nicey used to be a slave. She's a tiny little woman and doesn't talk right anymore, so she can't tell you what it was like. She sits in a chair on her front porch and watches people go by.

My family always gives her a gift at Christmas and on her birthday. She still has a lot of strength. When we went to see her last Christmas, she hugged me so hard I could hardly breathe.

I can't fool Dink. He knows about my cedar tree, and he'll stop to see if I'm up here. He likes birds because they can fly. He'll tell me that I am going to fall out of the tree and hurt myself because I can't fly. He always tells me the same thing. Maybe he won't notice. Maybe I can get rid of him real fast. If Max sees him talking to the tree, he'll be curious, and my plans for Max will be ruined forever.

Dangit, ol' Max is coming down the sidewalk behind Dink. I'll never be able to pull this off. Maybe I should get down the tree before Dink gets here. Max will never notice. No. I've waited too long to give up now. I'll move around to the other side. Maybe Dink will forget about my hideout.

Dink is almost at the tree, and so far he hasn't looked up to see me. I get my blowgun ready for Max. A green 1939 Hudson Terraplane comes down the street behind Dink and Max. I know whose car it is because there's only one like it in Coosa County. The car slows down almost to a stop. A man sticks a tattooed arm out the passenger side window. Oh, Lord! He has a gun in his hand. *BAM!* My god! My god! They just shot Dink. Oh, god! I hear someone from the car laugh as it speeds down Walnut Street.

2

SPORT

My stomach knots up and my muscles stiffen as I hold onto a limb. I have to do something. I drop out of the tree onto the ground. Dink lies on the sidewalk, and Max stands there like an idiot. Oh, god, they shot Dink in the leg. Boy, is he bleeding, and he's crying.

"Don't worry, Dink. You gonna be all right," I tell him. Dink caught the shot in his thigh, and every time his heart beats, blood spurts out of his leg.

"Go for help!" I yell at Max, who stands there with eyes as big as Ford hubcaps. He lost his breakfast, lunch, and snack in the gutter.

"Don't just stand there; go for help!"

Dink's wound looks like a busted artery. According to the Red Cross first aid class I took last year, the best thing to do is put a tourniquet on it. I pull my belt out of the loops and wrap it around Dink's leg just above the wound. I push the belt end through the buckle and tighten it. The bleeding doesn't stop, and blood flows around his leg onto the sidewalk.

"Max, go get help! You hear me?"

Max nods his head and runs toward the nearest house. Dink is lying on hard concrete, and I don't have nothing to put under his head. If I had my jacket, I could use it as a pillow. I didn't wear it today because it's a warm March day. Dink is silent, and his eyes are closed. I know he's not dead because he's breathing hard.

I've got to stop the bleeding. Hey, here's a block of wood. My hands shake as I loosen the belt and slip the block of wood right over the artery above the worsening bleeding. I tighten the belt again. I saw this in a picture show about a wounded marine in the war. Blood oozes out of the wound, but it's not spurting out. If help doesn't come soon, Dink will die.

I don't know what I can do. I can't leave Dink alone. I look around to see if Max is coming back. But instead of Max, I see a police car pull up next to the curb. Dan Wills, a city policeman and an ex-MP, gets out and comes around to where we are.

"What's happened here, Sport?"

"Dink's been shot! He's bleeding to death!"

Officer Wills kneels down and looks at Dink's wound. "It's pretty bad. Good job on the tourniquet. Gotta get him to a doctor and fast. Dr. Styles' place is the closest. Stay there."

The policeman walks to the back of his car and opens the trunk. He takes out an olive green tarp and unfolds it. He opens the back car door and spreads the tarp over the back seat. I watch as I hold onto Dink.

Dan Wills comes back to where we are and says, "I'm gonna pick him up and put him in the back seat. You gotta help. Get in the car and move to the far side, then grab his shoulders and pull."

I do what he tells me. By this time, a small crowd of curious people gathers and looks at us. They are all neighborhood women, children, and maids. Nobody says anything or offers to help. They just stare at Dan Wills, Dink, and me.

Dan Wills, with arms the size of a man's thigh, lifts Dink up and sets him on the edge of the seat. I take Dink's shoulders and pull him into the seat while he gently pushes. Satisfied with the way he's placed, he shuts the door, and then gets into the car and starts it up. He glances back and says, "Hope to hell the doctor's in."

The siren screams as we pull away from the curb and ride down Walnut Street, turn left onto Main, and go to Dr. Styles' office. His office is really a house with two beds for sick people. He's been a doctor around here for years and years, and his son, Jim, is a doctor too. Jim came home from the army about three months ago after serving at a field hospital in Italy during the war.

Dr. Bolton is my doctor, and I like his office better. It's new and not as spooky, and I don't think anybody has ever died there.

We pull up in the doctor's driveway. Dan Wills tells me to wait in the car with Dink and runs up to the house and through the door. Jim, the doctor's son, comes out of the house with him. They get Dink out of the car and into the house. Officer Wills motions for me to follow. I go into the house and see them lay Dink on a table. The young Doctor Styles cuts Dink's pant's leg off, and a nurse is there with some kind of instruments. I can't keep from watching them work on Dink. His eyes are open now, and he lies there without making a sound. He looks dead. Dan Wills clasps two big hands on my shoulders, turns me around, and pushes me back into the waiting room.

"That's all we can do. It's left up to the doctor now."

"Will Dink be all right?"

"Still alive. Thanks to you. Probably make it. Styles is a combat doctor. Worked on worse wounds than that one. Now what did you see? How'd it happened?"

I look down and see that blood has soaked my pants and shirt. I hope blood comes off because my mama ain't goin' to be pleased with this mess. Dan Wills sees me looking at the blood.

"Go to the bathroom and wash up as best as you can," he says, pointing to a door outside the waiting room. "Then tell me what you saw."

The bathroom is larger than I'm used to. It has a commode and a large washbasin but no bathtub. I see my blood-covered face in the mirror over the washbasin, and I can't keep from gagging as I wash my face and hands. My right leg begins to shake uncontrollably. I try to hold it still with both hands, but I can't. My hands are trembling, so I grab onto the washbasin, but I keep shaking and shaking. The bathroom door opens, and Officer Wills looks in on me.

"Can't keep from shaking."

"It's okay. It'll pass. Come out here and sit on the couch. Chief is here. Wants to hear whatcha have to say."

He takes my arm and leads me to the couch. Chief Manners stands in the middle of the room. He doesn't look happy, not that he ever does. Maybe a chief of police isn't supposed to look happy.

"You feel like telling us what happened?" Chief Manners asks.

"Yes, sir. I think I can."

"Let's hear it from the beginning."

"I was playin' up in that old cedar tree close to the footbridge on Walnut Street when I see Dink walkin' down the sidewalk. A green 1939 Hudson Terraplane comes down the street and slows down almost to a stop. I see a man aim a pistol out the window and fire at Dink. He goes down real fast. Then the car drives off."

"How many in the car? Two, three, or more?"

"Two men. The Thompson brothers. And I could see them real clear when they slowed down. The one that shot Dink had a snake tattoo on his arm."

The room begins to spin. I feel like I just got off a carnival Tilt-A-Whirl.

"By god, them Thompson scum done it this time. Nobody shoots down an innocent person in my town. Their asses are gonna go to the chain gang for a long time on this one. Dan, go tell the sheriff our situation and get a warrant. If ya can find them in town, arrest them. If they ain't in town, go out to their place with a sheriff's deputy and bring 'em in."

As Dan Wills turns to go, my granddaddy walks in.

"Granddaddy!" I shout.

3

JACK

Mom calls me from work. "Jack Copeland, don't you dare go near Sport's house today. He's involved in a shooting incident on Walnut Street. You stay away."

"Why? What happened?"

"Somebody shot the idiot colored boy that's always wandering around town. Sport kept him from bleeding to death until help came."

She's talking about Dink Roberts, and I don't think of him as a colored boy. Not like I do other Negroes. And he's not an idiot; he's just slow. I promise my mom I won't go over to Sport's house.

Either by chance or will of the gods, trouble finds Sport. A shootout on our street is pretty exciting stuff. As much as I want to, I don't dare go over there because Mom would skin me alive if she finds out. I should have been with Sport, but I had to study for my history test. Maybe I can go over to Ben Lloyd's house after supper. He probably knows more about what happened.

I can't imagine how my best friend, Nathan Bedford Kirk, saved Dink Roberts' life on Walnut Street. Everyone calls him Sport. I'm the only one he allows to call him by his real name and only if we're alone. When we were in third grade, I asked Sport if that was his real name.

"If you swear to the utmost secrecy, cross your heart and hope to die, that you'll never tell anyone else, then I'll tell you. I'll tell you my real name, and you'd better not laugh," Sport answered, fixing his steel gray eyes on me.

"I'll swear then," I said, crossing my heart with my right hand. And I didn't cross my fingers on my left hand.

"My daddy's name is Joe Wheeler. Granddaddy named him after Joe Wheeler, a Civil War general and a U.S. senator from Alabama. Granddaddy says he was one of the best cavalry officers in the war. When I was born, Mama and Daddy let my granddaddy name me. They thought he would choose George, his name. But he didn't. He picked another Civil War cavalry general to name me after, Nathan Bedford Forrest. So my given name's Nathan Bedford."

"Why don't people call you by your real name?"

"Okay. I'm gettin' to that. But if you ever tell anybody, I'll beat you up so bad you'll be in bed for a week," he threatened. "When I was one or two years old, every time Mama or Daddy called me Nathan Bedford or Nathan or Bedford, I cried. So they started calling me Sport. I know it's silly, but I don't mind the name."

"Nathan Bedford's not a bad name,"

"I'll use my real name if and when I ever leave Laceola. Until then, my name's Sport," he said.

On rare occasions and in private, I call him Nathan Bedford just to tease him. He acts like he gets mad at me, but I see him grin, so it's okay. Sport is always around where things happen. More often than not, he causes it. Like the time we almost got caught for dumping a sackful of frogs upstream from where the preacher of Mount Zion Primitive Baptist Church planned to baptize new Christians in Little Snake Creek. Sport wanted to catch water snakes, but I talked him out of it. He and I gathered up over a hundred frogs, large and small, on Saturday and put them in a tow sack made of burlap. Sport's plan was to dump them in the creek and to let them wash down to where the preacher did the baptizing just as the people entered the water.

On Sunday afternoon, the small congregation gathered on the bank of the creek as Sport and I waited upstream. When the newly converted, most were women and girls, waded into the creek up to their thighs, we dumped the sack of frogs. The frogs were swept downstream by a fairly swift current and settled in the still water of the baptismal pool. We hid back in the trees and waited for a reaction.

It came fast. One of the women yelled, "Snakes!"

Women and girls screamed and fell into the water as they tried to run out of the creek. Sport said we were doing God's work because he saw a miracle. A big fat woman walked on water right out onto the creek bank. One deacon lost his religion when he screamed, "If I catch the son of a bitch that did this, I'm a gonna kill 'em."

Mama thinks Sport is a bad influence on me, but she tolerates our friendship. When I was little, I stayed with Sport and his mother while Mama worked during the day. Sport's family has been good friends to us since my dad's plane went down in Germany. Sport has a creative mind, but he doesn't study or read as much as I do. I like to read, and I know that makes me kind of strange. Sport says he's proud to be my friend because I'm smart. Being his best friend is an adventure. Sometimes when we don't want to go to the picture show on Saturday, we ride our bicycles to the airfield at the edge of town and watch mechanics work on airplanes in the hangar. We talk to the pilots and owners of the airplanes and listen to their war stories. Four Piper Cubs are hangared there, but there are also a Stearman, a De Havilland and an Aeronca. Occasionally a DC-3 flies in and lands at the airfield.

We've memorized the silhouettes of almost every aircraft flown in the war: American, British, German, and Japanese. We never see a British, German, or Japanese airplane, but sometimes an American warplane flies over. We identify more F4U Corsairs than anything. They fly out of the naval air station in Atlanta. Once we saw a B-29.

Last summer I told Sport I would give anything to go up in an airplane. He said, "I don't see why we can't do that. All we need is ten dollars a piece for a ride."

"Yeah, where we gonna get ten dollars?"

"Not by selling Cloverine or Rosebud Salve."

"And not by selling *Grit,* America's only national weekly newspaper."

Sport once sold Cloverine Salve. His mother wound up with almost a whole case of the stuff. It seems our neighbors had bought enough salve from kid salesmen to last into the '50s. I signed up to sell *Grit.* Then I found out too late I had competition from at least five other kids with the same money-making idea.

"Why don't we sell Christmas cards? I saw an advertisement in a comic book about selling cards. They print people's names on them," I suggested.

"Naw, raking leaves is where the money is. We'll go to all those old ladies with big oak trees in their yards and charge them a dollar for cleaning up the leaves. They'll think we're cute and industrious. Let's do it now before somebody else thinks of it."

By the end of the day, six people promised to hire us to rake their yards and burn leaves in the fall. By the end of October, we had $10 between us.

"Don't worry about the money. I'll talk Ed Spiers into taking us up for $5 a ride."

On a cool, crisp Saturday afternoon in November, we rode our bicycles down to the airfield. Sport bargained with Ed Spiers, and he agreed to take us up in his Piper Cub for $5 a ride. Sport went up first just to show me there was no danger. When my turn came, I really wasn't afraid. I did have a few butterflies, but I loved flying. Mr. Spiers, who is a qualified instructor, promised to teach us to fly when we turn fifteen. Sport didn't tell his parents about our adventure, and my mom never found out, or she would've locked me in my room forever. She doesn't want me to have anything to do with airplanes or flying just because Dad died in a B-17. I nagged her enough until she finally let me build model airplanes. But I'll probably have to wait until I'm in college before I learn to fly. Believe me, I will someday.

It's just like Sport to rush in and help somebody without thinking. Helping a colored boy won't be popular with some people around Laceola. I hear grownups say colored people are okay as long as they stay in their place. I guess that means as long as they stay in Ducktown.

Boy, if there is ever another war, I'm not sure I want to be in Sport's platoon. He will either get you killed or make you a hero. I'll get the real skinny from him at school tomorrow.

4

SPORT

I wake up in my bed with clean pj's, and I'm all cleaned up. Dadgum it, I guess I fainted or something. It's almost dark already. Did I have a nightmare? No, I remember Chief Manners at the doctor's office. I remember Dink bleeding. Did I leave my belt at the doctor's office? I remember Granddaddy coming in, but I can't remember anything after I saw him. I hear my dad, Granddaddy, and Uncle Earl in the living room. I feel that my mama is in the kitchen. Hey, I'm not shaking anymore. I'm hungry. I get out of bed and walk down the hall to the living room.

Daddy sees me. "Hey, Sport. Have a nice nap? You feelin' okay now?"

Granddaddy and Uncle Earl greet me with smiles and a *hey, kid.*

"Yes, sir. Did I pass out? What happened to Dink? Did he die?"

"Dink is okay. You fainted. Been out about an hour or so. Young Styles told your granddaddy to bring you home and put you to bed. They took Dink up to the hospital in Palatine. He lost a lot of blood, but they'll give him transfusions."

"Gee, I'm glad. He was bleeding, and I couldn't stop the blood. I was so scared, and my hands were shaking," I say, remembering Dink lying on the sidewalk. "What time is it? I'm hungry."

"That's a good sign. Go on to the kitchen. Your mama cooked hamburgers for you, and she's been waiting for you to wake up. When you finish, we want to talk to you about what happened today."

In the kitchen, Mama hugs me and tells me I did the right thing, and she fusses over me until Ted wakes up from a nap. My one-year-old baby brother sure does sleep a lot, except at night. Sometimes he'll be going strong at one in the morning.

I hear Daddy, Granddaddy, and Uncle Earl talking in the living room. I wonder if they discovered what I had planned for Max. I don't know what happened to my blowgun and darts. I guess I'll catch hell, that is, heck, for trying to get ol' Max. The bad part is I never had a chance to carry out my ambush. I eat slow, chewing each bite twenty-five times like you're supposed to do, two hamburgers with Lay's potato chips and a glass of milk. I take small sips of the milk to make it last longer. Sooner or later, I'll have to face the music. They can't prove I was trying to drive a dart into Max's butt. I'll get a good talking to if I tell Daddy the truth, and that's all I'll get. I close my eyes and see Dink lying on the table with his eyes open but not making a sound. Lord, he must have been scared.

"Sport! You finished eating? We need to talk," Daddy calls.

"Yes, sir. I'm coming." My stomach does a double churn.

I go into the living room and sit down on the sofa next to Granddaddy. I always feel safe when I'm close to him because, most of the time, he sides with me in fights with my parents. Granddaddy takes out a fresh plug of Apple Sun Cured chewing tobacco, cuts off a small piece, and says, "You give a good account of yo'self today, kid. Showed some backbone and used yore head in saving that boy's life. But you'll have stiffen up in the days to come."

The Apple Sun Cured smells strong and sweet and inviting as he slowly places the piece of tobacco in his mouth and takes one chew. I don't understand what he's talking about, so I don't say anything.

"Sport, you look guilty of something. You didn't do anything wrong," Daddy says. He should have been a detective because he knows about my plan for Max. I take a deep breath and wait for him to ask for an explanation.

"Ah hell, kid. You don't have to feel guilty about passing out," Uncle Earl says. "Why, I've seen the toughest men in the world faint at the sight of a hypodermic needle. You've gone through a lot for a twelve-year-old."

Thanks, Uncle Earl. I breathe normal again. They don't know about the ambush I planned for Max.

"First," Daddy says, "you'll have to point a finger at the Thompson brothers. If they're prosecuted, you'll have to testify in an open court. What you did was right. However, there'll be people who'll say it wasn't any of your business, and they'll say you shouldn't have interfered. Can you face those men, Sport?"

"Yes, sir. I think I can. They shot Dink for no reason," I say without really knowing what he means.

"They shot Dink because he was a convenient nigger," Uncle Earl says, waving a Lucky Strike in the air.

I'm shocked. I have never heard the word *nigger* used in our house. My parents tell me again and again to never use that word anywhere. Only white trash talk like that.

"Earl!" Daddy says.

"Wheeler, you know I didn't mean it the way it sounded. You also know the Thompsons are Klan from way back, and Lawson Hill Community has been a festering sore in Coosa County since Dad gave up the sheriff's office. The law's too scared to go after that bunch of gangsters. I feel like goin' down there with an M-1 and cleanin' out that crowd myself 'cause I didn't fight the Japs just to come back home and live with low-life, draft-dodging white trash."

"Earl, y'all cain't take the law into yore own hands," Granddaddy says. "You'd be sinking to their level. They's good people in this county, and they ain't gonna let the Thompsons run wild. Let the law take care of them. Billy Macwain's one of the best sheriffs Coosa County ever had. He's a fair man. Besides, he ain't gonna side with no Ku Kluxers. The colored vote keeps him in office."

Granddaddy served two terms as sheriff of Coosa County during the '20s and '30s. He said he gave it up because he had to arrest some of his friends for making moonshine and that our kinfolks were next in line.

"Billy Macwain won't go up against the Klan," Uncle Earl says under his breath. Uncle Earl is a chain-smoker. He's real skinny and has this GI haircut. I don't remember much about him before he went into the army. I know he played right tackle for the Laceola High School football team and weighed 180 pounds. It's funny to imagine him going up against a gang of outlaws. He doesn't say much to anybody, not even to me. He's been kind of a loner, and everybody keeps their distance from him.

"Listen, Sport," Daddy says. "You remember seeing the Ku Klux Klan meeting about two years ago? Remember the cross burnin' in the vacant lot next to Mr. Wright's place? The Thompsons were part of that little spectacle, and there's gonna be pressure on you not to testify against them. I don't want to scare you, and believe me, nobody's gonna hurt you. Your granddaddy's right about there being more good people in Coosa County than bad. But you know you'll have to tell the truth to the police. You have to do what's right and honorable. You tell the police what you saw. Now, take the day off from school tomorrow. Your mother will write you an excuse."

"Will the good people of Coosa County do what's right?" Uncle Earl mumbles.

5

SPORT

I remember the Ku Klux Klan meeting all right. Kids, black and white, play pickup softball or football together on that vacant lot. On this night, a bunch of men carrying Confederate battle flags stood in front of a burning cross. They dressed in white robes and wore masks with eye holes cut out and white hats shaped like dunce caps. The men talked to a small crowd of people. I didn't hear what they said because we rode by in our car. We were spectators like just about everybody else in town. The burning cross and white robes made the hair stand up on the back of my neck, like it does when I walk through the city cemetery.

Daddy moves one of our radios into my bedroom. I listen to *Suspense* at ten o'clock. After I turn the radio off, I think about the cross burning on the vacant lot. I shiver and then drift off to sleep.

The fire leaps from pine tree to pine tree. The straw beneath the trees glows red with flames, and smoke curls up thick and heavy. I beat the flames with a wet blanket, but it flares up again and again as I retreat. The fire surrounds me, and acid smoke chokes me. I try to get away from the smoke by crawling along the ground. I call for help. There's no one to hear me. I feel the heat on my face and arms. The fire crackles overhead. My throat is parched dry. I try to scream, but nothing comes out. I know I'm going to die as I draw the blanket over my head.

"Wake up, son. You're having a bad dream," Mama tells me as she hugs me to her, and I wake up safe from fire.

Boy, that's a dilly of a dream. I still feel hot.

"What time is it?" I ask.

"It's three thirty in the morning. Go back to sleep. I'll sit right here by your bed."

"Okay, Mama." I turn over and go to sleep.

I get out of bed at seven thirty. Daddy is already at work. It's Friday, a school day, and I feel guilty. I always feel guilty when I'm not sick and I don't go to school. I'm not hungry, but Mama forces me to eat toast and jelly. Someone knocks at our front door. Mama goes to the door, and I hear her say, "Come in, Miss Sally. He's just finishing breakfast."

I go into the living room and see Miss Sally, Dink's grandmother, standing with Mama. "Spo't, you da young man dat saved my Dink. Law, you som'in else. Come here and let Sally give you a hug," she says. Miss Sally has her Sunday hat and dress on. She usually wears her cook's uniform for work in the high school cafeteria.

After the hug, I picture Dink lying on the doctor's table, and I ask, "How's Dink doing? Will he be coming home anytime soon?"

"Dat boy doin' just fine. Doctor say he be comin' home in a day or two. He don't like no hospital 'cause it scare him. He goin' be fine. I goin' back up to Palatine dis afternoon and stay wif him. He mama and daddy are drivin' down from Chicago today. Dey say dey goin' take my Dink back up no'th. Dey say it ain't safe down here no mo'."

After Miss Sally leaves, I have nothing to do. I watch the clock click off minute after minute. I stay in my room and listen to stupid soap operas: *Pepper Young's Family, Stella Dallas,* and *Mary Noble, Backstage Wife.* Actually *Mary Noble* isn't too bad. I wait until school is out. I'll bet Jack Copeland will come by. We'll listen to *The Lone Ranger* and *Straight Arrow.* Or we can go down to the creek and throw rocks at frogs or something.

It's five o'clock, and Jack doesn't come. I can't believe he hasn't come by. I'm beginning to think that he doesn't want to see me because I saved Dink's life. He's probably at the library. When I want to find Jack, I check the library first. I guess I can play peek-a-boo with my brother, Ted. He's almost two, and he can't understand a thing I tell him. I've got to catch up on homework I didn't do yesterday. I also have to finish my history presentation. Jack has already finished his project.

6

SPORT

I sleep late and wake up to a breakfast of grits, bacon, and eggs Mama fixed. Today, I have a big hunger, and I clean my plate, thinking about how kids in China or some place in India are starving. Daddy finishes hanging new screens on the front windows and comes into the house. When he sees me at the breakfast table, he says, "Sport, Sheriff Macwain called and wants you to come down to the jail to identify the Thompson brothers as the ones who shot Dink."

"What'll I have to do?"

"Well, you'll have to face the Thompsons and say they're the shooters."

"I'll tell the truth. They shot Dink for no reason, and they shouldn't get away with it. Can I go over to Jack Copeland's house when we get back? Then maybe we can go downtown?"

"No, it's best you stay around the house for a couple of days. Jack can come over here," Daddy says. I'm disappointed, but I don't say anything.

We get into Daddy's 1948 maroon Chevy coupe; he starts the car and backs out of our drive on Walnut Street.

A lot of colored folks live in Coosa County and in Laceola. They are farmers or sharecroppers, or they work at the cotton mill. Some are janitors for stores and buildings. We see them shopping at the grocery stores, at the drugstore, or at Rose's Five and Dime Store, but never at Pete Kelley's Diner, except at the side window where they buy food to go. The Maple Street Soda Shoppe has a to-go window also. Occasionally me and Jack will buy ice cream cones and take them out to colored kids we play ball with. Most colored people live in Ducktown or along the Seaboard Railroad tracks. Wash Ingram has a barbecue place in Ducktown. His sauce is rich, clear, and flavored with spices and herbs unlike that heavy tomato mixture all the other barbecue places serve. Everybody says Wash Ingram has the best pit barbecue within a fifty-mile radius.

The colored kids from Ducktown, which is really a part of Laceola, go to the picture show and sit in the balcony. We can hear them laughing, but we never see them because they go into the theater by the side door. I tried to sneak into the balcony seats one time but was caught and made to leave. I've never heard of a colored kid trying to sneak into our section of the theater.

Before we turn onto Main Street, I dial in 750, WSB in Atlanta instead of WGWG, our local radio station, which plays goofy music on Saturday morning. WSB broadcasts *The Buster Brown Show* with funny Froggy the Gremlin, followed by *Frank Merriwell* at eleven o'clock.

The Buster Brown Show goes off the air as we park in front of the Coosa County Courthouse. The sheriff's office and county jail where the Thompsons are held is on the second floor of the courthouse. Chief Manners and Sheriff Macwain wait for us at the side door.

"Hey, young fellow!" Chief Manners greets me, a lot friendlier than the last time we met, but his smile is still no better than a scowl.

"You doin' all right, Sport?" Sheriff Macwain inquires and says *how you* to Daddy.

"Yes, sir," I say.

"Okay, here's what we gonna do," the sheriff says. "We're goin' upstairs to the jail. I want you to look at the Thompson brothers and tell me if they're the ones you saw shoot that boy on Thursday. Think you kin do that?"

"Yes, sir."

I don't feel brave like I thought I would. My heart tries to come out of my chest, and I have this empty feeling in the pit of my stomach. I look down to make sure my fly is zipped. We go up to the top floor and pass the sheriff's office where Deputy Miller sits at a desk. He waves at me, and I wave back. The Sheriff opens a large steel door with a thick glass window and motions for us to go through. There are cells with bars on each side of this long passageway, and it smells of Clorox and other unpleasant odors. Chief Manners leads the way to the last cell on the left. Through the bars, I see the Thompson brothers, and they see me. The hair on the back of my neck gets all tingly when they look at me. Maybe I shouldn't do this.

Frank, the oldest brother, is big and mean-looking, and he has a tattoo of a snake wrapped around his right arm. He looks up at me from his seat on a cot and waves a finger at me and grins. His brother, the one they call Egg, stands in the middle of the cell and stares at me with a sad, lopsided smile. He has dirty blond hair like his brother, but he's fatter and softer. The shape of his head sorta looks like an egg. Both have been on a chain gang. Frank almost killed a man in a poolroom fight, and Egg robbed a store in Alabama. They don't say nothing. Frank lights a cigarette and blows smoke in my direction. Egg turns and walks to the cell window to watch something in the street below.

"Okay, son. Are these the men you saw shoot that boy?" the sheriff asks.

"Ah, ah."

Frank looks like he's going to tear my head off.

"Come on, boy. Are they or ain't they?"

I finally find my voice. "Yes, sir. They were in a green 1939 Hudson Terraplane, and the one with the tattoos fired the gun. I saw his tattoos. The other one was driving."

"That's all we need," Sheriff Macwain says. "Wheeler, we gotta strong case here, but I don't want anybody to get cold feet. Do you understand me?"

"My boy knows what's right."

"Chief, why don't cha take Sport and Wheeler out of the jail," the sheriff says.

Chief Manners scowls his smile and says, "I'll do that, Billy. See ya back here in a few minutes."

Chief Manners leads me and Daddy down the backstairs and out to our car. He tells us that he'll check by the house off and on for the next few days just in case someone gets any foolish ideas. I think I know why he said this, but I didn't say anything to Daddy.

Last year somebody shot two of Mr. Witcher's dogs after he agreed to testify against two of Frank's friends, who stole six cows from a farmer's pasture on the south end of the county. Mr. Witcher saw them while he hunted in the woods next to the farm. They gutted his dogs and left them on his porch. People said Frank, Egg, and their drinking buddies killed the dogs. Mr. Witcher refused to testify.

Jack comes over because my parents won't let me leave my house unless they or my granddaddy are with me. That means we can't go to the Saturday afternoon matinee. That's okay. I don't much feel like seeing *National Velvet* with that whiney Elizabeth Taylor anyway.

When we were alone, Jack said, "Tell me what happened when Dink got shot."

I give Jack a detailed description, but I carefully leave out the reason I was up in the cedar tree, knowing that he's not all that hot on revenge against Max.

"Listen, Jack. I'll tell you and nobody else. I was so scared I almost wet my pants. I fainted, you know."

"All the kids at school are talking about the incident on Walnut Street. That's what everybody calls it. I'll bet you'll have to tell the same story about a million times when you get back to school. Are you going to school on Monday?"

"Yeah, but I'm not gonna tell anything to anybody, Jack. I'll just say I can't talk about it."

"Why?"

"Oh, I dunno. It ain't no big deal."

I decide to tell him about my dream. "Jack, I had this nightmare about bein' caught out in the piney woods. The woods were on fire, and I couldn't escape. I knew I'd suffocate or burn to death, and I wrapped this blanket around me and just lay there waiting for the fire to come over me. The dream's pressed into my memory like it's real. This time I'm not makin' it up. It's real."

"Dreaming about fire's not a good sign. Fire means danger. You best watch out and not play with matches or firecrackers."

Jack interprets dreams. He read this book on the meaning of dreams, and I sometimes make up dreams so he can interpret them. I once made up a dream about Max Mendeaux running down the street without a stitch of clothes on, and his bare butt shining in the sun. That made Jack laugh, but he knew I made it up.

"Are you afraid of the Thompson brothers?" Jack asks.

"I'll tell you and nobody else. I'm scared all right. Just thinkin' about them gives me the creeps, but they're in jail. Chief Manners and Sheriff Macwain'll keep them there where they can't bother me or anybody else."

"You got more guts than I have. I'd be scared. I'd be so scared I'd find a place to hide and not come out until they went to prison or left the county."

Me and Jack go outside to fly balsa wood gliders in my backyard. They're biplanes like World War I Spads and Jennys, and we try to make them dogfight. The gliders don't stay in the air very long, and sometimes they crash into each other and break. But they only cost a quarter each at Greer's store. Jack gets a real good flight with his plane. It goes high, loops, dives, and slowly loses altitude as it glides across the yard. I push my biplane to go in behind Jack's, but it goes up, comes back down in a steep dive, and hits the ground hard.

"Hello, fellows," Max Mendeaux says as he comes around the corner of the house. Jack and I stop and look at him. "That was a good flight, Jack. I can't get a glider to do that good."

"You fly gliders?" Jack asks.

"Yeah, and kites too when the wind's right. You guys ought to get a couple of kites and come with me to the vacant lot next to Mr. Wright's store. That's a good place because the electric and telephone lines are all on one side."

Like bad money, Max always turns up unexpectedly. It's just like him to show up and start talking as if he never insulted us. He must be up to something, so I hang back and listen.

"The reason I've come over here is to apologize to both of you. Especially to you, Sport," Max says. "You did a brave thing, and I froze. My Boy Scout training didn't do me any good, and I found out I can't stand the sight of blood. I've never seen anyone bleeding like that before. And I should've helped, but I couldn't. I know you guys've been real mad at me for some time, and I want to set it right. Sport, let's bury the hatchet about Jeb Stuart and Forrest. They were both great cavalry officers and fighting in different sections of the country. There's no way of comparing them. I don't think either of you are plebeian at all, and I promise not to call you names again. Okay?"

"Sure, Max. And I won't call you a turd anymore unless you act like one," I tell him, but he's still wrong about the Confederate generals. Nathan Bedford Forrest was the greatest cavalry officer in the War Between the States. Joe Wheeler comes in pretty high.

"Well, that's good enough for me. By the way, did you say anything to anybody about my being there when Dink was, ah, shot?"

"No, I forgot until just now."

"Nobody needs to know I was there. Let's just keep it between us," Max says. "I understand you'll be cooped up here for a while, Sport. If there's anything I can do for you, like getting books from the library or something, you let me know. And when you can, you and Jack come over to my house, and I'll show you an electric experiment I'm working on."

If he thinks I'm going to be cooped up, he's full of horse hockey. But I will say that it's something to see him eat crow. I bet ol' Max never apologized for anything in his life. He must've been saved at the Baptist Church again. I tell Jack we'll just keep watching Max in case he drifts back to his old stuck-up self. Jack says that Max is not a bad fellow at all and that maybe we've misjudged him somewhat.

"Jack Copeland, you're one of the nicest guys I know. You never hold a grudge or anything. As for me, I'll not turn my back on Max, the turd."

7

SPORT

Mama wakes me up, and I roll over and go back to sleep. Boy, do I hate to get up on Sunday morning. Especially when we go to church. Jack gets to sleep late just about every Sunday because he and his mama seldom go to church. They're Presbyterian. For me, this Sunday is no exception. By the time I rouse myself up, Daddy has read the *Sunday Constitution,* Mama has already fed Ted some of that horrible carrot stuff. All I want is toast and jelly. I don't feel hungry like I usually do.

I used to go to Sunday school regularly, but I've been backsliding since my confirmation last year. I don't know why. Maybe it's because all the stories and Bible readings are beginning to be repeated. To tell the truth, we have not been attending church or Sunday school as much as we did before my little brother joined the family. We're not going to Sunday school today. We're just going to church.

I take small bites from my toast and jelly and chew as slow as I can. Then I dress at about the same speed, hoping against hope I'll delay enough so we'll miss church altogether. I think about praying for a flat tire on our Chevy, but I can't do that. It would be blasphemy.

Dressing up for church is a given. Even Granddaddy wears his blue serge suit to church on Sunday. So I put on my navy blue Sunday suit and stand before Mama for inspection.

"Oh, Sport, you got somethin' on your coat sleeve. Stand right there!"

Mama gets a damp washcloth and wipes whatever it is off my sleeve. No, it is not snot. I don't wipe my nose on my sleeve, and I carry a clean handkerchief all the time.

We drive to church in silence, except for my little brother. He's saying something only God can understand. The day is nice, and the ride ain't bad.

The jonquils are blooming everywhere. Granddaddy says spring will be late. March sure came in like a lion, and it looks like it will go out like a lamb. Dogwood trees are covered with swollen buds straining to burst open.

When fully opened, the dogwood bloom forms a beautiful white cross. On the end of each white petal there is an indentation, which sorta looks like an impression of a nail. The indentations are the color of dried blood. Granddaddy says that Jesus's cross was made from a dogwood tree, and ever since the dogwood can never grow large enough or strong enough to be made into a cross. And the dogwood blossom will always be in the shape of a cross with traces of Christ's blood on the edge of the petals. I don't believe this because the Bible doesn't say nothing about dogwood trees.

Our church's small parking lot fills up fast, so we park on the street. Daddy holds my little brother while Mama gets out of the car. Sitting in the backseat of a 1948 Chevy coupe is like hunkering down in a cave, and I have to crawl over the front seat to get out. I look up at the bell tower of our church.

The St. Luke's Methodist Church looks old and solid with red bricks. English ivy grows up the side. The First Baptist Church, where Max Mendeaux goes to church, is modern and white. The original Methodist Church was made of wood. An Irish company of Sherman's Union Army burned it to the ground in 1864. It took ten years to rebuild. Granddaddy says the congregation decided to rebuild with red brick so, if Sherman ever came back, he would have to blast it down with a cannon. My great-granddaddy laid bricks for the walls of the sanctuary. And every time I enter, I feel a sense of belonging and comfort just like when I'm in my cedar tree. I guess everyone feels that way about his own church. And I can't say who are the best Christians, but I think the hard-shell Baptist might be. I went to one of their revivals last summer, and their preacher scared the hell out of me along with most of the people in the congregation.

Mr. Thurston Burgess greets us at the sanctuary door and hands us the order of worship. I quickly find Granddaddy and slip into the seat beside him. He interrupts his meditation to give me an elbow in the ribs and smiles at Mama and Daddy as they sit down with my little brother. Uncle Earl is not there. He lost his religion in the Pacific. He attends church only on holy days.

Services begin with the processional. We stand and sing the third stanza of the hymn. "Thy world is weary of its pain / Of selfish greed and fruitless gain / Of tarnished honor, falsely strong / And all its ancient deeds of wrong." I listen to Mama's voice. It's sweet and soothing. Daddy doesn't sing, but Granddaddy makes up for Daddy with a rough top sergeant's voice.

During the Apostles' Creed I think about Pontius Pilate. Julius Caesar may be the noblest Roman of them all, but old Pontius Pilate is remembered by name every Sunday by Christians all over the world. The Bible talks about Augustus Caesar. I guess Julius lived during the Old Testament, but I don't think he is ever mentioned. I wave at Ben Lloyd who sits two rows down from us, and he waves back. I see Cindy Snow looking at me, and I stick my tongue out at her. She blushes and looks away.

After the congregation chants the Gloria Patria, Reverend Sommers reads from the holy scriptures, *"But he, willing to justify himself, said unto Jesus, And who is my neighbor? And Jesus answering, said, A certain man went down from Jerusalem to Jericho, and fell among thieves, which stripped him of his raiment, and wounded him, and departed, leaving him half dead."*

My mind wanders back to how Frank Thompson looked at me in the jail, and I shiver. The minister finishes his story about the Good Samaritan. I don't really have to listen because I heard it about a hundred times.

When the congregation sits down, Reverend Sommers prays for just about everything and everybody. I like him because he's a lot younger than Reverend Ball, our last minister, and not as serious.

Granddaddy says it's a good thing the bishop appointed a fresh preacher. He says Reverend Ball should have retired years ago but couldn't because the war took the younger ministers and left the church in short supply of new blood. Reverend Ball got pretty grumpy the last year he served our congregation. And he couldn't remember names. He always called me Clyde. I was afraid of him and avoided him whenever I could.

Reverend Sommers tells funny jokes, and he doesn't put me to sleep like he does Mr. Christian. Mr. Christian sleeps through most of everybody's sermons. He puts his head down on his chest and pretends to be praying or meditating, but occasionally a short snort or snore slips out.

We may have a softball league this year. Reverend Sommers is organizing a church league for the kids to play in this summer. Maybe I can get Jack Copeland to join. Jack can play softball; he just can't play basketball. He can't dribble. If we have a softball league, we can have real umpires instead of somebody who doesn't know a strike from a ball.

After the offertory, the congregation stands for a hymn—all but Mrs. Shires and Mr. Christian. Rheumatism has Mrs. Shires all bent over, and Mr. Christian continues his meditation.

Reverend Sommers stands in the pulpit and clears his throat. "As most of you know, and my wife will attest, I struggle to find a message for my Sunday sermon. I know the subject, but I fret and pray for just the right words. Many times I burn the Saturday midnight oil. Not so this week. I take my sermon from a parable told by Jesus to a lawyer who had asked, 'What shall I do to inherit eternal life?'

"Jesus asked him, 'What is written in the law?'

"The lawyer answered him correctly, but then asked, 'Who is my neighbor?'

"Jesus answered the lawyer with the parable of the Good Samaritan." Reverend Sommers goes on, "Now y'all know this story. You've studied it in

Sunday school. You've heard it all your lives. At times many of us get too busy to ask, who is my neighbor? There is one among us who knows this better than most. This past Thursday, he demonstrated how to treat a neighbor by saving a life. I know the Kirk family is very proud of him, as should be this whole congregation, because he is one of our own children. Sport, please stand and be recognized as a good neighbor."

Oh, Lord! I didn't expect this. Granddaddy pushes me to my feet, and I stand there like an idiot. I feel my face go red. I am embarrassed, and I want to shrink to the size of a peanut. I hear a low murmur from the congregation. Somebody starts to applaud. I think it is Ben Lloyd and his family. As I slink back down beside Mama and Granddaddy, I see the Gaineses, the Wilkeys, and the Mulinaxes stare straight ahead. They are not applauding. Well, as Granddaddy says, "You can't please everybody." Yeah. Like I want to please them.

I don't know what else Reverend Sommers says. I don't hear the rest of the sermon. All I want to do is be a face in the crowd, but it seems like it's always my fate to call attention to myself. It's not my fault that things happen to put me before a bunch of people. I see Dink shot in my mind's camera. I see the Thompson brothers driving off in their green Hudson Terraplane. Dink is bleeding. It hardly seems that it really happened.

Thank God, church service is over. The acolytes, with Reverend Sommers behind them, carry the light out into the world. Mama, holding my little brother, Daddy, Granddaddy, and I follow the rest of the congregation outside. Ben Lloyd's daddy shakes my hand, and his mama pats me on the shoulder. Ben gives me a quick jab in the arm. Mr. Thurston Burgess and his wife shake my hand. Tom and Millie Snow, with their stupid, wormy daughter, Cindy, stop to chat with Mama and Daddy. Tom Snow is the prosecutor for Coosa County.

Granddaddy says that to disarm someone you don't like, give them a compliment. I say to Cindy, "You look real nice today." *For a skinny girl*, I silently tell myself.

"You really think so?" she says, but it's more of a statement than a question.

"I shore do," I say with my fingers crossed and hidden behind my back.

"That's awfully nice of you, Sport. Well, I'll see you at school tomorrow."

"Okay," I say, and then to myself, *Not if I see you first.*

I ask Mama if I can ride home with Granddaddy. "If he doesn't mind," she answers. Granddaddy never minds. Although his old Buick is like a tank, it's a lot better to ride in the front seat of it than to ride the backseat of our Chevy coupe.

On the way home, I ask Granddaddy, "Were you ever in danger during the war?"

He never tells me very much about his service in France, and I always try to get him to tell me more. He plays down his part in the Great War by saying he had it pretty easy.

He said the real heroes are the ones who never came back. But I've seen his Distinguished Service Cross and other ribbons.

"Yap, mostly from artillery shells," Granddaddy answers. "Got nicked one time when I did a short stint as a runner, and that was plenty fearsome. Communications was just awful even with field telephones. I took care of army horses and mules. Blacksmithing mostly."

Granddaddy is proud of his service in the cavalry. He keeps all his cavalry stuff in a special room, which he calls his tack room. There are saddles, bridles, and his highly polished boots and spurs. He also keeps an old Enfield rifle that looks almost new. He served over twenty years in the army and retired at Fort Oglethorpe, Georgia, in 1922. He came back to Coosa County and set up a blacksmith shop because, according to him, there were more horses and mules in the county than there were people. Granddaddy knows animals and made a good bit of money doctoring horses and mules.

"Did you ever kill a man, Granddaddy?"

"I shot at a German one time, but I don't know if I hit him or not. I was runnin' too fast to pay much attention. I did shoot ol' Sims Laney in the leg when I was sheriff. It happened when he ran away from me as I arrested him for stealing a pig. Ol' Sims would steal the nickels off a dead man's eyes. I tried to do him a favor by not placin' him in handcuffs, but the damned fool ran. He should've knowed better, and now when he sees me, he limps around something pitiful like I broke his leg. It was just a flesh wound, but he wants me to feel sorry for him. When yore a law officer, ya can't trust nobody, especially if ya know they committed a criminal act."

He changes the subject and talks about the *Jack Benny Show*. Van Johnson was Jack Benny's guest last week. In that episode, Jack and Van went on a double date. Of course, Jack is as stingy as ever. Granddaddy never misses *Jack Benny* on Sunday night. I like Van Johnson. He's real good in World War II pictures. He played in *Command Decision*.

I keep thinking about what Reverend Sommers said about me saving Dink's life. I didn't do anything special. And I don't feel like a Good Samaritan 'cause I didn't even think about what I was doing. If I had, I probably wouldn't have done it. At least I don't have a yellow streak down my back like Max Mendeaux.

Would I try to save Dink's life again? You damn, I mean, dadgum right I would.

I can relax with *Jack Benny* and *Our Miss Brooks* tonight. I finished my homework last Friday.

8

SPORT

Jack is right about the attention I get at school. Everybody stares and whispers about me before classes begin. Boy, this is Monday, and I'll have to put up with this a whole week. Mr. Grant, the principal, tells me what a fine thing I did. A couple of kids ask me about what happened. True to my word to Jack, I say I can't talk about it.

Mr. Pritchard tells my seventh-grade class not to ask me any questions about the incident. "If he . . . ah . . . ah . . . doesn't want to talk about it, it's his right to remain silent," he says. That stops the questions from all except Eugene Laney. Mr. Pritchard shuts him up and says, "Ah . . . Ah . . . Y'all put your books away. I'm . . . ah . . . ah . . . going to tell you a story."

"I come from the Blue Ridge Mountains," he begins. "In 1942 I volunteered for service in the army. I arrived at Camp Gordon, Georgia, for basic training not knowing anyone. Men from New York, New Jersey, Pennsylvania, Ohio, and North Carolina, Americans from all parts of the eastern United States were there for basic training. One of the first boys I met came from New Jersey. He was a redhead like me. I guess that's what threw us together. I took the usual ribbing about the army giving me my first pair of shoes. I didn't mind that because I thought these fellows were just showing their ignorance. Anyway, this redheaded fellow and I became fast friends. We trained together and supported each other. When we received passes, we went together to Augusta. A few days before we completed basic training, one of our fellow soldiers took me aside and whispered, "Did you know you were running around with a Jew?"

Mr. Pritchard pauses, then continues, "I had never seen a Jew before, so I didn't know what he was talking about. I only knew he was talking about my friend, the finest man I ever had the privilege to know. 'I don't care,' I told the soldier. Heck, I'm a Jew too. The soldier looked at me real strange and walked away. From that point on, nobody in our unit ever said anything about Jews or any other religious group."

"What're you trying to tell us?" Carl Lopez asks.

One time Granddaddy told me the Lopes family is one of two Jewish families in Laceola. According to Granddaddy, Jews have had a long and distinguished history in the South. Carl's family descended from Spanish Jews who settled in Florida before the Revolution.

"Ah . . . ah . . . Carl, I'm telling you not to judge a person by his religion or his color. What matters most is your good character and what's in your heart. After all is said and done, we're all equal under the United States Constitution. Now . . . ah . . . ah . . . do y'all understand me?" Mr. Pritchard asks.

"I understand," Jim Washington spoke up. "It's like Andrew Jackson saying the Creek Indians were nothing but animals."

"You pegged it, Jim."

At lunch Eugene Laney asks me to tell him about Dink's blood. He wants to know if it was hot and how much came out and did I pass out when I saw the blood. Eugene always wants to know about real nasty stuff like cat puke. He likes to describe what a snake looks like after being smashed in the street by a truck. He'll probably become a doctor.

I tell Eugene I won't talk about what happened except to say that blood ran into the gutter like water and a dog came along and licked it up. Eugene gets excited when he hears this and goes around telling everybody about the blood and gore in the gutter and about a pack of dogs lapping up the blood.

At afternoon recess, me, Jack Copeland, Weasel Devoe, and Ben Lloyd sit around the base of an old water oak tree on the side of the playground. We talk about knives. Ben says he doesn't need a switchblade because he can open his single-blade case knife as fast as it comes out of his pocket. He shows us how he does it, and he's fast.

Johnny Adkins walks up and says, "Why didn't cha let that nigger die? Be one less we'd have to put up with. I guess yere just a danged nigger lover."

I get up and begin to tremble with rage. I'm fixin' to ram my fist down his throat. Jack Copeland stands beside me and says, "Johnny, you're just plain stupid. I'll bet that's what your daddy told you. If you were bleeding to death, I bet you'd say, 'Go away, colored boy. I'd rather bleed to death than have you save me.' Is that what you'd say?"

"I don't know. Maybe."

"No, you wouldn't. You'd be crying for help from anybody, black or white, who'd save your worthless life. Now, why don't you leave us alone before we get riled enough to beat your ass," Jack finishes with a cold stare at Johnny.

He doesn't like to fight, but he knows Johnny Adkins is a lily-livered coward. Johnny is lucky that Jack is with me. I'm not so particular about slapping a polecat up side the head.

After school Granddaddy picks me and Jack up in his old Buick and takes us home. That's when he explains to me about the bail. The Thompsons were brought up before Judge Morris for arraignment. The judge set bail at $5,000 each. Somebody put up money to get them out of jail until they are called to trial.

My stomach did a couple of flip-flops. Oh, dog crap. They're out of jail. Why did the judge let them out? Those crumbs are dangerous.

"What am I suppose to do now? They scare me to death, and I don't want to see them."

"I don't think you have to worry about the Thompson brothers. They'll be on their best behavior before the trial. Superior Court convenes in June. Their trial date will be on the docket sometime during the next session," Granddaddy says.

"Then they won't bother me."

"I didn't say that. It's not just the Thompsons. It's also the people they run with. The brothers won't do nothing alone. They like a nasty crowd, and they'll talk it up amongst the people that think like 'em. And them's the ones we have to watch out fur."

I'll be out of school by the time they go to trial, and I don't know how long a trial lasts. It better not cut into my vacation 'cause I'm looking forward to being out of school. I spend two weeks with my aunt Minnie, uncle Luke, and my cousins in Alabama every summer. They live on a farm with a lake full of fish. You can swim in the lake too. Sometimes we'll take a bateau out to the middle of the lake and dive off the back of it into the water. Aunt Minnie fusses about the danger, but she lets us do it anyway. Uncle Luke sets up targets for us to shoot at with our .22 rifles. I hope Jack's mama will let him come with me this summer. It'll be great fun even if we do have to do some work for Uncle Luke.

9

JACK

Either by chance or will of the gods, Sport hasn't run into any trouble for the past week. His family has been very cautious because they expect the Thompsons to do something. So far the Thompsons and their Klan friends have left him alone. I personally don't think those people are stupid enough to try anything. Mom says the talk around town about Sport from both sides has stopped and that the incident was blown out of proportion. It's okay for me to hang around with Sport, but Mom warns me to be careful.

Sport has permission from his parents to go downtown today. Saturday is a great time to meet our friends at the Maple Street Soda Shoppe or go to the picture show. I walk over to Sport's house.

"You wanna go to the picture show, Sport?" I ask.

"What's playing?"

"Tarzan's New York Adventure."

"Naw, it's pretty boring. But I'll go if you want to. I'm sure Ulene'll be disappointed if Jack Copeland doesn't show up."

"Ahwww, she's just a danged ol' girl. Why don't we just hang around town? We can go to the soda shop and get an orange smash or a Cherry Coke," I say trying to get Sport off the Ulene thing.

We walk down Walnut Street and pass Sport's cedar tree.

"You haven't been climbing that old cedar lately," I say.

"No, I don't have time to climb any kinda tree. That poor old tree is gettin' run down. Its limbs aren't as strong as they used to be, and I gotta take care of it."

We walk over Little Snake Creek on the footbridge, cut across the vacant lot, and head downtown on Main Street. Charles Jackson, a big colored man who works at the steel furnace, meets us.

He tips his gray felt hat and says to Sport, "How y'all doin', young mister?"

"Fine. Fine as frog hair," answers Sport.

"Where y'all headed to?" Charles inquires.

"Going downtown, maybe to the soda shop. You shore do look all spruced up in that suit. You going to a wedding or a funeral?" Sport asks.

We have never seen Charles Jackson wear anything but work clothes. Today he wears a gray pinstripe suit and white shirt with a red- and silver gray-striped tie. His shoes are black wing tips.

"I thank y'all for dat com-ply-mint. Preacher call dis meeting over at da church. And since I'se a deacon, thought I need to look like a deacon should."

"Well, it's nice seein' you, Mr. Charles," Sport says.

We start to move on down the street when Charles Jackson stops us. We turn back to see him showing lots of teeth in a big wide smile.

"Mr. Sport, if'n y'all needs anything from me, all's you has to do is call. Listen, you got a heap of friends in these parts. Now go on and take care of yo'self."

"Yessir, Mr. Charles."

"Did you see how big that man is?"

"Yeah, he looks like a football player dressed out with shoulder pads and everything," Sport says.

"He looks scary to me. I'll bet he could take Joe Lewis."

Out of habit, the first place Sport and I go is Greer's Hardware Store, which sets at the beginning of the business district on south Main. We buy our BBs, balsawood gliders, and model airplanes there. And we're always interested in the tools and things Mr. Greer sells.

"Howdy, boys," Mr. Greer greets us as we enter the store. "Y'all come for a supply of BBs?"

"No, sir," Sport says. "My daddy took our BB guns away from us when he saw us shootin' at a street light. Heck, that old streetlight wasn't working anyway. We wanna see if you have any new model airplanes."

"Well, that's too bad. I guess you won't be shootin' at snakes and frogs in Little Snake Creek."

"Daddy took our guns. I didn't say he took our weapons. Me and Jack made rubber flips. With small rocks or lead balls, they do just as well as BBs against frogs. Of course, they ain't as accurate, and you can't hit a snake doctor with one. It's hard to find real red rubber anymore. Just about the only thing we get these days is that old black synthetic stuff," Sport explains.

"Do you sell old red rubber inner tubes?" I ask Mr. Greer.

"No, but you might try the rubber bands that go into model airplanes."

"Doesn't work as well. We tried 'em," I say.

"Have y'all seen the new P-51 Mustang model?"

"Yes, sir. We built one and a F4U Corsair too," Sport says.

"I'll bet you boys ain't seen the navy Douglas A-1 Skyraider. I just got it in. It's a nice-lookin' plane."

Sport and I look it over. The A-1 is a beauty. It costs $2.35. Together we don't have that much money.

"We're goin' down to the soda shop," Sport tells Mr. Greer. "We don't wanna carry a model airplane around with us all day. If we have enough money left over, we'll come back and get one."

"That's fine, boys," Mr. Greer says. "Remember, this is Saturday. We close at five o'clock today."

Before we get to the drugstore at the corner of Main Street and Greene Avenue, Sport and I stop to listen to Mose, a colored street musician. He plays his guitar either here or on the courthouse square for donations almost every Saturday.

Mose uses a case knife to chord his guitar, and it sounds as if the strings are hanging down to his knees. Steel on steel is kind of exciting. He's singing:

> My baby don't 'llow no cheatin', my babe
> My baby don't 'llow no cheatin', my babe
> My baby don't 'llow no cheatin'
> She don't 'llow no midnight creepin'
> Pretty little baby, my babe

Then he drifts into his lonesome and blue rendition of "Macon County Chain Gang Blues" and finishes up with "My Baby Left Me in Clarkesville."

A few people, white and colored, stop to listen. After his last song, one or two people drop a dollar or fifty cents in a hat he placed on the sidewalk. He thanks them. The little crowd moves off, leaving Sport and me as his only audience.

Sport reaches into his pocket and pulls out a quarter. "This is shore not enough for your fine songs, Mose. But it's all I can afford. We're goin' up to the soda shop for an orange smash."

"I 'preciates anything I gets. Most people just don't cotton to the blues. I guess dey wants to forget 'bout hard times and the Depression. 'Cos colored folk ain't the onliest ones to sing da blues. Y'all listen to dis one from a white man from Mississippi. He name was Jimmie Rodgers. Now I cain't yodel, and I ain't gonna try. Dust stand there and listen 'cause dis one's for y'all."

Mose slips his case knife into his pocket, picks out the introduction on his scarred-up guitar, and sings: "All around the water tank, waiting for a train."

Mose finishes with a flourish. "I'm a thousand miles away from home just waiting for a train."

Sport and I applaud and shout, "Yeah, Yeah." This attracts the attention of some passersby, but they don't stop.

"I ain't ever heard that one before," Sport says.

"Peoples is just too busy to remember dez days. Dey needs to slow down. Dat's what dey needs to do."

"We'll see ya later, Mose," Sport says.

As we walk away, I whisper to Sport. "Did you give Mose your last quarter? You won't have enough to buy anything."

"You gotta know this about me, my friend. I always have a backup. Granddaddy gave me a dollar, and I keep it in my shoe in case of emergencies, and I deem this to be such an emergency. Let's cross the street at Blount's Drug Store before we get to Cobb Street."

"Why?" I ask.

"The preacher. I don't wanna be told I'm goin' to hell."

"Oh yeah. I forgot."

A hellfire-and-brimstone preacher gives his fiery sermons on the corner of Cobb and Main streets every Saturday. He tells everyone walking past they are going to hell unless they repent right now, right on the spot. At times he picks out someone and follows them down the street a few steps.

"Yere sinners, and yere going straight to hell," he'll scream at his target. Sport and I avoid him unless we forget he's there. We look both ways and wait for a break in the traffic.

"Hey, kid!" a rough-looking man shouts across Main Street from the front of the pool hall.

Sport looks at the man and freezes. The man points his finger at him like he's shooting a gun. He pretends to fire straight at Sport, and then he makes a gesture with his middle finger. Sport's right eyelid begins to twitch, and he's breathing real hard but stands looking at the man grinning at him. There are goose bumps on his arms, and he shudders, but he still doesn't move. I grab his shoulder and turn him around.

"Hey, buddy, what's the matter. Come on, let's go."

Sport's eyes come back into focus.

"That's Frank Thompson."

"Come on," I say and pull him down the sidewalk "We'll stay on this side of the street. The preacher ain't that bad."

Sport walks like his in a trance. The preacher doesn't notice us when we pass by and go across Main.

I grab Sport by the arm, "Come on, let's run."

Sport is a celebrity of sorts since the *Coosa County News* printed the story about the shooting, and people stare at us as we run down the street. Sport's scared after seeing Frank Thompson, and it scared me when he froze up like that.

We enter the soda shop, and Marshall Biggers, the owner, says, "Hey, Sport! You come for one of them orange smashes?"

"Huh, ah, yes, sir."

"Myrtle, give Sport an orange smash on the house," Mr. Biggers orders.

Sport gives me an elbow in the side and whispers, "The Lord does protect us from harm, doesn't he?"

I say hello to our friends: Weasel Devoe, Eugene Laney, Ben Lloyd, and Pow-Pow Johnson. Johnny Adkins is there and so is Max Mendeaux. I ignore Johnny. Max reads a book in a booth at the back of the soda shop. He either ignores us or is unaware we're here.

We sit down in a booth across from our friends.

"What's the matter with Sport?" Ben asks

"Ah, he's just out of sorts," I say.

Eugene Laney is describing every gory detail of how the lions ate Christians in the Roman circus. "They'd tear off arms. Blood gushed out. Then the lions would grab them in the belly and rip out their guts while they were still alive and screamin'." Most of the kids pretend interest in his story.

Myrtle serves the orange smash to Sport. I order a Cherry Coke. Sport comes out of his shell and says, "Eugene, can't you stop talking about those danged ol' gory stories?"

"Naw. People like to hear ma stories. Doncha, fellows?"

"Well, I don't, so stop talking about it."

"Hey, I'll bet I could be a radio announcer. Maybe I could get a job at WGWG. I'll bet I could be a popular storyteller," Eugene says as he launches into his imitation of a newscaster doing a play-by-play of the Christians and the lions.

Sport and I finish our drinks. Carl Lopez comes in and is cornered by Eugene Laney. Weasel, Ben, Pow-Pow, and I discuss our plans for summer vacation.

"What about you, Sport? What you gonna do?" Pow-Pow asks.

Sport livens up a bit. "I want to go to my aunt and uncle's farm in Alabama. Maybe me and Jack will go together. But it looks like I'll have to testify in this trial, and I don't know how long it will last."

Weasel says he has to go to some god-awful camp in North Carolina.

"I ain't goin' nowhere," Ben declares.

"I'm staying right here with Ben," Pow-Pow says. "We'll get us a bateau and float down Little Snake Creek 'til it runs into the Coosa. We gonna camp out and fish along the river 'til we get good and ready to come home. Ain't that right, Ben?"

When he was a little kid, Ronald Johnson ran around pretending to shoot a wooden gun. Most toys were made of wood during the war. He made the noise *pow-pow* to mimic the sound of a gun. Older kids started calling him Pow-Pow, and the nickname stuck.

"If you say so, Pow-Pow. Except I can't stand mosquitoes. If I have to put up with mosquitoes, I ain't goin'," Ben says.

Sport perks up. "Ya can keep mosquitoes away by rubbin' garlic juice all over yore body. The scent of a human attracts mosquitoes, but garlic juice confuses them."

"I thought garlic keeps vampires away," Pow-Pow says.

"Mosquitoes're kinda like vampires," Sport answers.

"Smoke keeps them away," Ben says.

"Why don't we ask Max Mendeaux? He's just about an Eagle Scout," I say.

"Max ain't never been in the real woods," Sport says. "Cal Slowman can give ya the real remedy to keep mosquitoes away." We nod our heads in agreement. "But I'll betcha he'll tell ya I'm right about the garlic juice."

"D'you think he has a remedy for chiggers too?" Ben asks.

Pow-Pow begins to explain how kerosene is used to kill chiggers when I interrupt. "Oops. Hey, Sport. We gotta go."

"Why? Now, Jack, we don't have to rush. Heck, I'm enjoying this discussion about nature. Besides we've got another hour or so."

Ulene MacFadden, Fiona Burns, Lucy Renfoe, and Myrna Clayton come into the soda shop.

"Come on, let's go," I say to Sport under my breath as I nod a greeting to the girls.

"Hey, Myrna. Hey, Fiona. Hey, Lucy. Hey, Ulene. Jack's gotta go home and study about jet planes cracking the sound barrier and such. We'll see y'all later," Sport says.

"You shore are shy around girls," Sport tells me when we leave the soda shop.

"No. That's not right. Ulene makes me nervous."

"Because she's sweet on you?"

"Awhh, she's just a danged ol' girl." The truth is I feel kind of proud to have Ulene like me. But she does make me nervous because I don't know what to say to her.

We decide not to go down to the Confederate memorial on the courthouse square and listen to the old men tell tall tales. Instead we head for home.

"The Metropolitan Opera should be off the air by the time we get home," Sport says. "There's bound to be something on WSB out of Atlanta or WPLT out of Palatine. The grits, bacon, and eggs I ate for breakfast have been used up. We'll get something to eat at my house."

"That's okay by me. But I gotta be home by supper, and I gotta go over my history project for tomorrow."

I didn't say anything about Frank Thompson, and neither did Sport.

10

SPORT

For the next two days, each of us in my seventh-grade class will give our American history project presentation. It has to be two to three minutes long, and everyone has to face a bunch of stupid nudging-and-giggling twelve-year-olds with whatever he or she chooses to tell about. Mr. Pritchard will listen at the back of the classroom with his timer and grade book.

My project is on Morgan's Raiders. John Hunt Morgan and his two thousand men raided Kentucky and Indiana. The "blue bellies" captured him in Indiana. Then he escaped from prison and continued raiding. Finally a company of Federals surrounded and murdered him in Greeneville, Tennessee.

Jack has really worked on his presentation, and it's sharp. He traces the history of aviation from WWI to the present. He has some great pictures of airplanes and deserves to get the best grade in class.

Eugene Laney is first. He jumps up from his desk and runs to the front of the classroom. He tells the story of the Salem witch trials. What I get out of it is a bunch of people was accused of using witchcraft to make cows go dry and things like that. Eugene doesn't care if they were guilty or not. He just likes to describe how they were tortured into confessing and how they dangled at the end of a rope until they choked to death.

Mr. Pritchard stops Eugene after three long minutes.

"But I ain't finished," Eugene protests.

"Yes, you are, Eugene. Now . . . ah . . . ah . . . sit down."

"But I didn't get to tell how the witches were burned at the stake."

"Sit down, Eugene. Now we'll hear from Fiona."

Fiona Burns rises from her desk and walks slowly to the front of the classroom. As she passes by the window, a ray of morning sun illuminates her honey blonde hair and silhouettes her profile. My heart tumbles over and hits the pit of my stomach, then bounces back up to hang like a piece of green apple in my throat. I have never seen this girl before. Could this be Fiona? She's pretty. She faces the class and clears her throat. Someone giggles in the back of the room, and Fiona smiles.

"The subject of my history project is Laceola," she says. "We know Creek and Cherokee Indians lived here long before the white man came. This was a meeting place where both tribes gathered to settle their disputes and trade. The area where The Three Springs empty into Little Snake Creek had been designated neutral territory. Individuals of both tribes could come and go as they pleased without reprisal. The first white man arrived in . . ."

I hear her voice for the first time. Like Tibetan temple bells, it softly lilts across the classroom. I know, I know. I have never heard real Tibetan temple bells, but after reading Rudyard Kipling, that's how I imagined temple bells sound. I stare at Fiona and listen to her voice. I am bumfuzzled.

"After the French traders, Joshua Middleton set up a trading post near The Three Springs in 1796. He married a Creek Indian woman and raised a family. Mr. Middleton left with his family after he sold his trading post in 1811 to Elija Brown, who was part Cherokee. During the War of 1812, a group of Creeks and Cherokees joined General Andrew Jackson to fight against the British . . ."

What's happening to me? I have never thought about Fiona Burns. Never. What am I thinking? Did I just realize she's pretty? Damn, that is, dadgum pretty? She has a perfect nose, and it doesn't twitch when she talks, like Lucy Renfoe's. Her lips ain't crooked like Nola Greene's. Although Nola Greene ain't that bad. I slap the side of my face to clear my head. Fiona pauses and smiles at me. Wow!

"The people living here petitioned the state legislature for a charter in 1839 and named their village Laceola for a Cherokee Indian who had helped early settlers in Coosa County. By 1860 there were about 750 people living in Laceola and about two thousand in the whole county . . ."

I don't take my eyes off Fiona as she continues her history of Laceola up to the present day.

"Approximately 1,500 men and women from Coosa County served on all fronts during World War II. And that completes my history of Laceola," Fiona smiles at the class.

For some stupid reason, I applaud. Everybody, including Fiona, looks at me.

"Now . . . ah . . . ah . . . Sport. I appreciate your exuberance for Fiona's excellent work, but it would . . . ah . . . ah . . . behoove us to wait until all have presented their project before we applaud," Mr. Pritchard announces from the back of the classroom. "Thank you, Fiona, for a fine report."

I sink into my desk as low as I can get. Fool! Why did you do that? Oh, Lord. I'll never live this down. I glance at Jack, and he grins like a mule eating briars. He's got me, dang it. He's got me. I'll propose a pact that we won't kid each other about girls and things like that.

11

SPORT

Miss Sally calls Mama to tell her Dink came home from the Palatine hospital this afternoon, and his parents are back in Chicago. Mama tells me when I get home from school. Yes, it's Friday, and I made it through school this week without too much ribbing. Before this weekend is over, everyone but Eugene Laney and Jack would have forgotten my outburst of applause. Eugene forgets nothing. Me and Jack made a pact not to kid each other about Fiona and Ulene, but I'm not sure I can keep it. Jack is just too good a target. He blushes too much.

After supper Mama, Daddy, my little brother, and I load up in the Chevy and drive over to Miss Sally's house. It's a big rambling white house, the kind you see on farms around Coosa County. It's the largest and oldest house in Ducktown. Miss Sally meets us at the door.

"Dink will sho' be glad to see you, young Spo't. He been axing for you since he got home," Miss Sally says. "Y'all go on back to his room. It the one on the left down the hall."

I pass through the living room and see Aunt Nicey sitting in a straight-back chair near the fireplace. She is saying something that sounds like, "Is that you, little George?"

Miss Sally says, "No, Mama Nicey, dat's his grandson."

Dink's door is open, so I walk in.

"Did you fall outta dat tree, Spo't?"

"Whatcha talkin' about Dink?"

"When y'all save me dat day."

"No, Dink. But I'm glad I was there. How ya doing?" I ask.

"I so' but not too bad. Cain't move my leg. I was scaredt."

"Me too, Dink. Hey, I brought cha a Captain Marvel comic book. He's the one that can fly. Shazam!"

"Yeah, yeah. Shazam! I likes Cappin' Marble. I'll read it tonight."

Surprisingly enough, Dink can read some. With pictures he can understand a lot in a book, and he takes pride in writing his name. Once he saw my name which my mama had written on the lining of my coat and asked, "Is tha' your name?"

"Shore is," I told him.

"Well, here's my name." He wrote his name on the sidewalk with a broken piece of rock. "I gonna 'member how to write yo' name, Spo't."

Mama and Daddy come to Dink's room. Miss Sally, holding on to my squirming little brother, tells them, "Dink don't have his strength back. He gets real tared real fast."

"It takes awhile to recover from a wound like his. He'll come around," Daddy tells her.

"Look at dis, Mama Sally. Spo't brought me a Cappin' Marble book."

"Now, ain't dat nice of him," she says.

Mama and Daddy talk to Dink a few minutes, and then Daddy tells Dink we'd better let him get some rest. I say goodbye to Dink. We all troop down the hall to the living room. As I pass Aunt Nicey, she plainly says, "Little George, you come here!"

"Mama Nicey, dat ain't little George. Dat Spo't."

Aunt Nicey grabs and hugs me. "Little George, you don't come to see yore old aunt Nicey ofen enough, you hear me."

"Yes, ma'am." I go along with her because I realize she thinks I'm Granddaddy. "I promise to come more often."

Aunt Nicey releases her grip on me and drifts off into her own world.

When we leave, Miss Sally tells me, "You can come down here to see Dink by yo'self. Y'all safer in Ducktown than you is up dere in Laceola."

"Yea, ma'am. I'll try to see Dink again real soon."

12

SPORT

Mama sends me to Mr. Wright's store for a loaf of bread. She fixes sandwiches for lunch on Saturday, and I always buy Merrita Bread because the company sponsors *The Lone Ranger*. I'm a loyal listener. But if you think about it, the Lone Ranger is kind of strange. Dan Reed, his nephew, is the Green Hornet. The way I figure, Dan Reed must be fifty or sixty years old, but he doesn't sound old.

Ulene MacFadden comes into the store as I pay Mr. Wright for the bread.

"Hey, Ulene," I say.

"Hi, Sport. Is Jack with you?"

A plan to see Fiona pops into my head, and I lie to her, "Naw, we're meeting this afternoon to go to the picture show."

"Oh, what time are you going?"

"I guess around two o'clock."

"I'm going this afternoon too."

"Really. Is Fiona going with you?"

"Yes. And Lucy too."

I don't care about Lucy, but Fiona will be there. I may have to hog-tie Jack and drag him out by hook or by crook, and whether he knows it or not, he's going to the picture show with me.

"Okay. Me and Jack'll see you around two."

As soon as I get home, I pick up the phone. "Number please," the operator says.

"952."

Jack's mama answers the phone. "Mrs. Copeland, this is Sport. Is Jack there?"

"Why, of course he is, Sport," she says.

"Does Jack have anything to do at home this afternoon? Can he go to the picture show with me?"

"No-o. But why are you asking my permission for Jack to go out? You don't usually do that."

"Oh, I don't wanna get Jack in trouble if he has anything to do."

"Well, he doesn't. Would you like to speak to Jack?"

"Yes, ma'am."

"Sport! What's goin' on?" Jack asks.

"I want you to go with me to see *The Babe Ruth Story* this afternoon. Your mother said you can go."

"We saw it last summer. Remember? I don't like William Bendix."

"Oh, come on, Jack. It's baseball season. We gotta get into the baseball spirit. It's that time of year."

"What do you mean? The only baseball games we can pick up on the radio are the Atlanta Crackers on WSB or the St. Louis Cardinals on KMOX. And that's only at night."

"So? I like the St. Louis Cardinals and the Atlanta Crackers too. Come on. It's not gonna hurt you to see *Babe Ruth* again."

"Okay. But if I get disgusted with it, I'm walking out."

"That's a deal."

We get to the picture show about fifteen minutes before the feature starts and settle into our favorite seats, eight rows down from the back on the right side. I slide in first and move down to a seat in the middle of the row.

"Why don't we sit on the end?" Jack asks.

"I can see better from here."

As the title, *The Babe Ruth Story,* flashes across the screen, I glance over my shoulder and see the three girls come in. I half-wave to Ulene. She waves back, makes her way to our row, and slides in beside Jack.

"Hi, Jack. Mind if we sit here?"

"It's a free country," Jack tells her and glares at me.

I whisper, "Hi, Ulene, Fiona, Lucy. You girls like baseball?"

"Oh, yes," Fiona says, and I melt.

Jack stares straight ahead and gives me an elbow in the ribs. I'm not sitting next to Fiona, but that's okay. She's close. Maybe I can persuade Jack to go to the Maple Street Soda Shoppe where I can sit in a booth with her.

As we watch the movie, Ulene asks Jack stuff like, "Was *Babe Ruth* really that good?" and "Why didn't he pitch?" Jack whispers short, direct answers. I wish I could talk to Fiona. Boy, Jack has it made.

When the credits come on the screen, Jack says, "I gotta go home."

"No, you don't, Jack. You said we were going to the soda shop. Hey, you girls wanna string along?"

The girls say, "Yes."

"I'm gonna kill you with my bare hands," Jack whispers under his breath.

Jack, the three girls, and I walk down to the soda shop. Before entering, Jack says, "Gee, I don't have any money. Maybe I should just go home."

"I have money," Ulene says.

"Jack, would I let my buddy sit around without a Cherry Coke? No, sir. I've got my emergency money, and you don't have a thing to worry about."

We go in and choose a booth next to the window. Me and Jack sit on one side of the table, and the girls face us on the other side. We order sodas. Ulene asks Jack about something, and he mumbles an answer. I'm concentrating on Fiona. Unlike Lucy, she takes small sips from her straw like a delicate hummingbird. I know she's a goddess.

"Fiona," I say, "your history presentation was real good. I didn't know Laceola had such a history. Where'd you find so much information?"

"That's awfully nice of you to think so. The library has some information about Laceola, but I talked to some of the old-timers around town. One was your grandfather."

"You talked to Granddaddy?" I am surprised he didn't tell me.

"Yes, I did. I like him. He told me some great stories when he served as county sheriff. He told me some things about you too."

"I'm glad you talked to Granddaddy. He knows a lot about Coosa County and Laceola. Listen, I guess me and Jack had better go."

Boy, this is hitting close to home. Granddaddy wouldn't dare tell her my real name or about me being scared of Santa Claus when I was little. I ain't scared of nothing now, well, maybe ghosts, but I still don't like Santa Claus. I just know Granddaddy wouldn't tell.

"You ready, Jack?" I ask.

"No, this is gettin' interesting. What did he tell you about Sport, Fiona?"

"Nothing really juicy. He said Sport was born during a thunderstorm. Dr. Styles delivered him. He also said Sport is a free spirit, much like himself at twelve years old. Sport loves to climb an old cedar tree, and he had rather walk or run than ride."

"I'll be thirteen on August twenty-third," I say.

"I know that. Tell us more, Fiona," Jack urged.

"That's about all he told me. Except that Sport's family settled in Coosa County in the 1840s after the Cherokees were forced out."

Good old Granddaddy. I'll have to thank him for not telling everything he knows like the time I got hung up in my cedar tree for half a day when my pants snagged a limb or the time I fell into Little Snake Creek, then pulled my clothes off and ran home naked as a baby jaybird.

"Is that all, Fiona?" Jack asks.

"My family's been here since before the War Between the States," Ulene says. "Would you like to see some of Daddy's Civil War collection, Jack? If you come over to my house, I'll show you."

"Yeah, maybe I'll do that. But Sport and I have to go now. Don't we, Sport?"

When we hit Main Street, I say, "Jack, old buddy, you just had yore first date with the lovely Ulene MacFadden, and ya didn't even know it."

"You and Ulene cooked up this whole mess, didn't you?" Jack frogs me on the arm, but I laugh so hard I don't feel the pain. All in all, it is a pretty good day. I get to sit close to Fiona at the soda shop. Okay, maybe it was across the table, but that's close. And I get to talk to her. That's the best part of the day. Maybe my lousy luck is changing for the better.

13

JACK

I'm not comfortable sitting across from Ulene. Sport and Ulene cooked this whole thing up with the picture show and soda shop. See if I ever trust Nathan Bedford Kirk again. He sits there mooning over Fiona Burns, who is just another danged ol' girl. She's a spoiled brat if I've ever seen one. He hangs on her every word like a lovesick jackass. Ah ha! Now she acts like Sport's granddad has let out a deep dark secret about Sport, and he blushes.

"You ready, Jack?" Sport asks.

"No, this is getting interesting. What did he tell you about Sport, Fiona?" I ask. I'll let Sport squirm just to get even for getting me into this mess. I watch him as Fiona goes on about what his granddad told her. I almost laugh at the way Sport looks around for a way to escape from Fiona's story.

Fiona finishes telling her great nothing secrets about Sport.

"Is that all, Fiona?" I ask. Maybe I should tell her about how Sport is afraid of Santa Claus. By the gods, that would turn his liver.

Ulene starts in about her daddy's Civil War collection. Man, I have to get out of here. Sport is obviously ready to go, and so am I.

When we turn the corner onto Main Street, Sport makes this stupid comment about it being my first date with Ulene, and I frog him as hard as I can. He laughs his ass off. At the footbridge at Little Snake Creek, we see Jimmy Banks, a colored boy who plays softball with us, trying to get something out of the creek.

"What you got, Jimmy?" Sport shouts.

"A big snappin' turtle," he shouts back.

"Let's go help," Sport says and takes off running down the levee. I follow.

The snapping turtle tries to escape into the creek. Jimmy Banks stands between it and freedom. The turtle hisses and snaps at the stick Jimmy pokes at it. It's one of the biggest turtles I've ever seen.

"You gonna take it home, Jimmy?" I ask.

"Naw, it ain't no good to eat. It's a nasty looking thing."

"Don't let it get a grip on your leg. It'll hold on 'til it thunders," Sport advises.

"It'll eat every fish in this creek including sun bream and catfish," Jimmy says.

The turtle stands his ground. Jimmy pokes his stick at it again, and the turtle grabs it and breaks about four inches off the end. Jimmy jumps back.

"If you ain't gonna eat it, let it go," Sport says.

Jimmy and the turtle eye each other. I hear something at the top of the levee. Three objects drop over the edge and roll down toward us.

"It's cherry bombs," Sport shouts as one explodes just to the left of where he stands. Another sends a plume of water up in a dull thud. The third lands five feet behind the turtle and bursts in a flash of light and smoke. Bits of mud and gravel hit my face and chest. The turtle scrambles past Jimmy and splashes into the creek.

"Run," screams Jimmy as three more cherry bombs arc over the levee. Sport leads off like a flash of light. Behind him, Jimmy and I slip and slide along the creek toward the footbridge. I concentrate on running as fast as I can as the cherry bombs go off one after the other. I hear laughing and whooping from the top of the levee.

"Hey, what the hell you boys tryin' to do? Kill somebody?" Mr. Lindsey, our neighbor, shouts from the middle of the footbridge.

The three of us pull up just short of the bridge and look back. I see four people disappear along the levee. My heart pounds from fear and running as we climb slowly up the bank to the bridge.

"Y'all all right?" Mr. Lindsey asks.

"Yes, sir," we answer.

"Bunch of damn idiots. Throwing cherry bombs like that. They could've put yere eyes out or busted yere eardrums. Ought to call the cops to 'em 'cause they ain't suppose to be shootin' off no fireworks in the city limits anyhow. Well, if y'all are okay, I'll be gettin' along home. Y'all just be careful who ya choose to play with," Mr. Lindsey says and walks off toward his house.

"Jimmy. Jack. Don't say nothin' about this to anybody. I'm in enough trouble, and I don't want Mama and Daddy to know," Sport says, breathing hard through his mouth. "They'll never let me come to the creek again."

Jimmy Banks looks at Sport in a strange way.

"Them peoples're serious crazy. I don't want no trouble, so I ain't saying nothin', and I ain't comin' down here to no creek no more. Spo't, I gonna stay away from you. You dangerous, man."

He isn't dangerous. It's those people who are after him. It sounded like teenage boys this time, but next time who knows?

Sport doesn't talk on the way home. I can tell he's steaming mad by the way he kicks at rocks and grass along the way. When we get to his house, he turns and looks at me with gunmetal gray eyes. His left eyelid twitches.

"I'll get even with 'em, by damn," he says.

"You don't know who they are, Sport."

"It won't take me long to find out. And when I do, I'll even the score one way or another."

14

SPORT

It's rained for three days straight. In Granddaddy's words, "It rained like pouring piss out of a boot." A ray of sunlight breaks through dark clouds and shines into our classroom window. Thank God, the rain has stopped. Me and Jack can go down to the creek this afternoon without worrying about school for the rest of the week. Our Easter holiday begins tomorrow, and we'll have two days to do nothing. The weather turned cold as if were January. But that won't stop us from having fun.

After school I tell Mama me and Jack are going up to a narrow part of Little Snake Creek near the railroad bridge to see what kind of things washed up on the creek bank. It happens almost every year. The creek rises to a flood stage. The levee, constructed during the '30s and '40s, holds the rushing water away from downtown Laceola, but the creek floods part of the countryside after it passes through town. Heavy rains bring a lot of stuff down with the water. One time we caught a rowboat. It wasn't much good because it had a hole in the bottom. Another time we pulled a bicycle out of the floodwater.

"You boys don't get too close to the water and don't get wet or you'll catch a cold," Mama warns. "Be back before it gets too dark to see where you're walking."

"Don't worry," I tell her. "We won't get our feet wet. Ha ha."

I pull on my heavy fur-lined jacket. Jack also wears a heavy coat. We walk down Walnut Street, and I salute my cedar tree as I pass by. At the footbridge, we check out the level of the creek. The water runs swift three or four feet below the middle of the bridge. We continue on to Main Street where Walnut Street dead-ends. A floodplain as big as two football fields lies on the east side of Main and the south side of the creek. Water stands a few inches deep on the floodplain and empties into the main stream. We cross the Main Street Bridge and take a footpath along the higher north bank of the creek. We reach the Seaboard Railroad Bridge. Water soaks through my brogans, and my socks are wet and uncomfortable.

"The water's too high for us to walk under the bridge," I tell Jack. "We'll have to climb the embankment and cross over the railroad."

"Right," he says.

We slip and slide up the bank. On the railroad, I stop and put my ear to a rail. Jack does the same.

"No trains coming," Jack says.

"Right."

We creep slowly down the other side of the tracks to the creek bank and cautiously continue upstream. About fifty yards beyond the railroad bridge, we stop at a cane break.

"Let's cut a cane so we can poke around in the water," I say to Jack as I open my case knife.

Jack says okay and takes out his knife.

I pick a bamboo cane about six feet long. It's tough and takes an effort to cut through the green cane. Jack has the same trouble, but we get the job done. We strip the small limbs off our bamboo and shape the large end to form a sharp point. Now me and Jack are armed with weapons and walking sticks.

"You think any snakes've washed down?" Jack asks.

"No doubt. Ground's soaked through and through, and snakes go to higher ground. They'll even climb trees to keep away from water. Remember the water moccasins we saw last year? They were holding on to that log like they have arms. I'll bet they made it too. But I'm not scared of them. They won't strike unless you step on 'em, and I don't intend to do that."

We walk down the bank to the edge of the creek and watch the stream swiftly flow toward the railroad bridge. We see a 'possum scramble up the bank on the other side.

"He made it," Jack says.

"Yeah. He'll probably dry off in the middle of a road."

Jack points to a clump of brush floating down the creek. "Look! What kind of animal is that?"

It takes me a couple of seconds to spot what Jack is pointing at. "Don't know. Hey, it looks like a dog. A puppy. Come on. Maybe we can get 'em before he gets to the bridge." I wade into the water and sink up to my knees.

"Hey, don't do that. You can be swept away."

"Naw, not if I'm careful."

"Here!" Jack offers me the end of his bamboo cane. He holds on to one end of the cane, and I hold the other. This gives me about six feet farther into the water. If the clump floats close enough, I can hook it with my cane. I wade thigh-deep in rushing water as the tan and white puppy clinging to brush floats toward me. It kinda looks like Granddaddy's old dog, Roland. When Roland died two years ago, Granddaddy swore he'd never get another dog. If I can catch this puppy, Granddaddy will take him. I can't keep him because Daddy says a dog needs roaming space and shouldn't be locked up in town. The brush holds the puppy half in and half out of the water, but if it hits the bridge, he'll be knocked loose. He won't make it out.

The puppy floats closer. I reach out with my cane. Just a little more, and I'll have him. Come on. Come on. My cane catches the brush and slips off. Dadgumit. The puppy floats by us toward the bridge.

"I missed 'em, Jack!"

Jack pulls me back toward the bank with his bamboo cane. It's hard for me to wade against the strong current to the bank, but I make it with Jack's help. I pull my jacket off and hand it along with my cane to Jack. This is something I have to do.

"Whatcha doin', Sport? Are ya crazy?"

I plunge into the swollen creek. The cold water sends a shiver up my body, and I half-wade and half-swim to the middle of the stream where the water reaches my armpits, then I let the current take me. I keep my eyes on the puppy. With a few hard strokes, I catch him and pull him out of the tangle of brush. The puppy whimpers as I put him on my shoulder and kick with my legs and pull with one arm trying to use the current. It's no use. Dang, my shoes are heavy. I should have taken them off. I can stop myself at the railroad bridge. I look at the bridge, and it's coming up faster than I think possible. I hear Jack screaming at me, but I can't understand him. I see a pylon on the right side of the bridge. I'll catch it and hold on until Jack can get me out.

The creek widens before it reaches the bridge. On my left, water gushes out of the floodplain, adding to the stream. It's swifter down here than it looks from above. I kick my legs to get into position to grab the pylon. The flow from the floodplain creates a swirl too strong for me to fight, and I miss the pylon. As I go under the bridge, I catch a glimpse of Jack running down the path. I come out on the other side fast. Even if I reach the creek bank, there's no way I can pull myself out. Come on, Nathan Bedford. Think. Forget the Main Street Bridge. There's nothing there to hold on to. My next chance is the footbridge, after that the Mason Avenue Bridge, and then the Highway 100 Bridge. That's my last chance to stop. After the Highway 100 Bridge, it's a long float to where the creek widens and the water is shallow enough to walk out.

I don't know how far that is. I once borrowed a boat from Cal Slowman, and me and Jack floated all the way to the Old Mill dam one or two miles down from the railroad bridge. I try to picture our trip. There has to be another bridge, but I can't remember it. The puppy is shaking, and so am I.

I see the footbridge. I'll go under the center of the bridge to keep from bashing my head in on the wooden frames. I gather my strength so I can jump far enough out of the water to grab the underside with one hand. It's only three, maybe four, feet above the water at that point. The stream speeds up, and I push down to find the creek bottom with my feet. Doggonit, I can't reach the bottom.

"Jack, Jack!" I scream as I break the surface. But the only thing I see when I look back is the bridge moving away from me. The puppy snorts water from his nose. I move fast now.

"Settle down," I tell myself. "You're a strong swimmer."

It seems like seconds before I see the Mason Avenue Bridge. The creek narrows as faster water smashes into the side of its concrete pylons. I know not to attempt a try at the bridge's edge. The concrete could knock me out so I slide under Mason Avenue. To keep my courage up, I silently sing Granddaddy's version of "The Yellow Rose of Texas." Water slips into my mouth as I try to whistle "Garry Owen," the Seventh Cavalry song that I heard in the movie *They Died with Their Boots On*. Dang it, I got myself into this, and I'll get myself out. I round a bend in the creek and see the Highway 100 Bridge. A man wearing a dark green raincoat with the hood pulled over his head stands in the middle of the bridge. He sees me and waves. I try to wave back, but I can't lift my arm. The man disappears. What lousy luck. He didn't see me after all. I look to see if there is anything I can grab onto, but the levee is bare on both sides of the creek. The water carries me to the left side, and I feel too tired to hold on to the puppy. My legs seem to have disappeared because I can't feel anything below my hips. I want be able to hold onto a bridge pylon. I don't think I'm going to make it.

15

JACK

The water swirls around Sport. He tries to grab the brush with the puppy but misses. Sport holds on to the bamboo cane, and I pull him back to the creek bank. When he reaches the edge of the water, he takes off his coat.

"Here, Jack, hold this for me."

Hesitating for a second, Sport says, "Ah hell," and plunges into the swollen creek after the puppy.

"Whatcha doin', Sport! Are ya crazy!" I shout at him. He swims out to the middle of the creek and lets the swift water take him toward the puppy. Carrying his coat, I scramble up the creek bank to the footpath. I run along the path, keeping Sport in sight.

"Catch the railroad bridge. I'll getcha there."

I move as fast as I can. My foot hits a patch of wet grass, and I lose my balance. Slipping down the bank, I stop just short of the water. *Come on, Jack,* I tell myself. *You gotta be more careful.* I climb back up to the footpath and look down the creek for Sport. There he is. He has the puppy and moves closer to the railroad bridge. If he can grab a pylon, he can hang on to it.

My heart pounds in my chest. Hurrying down the footpath, I lose sight of Sport for a few seconds. Why would anyone go into a flooding creek to get a nasty dog? Dogs carry fleas and all kinds of vermin on them, and they don't care where they go to the bathroom. Well, it's his choice. I stop to see where Sport is. He's almost at the railroad bridge. Oh no. The current carries him away from the pylon, and I watch him disappear beneath the bridge. The footbridge is his best chance to get out of the creek. I'll get him there.

Up the embankment of the railroad bridge, cross the tracks, slipping and sliding down the other side, I reach the Main Street Bridge and climb up the side to the street. Some fool scratches off with tires squealing. A green car makes a fast turn on Lancer Street. Making it to the middle of the bridge, I see Sport at the footbridge. He disappears under the water and comes up beneath the bridge, and then he's gone. The next bridge is at Mason Avenue. Realizing I can't get there on foot, I run to Mr. Wright's store for help.

Tim Beasley and Bernard Landrum, two sixth graders, come down Main Street on bicycles. They see me running toward them and brake to a stop.

"I need to borrow a bicycle," I scream. "Sport's in the creek. I've gotta chase him."

"What's he doin' in the creek?" Tim Beasley asks.

"He fell in," I shout. "Look, I don't have time to explain. I've gotta get to the Mason Avenue Bridge."

"You can take my bike, Jack," Bernard Landrum.

"Okay, thanks. You two guys wait for me at Wright's store. I'll be back."

I pull my coat off and toss it on the ground along with Sport's. "Here, watch our coats.

I push the bike down the street to gather speed, then jump on it and start peddling fast. I turn left on Lancer Street. I can make it to Mason Avenue Bridge in five minutes maybe. Sweat runs down from the edge of my hair to my face and hangs there. Thick air wraps around my body like wet cheesecloth.

Mason Avenue is in sight. I peddle faster and then make a sharp turn, almost too sharp. I reach the bridge, slam the pedals down, and slide to a stop. I look up the creek and see nothing. I run to the other side. Tree limbs and trash swirl around in the rushing water. Sport has already gone through here. The last place he can grab a pylon is at Highway 100 Bridge. I'll get help. God, I forgot—it's Wednesday afternoon. There won't be anybody around. I'll go back to Mr. Wright's store. Maybe I'll see a policeman on the way.

16

SPORT

I don't have the strength to catch on to the bridge pylons. The only thing I can do is keep my head above water and float. I look up and see the man reappear on the left side of the bridge.

He shouts, "Ho we dum thuk."

I don't understand a dang thing he's saying. He dumps something that looks like a fishnet over the side. It has ropes fastened to it. This is my chance. Somehow I find the last bit of strength and kick my legs to get in position to catch the net.

The bridge squeezes the creek into a funnel and makes it move faster. Oh no. I begin to turn to the right, back to the center of the creek. The man moves the net. My arms and legs are heavy. I guess my clothes and shoes are weighing me down. I don't feel cold anymore, and I'm comfortable, almost sleepy. I think, *Is it worth the energy to try for the net? Heck, yes,* I answer my own question. I kick a few times to get closer to the net. Here it comes. It catches me. The water pulls at me and tries to force me under the bridge, but the net holds. I push my hand and arm through a hole in the net and relax just a little. From the top of the bridge, the man pulls me and the puppy toward the bank. I bang into a concrete pillar a couple of times, but he keeps tugging until I'm away from the swift water. I can't help him because my legs won't move. I hang onto the net as the man drags me up the side of the levee. He gets me out of the water to a place where I won't slip back into the creek and loops the ropes around a steel signpost on the bridge. Then he disappears from the bridge.

My muscles ache, and I feel like I'm going to pass out. A puppy cuddles up to me, and my teeth chatter like I have a chill. I hear a car stop on the bridge. A farmer in overalls gets out of the truck and runs over to where I lay.

"You all right, son?"

I nod my head. "Yes. What am I doing here? Where am I?"

"I don't know what you doin' here, but you musta come out the creek. Damned if you and that dog ain't soaked to the skin. Can you tell me yore name?"

"Sport. Kirk."

My legs are so stiff I can hardly walk, so the farmer half-carries me to his truck and covers me and the puppy with a horse blanket. It's warm inside the truck, and I begin to feel better.

"Ain't ya George Kirk's grandboy?"

"Yes, sir. Where am I?"

"You're at the Highway 100 Bridge."

"You pulled me out with a fish net"

"No, boy." The farmer gives me a look.

"You're not the man that dragged me out of the water? Did you see who it was?"

"Didn't you see him?"

"Yes, but that's all I remember."

"Look, I'll take you home. Where you say you live?"

"On Walnut Street."

I tell the farmer about going into the creek to get the puppy and seeing the man on the bridge, but I can't remember anything else.

"I didn't see nobody. Only thang I saw comin' from the bridge was a green car that met me about a half mile down Highway 100."

As we passed Mr. Wright's store, I see Jack.

"I'll get out here."

"You sure you okay? I ought to take you home"

"No, sir. I see my friend. He's probably looking for me, and I feel all right now."

17

JACK

Oh, man. My leg muscles knot up with cramps. I sit on the curb and rub my Charlie horse on my left calves. Dadgumit, it hurts like the devil. The pain brings tears to my eyes, as if I'm not wet enough. I am beat, but I have to get back, cramps or no cramps. I hobble along, pushing the bicycle down Lancer Street until my muscles loosen up. I move as fast as I can with one stop to rest, half way to Mr. Wright's store. There's not a soul around. Guess everybody is staying in today. At Main Street, I get on the bicycle and ride down to the two boys waiting at the store.

"Did ya see Sport?" asks Bernard Landrum.

"How long have I been gone? You guys have any idea?"

"Been maybe forty-five minutes," Tim Beasley says.

Bernard Landrum looks at his watch. "It's been longer than that. Did ya find Sport?"

"Couldn't have taken me that long. He's probably at the Highway 100 Bridge."

"You'd better ask Mr. Wright to call the fire department," Tim Beasley says.

"Yeah. Yeah, I guess I'd better do that."

As I begin to hobble toward the store, an old pickup truck rolls by. "Look!" Bernard Landrum says. "There's Sport."

I turn to see him wrapped up in a blanket on the passenger side, with the puppy looking out the window. The truck crosses Main Street Bridge and slows to a stop at Walnut Street. Sport and the puppy get out. I grab Sport's coat and hobble down the street as fast as I can. A catch in my throat keeps me from finding my voice, and the cold wind brings tears to my eyes. No, I won't lie. I'm crying.

"Sport!" I scream. He turns and sees me. He gives me this half-ass British salute and waits 'til I walk up to him.

"Hey, Jack. I was on my way home 'til I saw you. Oh, you got my coat. Thanks, man. I'm freezing."

"Dang you, Sport. Dang you. That's the craziest stunt you've ever pulled. That nasty dog ain't worth it."

"Had you worried, didn't I? But not as much as me 'cause I thought I was a goner." He says with a silly grin spread all over his face. "Here, hold the puppy while I put my jacket on. Boy, am I'm tired."

I hold the puppy at arms length while he slips on his coat. "Don't piss on me, dog."

Sport takes the puppy and puts him under his coat.

"How'd you get out of the creek?"

"I remember floating down to Highway 100 Bridge. Some man threw a fishnet over the side, and I caught it. He pulled me up the bank to safety."

"Who was it?"

"Dadgumed, if I know. He tied off the rope on a steel pole at the end of the bridge and disappeared. I don't remember anything else until that farmer came along and saw me lying on the bank. Now, I'm gonna tell Mama and Daddy I got wet going into the creek after the dog. But I'm not gonna tell 'em how far down the creek I went. That's not a lie, okay."

"All right. But no more heroics. The gods were with you this time."

We slosh down Walnut Street toward home.

18

SPORT

I go through the back door onto our screened-in porch. For rainy days, we have a clothesline strung across one end of the porch. I'll shed my wet clothes and hang them up to dry.

"Mama! I'm wet, and I need a towel."

Mama opens the kitchen door. "Sport, I thought I told you not to stay outta the creek. What do you have there?"

"It's a little puppy. I rescued him from the creek." I hold the puppy so she can get a good look at him.

"He's pretty and just a baby. You can't keep him, Sport. Yore Daddy'll have a hissy. Now get out of those wet clothes while I get you some dry ones."

"Granddaddy'll take 'em," I tell her as she disappears into the house.

The puppy licks my face. "I'm glad I got you, little dog. I'll let Granddaddy name you since you'll be his dog. I'll bet you'll be brave and smart."

George, my cat, shows up. He takes one look at the puppy and runs off to hide. George doesn't like babies of any sort, not even my little brother. I guess he can't stand the crying.

Mama brings me a change of clothes, a towel, and a cardboard box stuffed with an old quilt. "Dry the puppy off before you put him in the box. He looks hungry. I'll get some ham scraps for him. I hope he's old enough to eat solid food."

"He's gonna be a big dog, and he'll eat. I have to call Granddaddy to tell him about his new dog. Boy, will he be surprised."

I dry the puppy off and put him in his box. Chill bumps pop up all over me as I change into dry clothes and hang my wet ones on the clothesline. I take the puppy into the kitchen and find the ham scraps Mama left in a bowl on the table. The puppy dives into the ham as if he hadn't eaten in a week. George sneaks into the kitchen and peeks around a cabinet at the puppy. The puppy sees George and stops eating long enough to growl just loud enough for George to hear. George disappears again.

Hey, no more school this week. Day after tomorrow is Good Friday. I can spend the day with Granddaddy and his new dog. But first I have to plan how to spring it on him. Maybe I'll tell Granddaddy that the puppy is a birthday present five months early. The phone rings in the living room, and Mama answers.

"Sport, it's Jack."

I grab the phone. "Jack, you okay?"

"I'm callin' to see how your nasty dog is doing. I'll bet he stinks. Wet dogs always stink."

"I can't understand why you don't like dogs."

"Dogs stink."

"Okay, but this puppy doesn't stink. He's probably as clean as he'll ever be."

"Listen. The puppy belongs to someone. What you intend to do with him?"

"I'm givin' him to Granddaddy. He needs a dog to keep him company. But if someone claims him, I guess he's theirs."

"You want to come over later?"

"I'd better not. I'll have to take care of the puppy."

"Well, I'll tell ya now that I won't be here for Easter. Mama and I are going down to visit my aunt in Columbus. We're leaving after the bank closes on Friday and won't be back until Sunday night."

"Okay. I'll see ya tomorrow. I gotta call Granddaddy now."

Granddaddy answers the phone with a gruff, "Hello."

"Is that you, Granddaddy?" We always go through this routine.

"Who were you expectin'? Harry Truman?"

"I've got a problem and need you to help me out? I pulled this little white and tan puppy out of Little Snake Creek. He washed down from somewhere east of Laceola, so I don't know who it belongs to. Couldcha keep it until we find the owner? I can't take care of it here."

"Old Roland was white and tan. Are ya tryin' to put somethin' over on me, boy?"

"No, sir. I wouldn't do that. He's a lonely little puppy, that's all."

"Want me to come over now?"

"Couldcha come tomorrow? I wanna keep him tonight,"

Granddaddy agrees, and I know I hooked him just like a catfish. When he sees the puppy, I'll reel him in. Old Roland was with him all the time, and after he died, Granddaddy got the blues so bad he hardly ate anything for a couple of weeks. That's why he swore he'd never get another dog.

"Sport," Mama calls. "Your dog piddled on the kitchen floor. Get in here and clean it up."

Oh, man. I don't think I'm ready to take care of a dog. At least old George goes in a box. I clean up the mess and take the puppy to my room. I try to think how long it takes food to go through a dog. If my experience with my little brother counts for anything, I calculate the puppy will get the urge to do number two in the middle of the night. I hope he can hold it until morning.

I watch the sun rise through white billowy clouds while the puppy does his business in our backyard. If I were a poet, this could inspire me. Not the puppy, the sun. Granddaddy drives up and walks around the house.

"Hey, boy. Does that dog bark at the moon?"

"You're the one who'll train 'em. Teach 'em not to bark at anything but 'possums. Look at his feet. He's gonna be a big dog."

"Yes, sir. He kinda looks like old Roland. He'll turn into a fine animal. Bring the dog and come on. I need a cup of your mother's strong coffee."

I leave the puppy in his box on the back porch. Daddy and Granddaddy sit at the kitchen table and talk about business.

"They're building a few houses north of town, but Coosa County's not growing fast enough. In fact we're losing people. I can name at least five families who've moved away since Christmas," Daddy says.

"We need more and better industries. Textile mills don't pay enough. Educated people won't settle for mill work."

"Are you taking that puppy, Pa?" Mama asks, interrupting the talk.

"Sure am. I'll see if anybody claims it. Otherwise it's gonna be Sport's and my dog, fifty-fifty. I get the front half and Sport can take care of the back half. Is that a deal, Sport?"

"I'll have to think about that."

"Have you heard anything about the Thompsons?" Daddy asks.

"Been quiet, and I don't expect 'em to raise their ugly heads. Billy Macwain keeps a watch on 'em. He'll let me know if he suspects anything.

Daddy tells us he has to get to work.

"You mind if Sport and the dog come with me, Missy?" Granddaddy asks Mama. She gives her permission.

Granddaddy motions to me. "It's too wet to plow, so we'll have plenty of time to start training your half of the dog. We'll name him too. Get the puppy and saddle up."

I think of Jack, and I know he's sleeping in, so I'll call him from Granddaddy's place. Maybe we can get together later today.

19

SPORT

Tomorrow is Easter. Because it comes on April 17, everybody says it's late this year. Last year it was in March, and I don't know why the date keeps changing. Jack says it's a moveable feast, so it moves to a different date every year while Christmas stays the same.

My family keeps Easter Sunday holy, but we never have what you would call a feast. All of us, me, Mama, Daddy, Granddaddy, Uncle Earl, and my little brother won't miss church on Easter. St. Luke's Methodist Church has two services on Sunday; one is at sunrise, which we never attend, and the other is the regular service at eleven o'clock. All the women and girls dress up in their newest outfits, and there's an Easter egg hunt after the service. I'm too old to hunt eggs, and my little brother doesn't know what an egg is, so Granddaddy is taking me to Pete Kelly's Diner for lunch after church. I love the gravy burgers Mr. Kelly makes, and Granddaddy will buy me two. I really miss Jack. Saturdays are not the same without him.

"Sport! Come in the house," Mama calls me from the back porch.

I go into the living room and see Miss Sally with Dink's mama and daddy waiting for me.

"Do you remember me, Sport?" Dink's daddy asks.

"I remember seeing you when y'all came to visit Miss Sally and Dink."

"We've come to thank you for what you did for Dink, and I want to give you a reward. Here's twenty-five dollars. I know you can put it to good use."

Hey, I can buy a new radio and have enough leftover to pay Mr. Spiers for more airplane rides. But it's not right for me to take the money.

"No, sir. Thank you, but I can't take it."

"What's the matter? Isn't my money good enough for you? Or is it you can't take money from a Negro?"

"No, sir. I didn't do nothing for any reward. What I did, I did because Dink needed help."

I think I made a bad decision. Oh well, I never do the right thing around grownups anyway. I look at Daddy, and his face is turning red. But he doesn't say anything.

"Buddy Roberts! You just shut yo' mouf," Miss Sally says. "Dis boy's as good as dey come. He don' want no reward fo' doin' da raht thang."

"You sound like an old Uncle Tom. You cozy up to the very people who held us in slavery and still keep us down. You'll never be out from under the thumb of the white man," Buddy Roberts tells Miss Sally.

"I'm still yo' mama. You don' talk to yo' mama dat way. You may be edjacated, but you ain't vera smart. Dis boy's great-great-granddaddy bought Mama Nicey when she was a little girl and about to be sent to some plantation in Mississippi. Dis fambly raised her just lak she be they own flesh and blood. Don' you talk to yo' mama dat way!"

"Mama, calm down, you'll have a stroke."

"After my mama died and my daddy was killed on da railroad, dis fambly fed Mama Nicey and me 'til we gets daddy's money from da railroad. Mama Nicey's part of dis fambly, and she love dis fambly," Miss Sally pauses for a deep breath. "You best 'member where you come from and how you got where you got. And whens you goes back up no'th, dis boy goin' be raht here. You thank it gon' be easy fo' him in dis mess?"

'I know wha—"

"Shut yo' mouf. I ain't thru. We've been sendin' up prayers for he safety every day. You ain't da one dat goin' be testifying against dem criminals. You take a good look at dat boy. You look at him and see da future, and you better get dat monkey off'n yo' shoulder befo' you dig yo'self a hole."

Buddy Roberts looks at Miss Sally sheepishly, then turns to me and says, "I guess I've been talking when I should have been listening, Sport. I sincerely apologize to you and your family for speaking the way I did, and I realize your good deed was from the heart. I want you to know that I sincerely appreciate what you did for Dink and what you're doing. Perhaps I can send you a little something from Chicago. A gift, not a reward."

"I'd like that."

Remind me never to get on the bad side of Miss Sally.

After Dink's folks leave, I ask, "Daddy, is it true what Miss Sally said about our family owning Aunt Nicey?"

"It's true. As I understand, she was a little girl when she came to live with our family, and she stayed with the family until she got married in the 1870s. Your great-great-granddaddy gave her about ten or fifteen acres of land in Ducktown as a wedding present. Of course, there was no Ducktown then.

They were the first family to settle there, and they raised ducks. You ought to ask your granddaddy about it because he knows more than I do."

I can't believe my family ever owned a slave, but I guess a lot of people owned slaves in the 1800s. In a strange way, our families are tied together. Maybe not by blood, but the ties are there. Now I know why Granddaddy visits Aunt Nicey about once a month, and she doesn't even recognize him anymore. I don't understand why he's never told me about our families.

20

SPORT

I wake up on Easter morning. The sun is a red ball against my window shade, but that can't be. The sun doesn't reach my window until midmorning. I get out of bed and lift the shade. Oh, Lord! Something is burning in our front yard. I run out of my bedroom and yell for Daddy and Mama to get up.

"There's a fire out in the yard," I scream.

Daddy stumbles out of his bedroom and goes into the living room. I'm right behind him, and Mama is behind me. Daddy slowly opens the door. The smell of kerosene floats into the house.

"Those sorry sons of bitches. I will kill every last one of them," Daddy screams.

In our front yard, a large cross blazes from top to bottom. I feel heat coming through the door, and I remember my nightmare. Mama grabs the phone and calls the fire department. I can hear sirens from fire trucks rumbling down Walnut Street. Someone has already made the call.

"Stay inside, Sport," Daddy says.

Mama gets my little brother out of bed and holds him. She's crying. Through the front window, I see firemen pump water on the burning cross. The flames die down, and the cross begins to smolder. Daddy talks with the fire chief. Our neighbors, in various stages of undress, watch from the street and then make way for a police car driven by Dan Wills. I go to Mama and try to keep her from crying. She's trembling, and I hug her. Daddy and Officer Wills come into the house.

"You want one of us ta stay with y'all?" He asks Daddy.

"No. I'll call my family. But I'm going to shoot the first son of a bitch that tries this again. They've warned me, and next time I'll be waiting for 'em."

"Now, Wheeler. Cool down before ya blow a gasket. I'll have Larry stay here for the rest of the night. Y'all go back to bed 'cause ain't nothing to worry about now."

"How the hell you expect us to sleep just knowin' that thing is in our yard? I'm calling Pa and Earl now."

"I'll have the firemen remove it directly. It'll only be a scorched place when y'all wake up."

Daddy comforts Mama and me. I feel sick to my stomach, and my hands are shaking. My little brother sleeps through the sirens, truck horns, and everything. A few minutes later, Granddaddy and Uncle Earl arrive.

"Don't worry, honey," Granddaddy tells Mama. "They won't be back tonight. They done their dirt, and they're too yellow to show up in daylight."

"I say we strike them now, tonight," Uncle Earl says as he lights up a Lucky Strike. "They won't be expectin' it. We can be in and out of there before daylight."

"We don't know for sure who did this," Granddaddy says.

"That's just the lawman talking. Hell, you know it's the Thompsons and their low-life Klan buddies. I say we go down to Lawson Hill and kick the shit out of 'em."

"Pa's right, Earl. Maybe it wasn't the Thompsons. We can't know for sure," Daddy says. "I'm mad as hell, but let's think this thing through. Besides, there's only the three of us."

"And we can't just go off without a plan," Granddaddy says. "You know that anybody can be a Klansman. All ya need is a sheet, a wooden cross, kerosene, and a match. Let's think about this for awhile."

Daddy persuades Mama and me to go back to bed, but I don't sleep. I listen to the three men talking in the living room. Before my eyes get too heavy to keep open, I hear Daddy say, "I'm confident the law'll take care of 'em, and we don't want to stir up any more trouble than we already have. I can protect my home and family, and that's all that matters to me. If anybody tries anything around here, I'll shoot to kill. But I'm not goin' out after 'em."

We don't go to Easter service, and Granddaddy and me don't get to eat at Pete Kelly's Diner. A lot of friends and neighbors, including Sheriff Macwain and Chief Manners, come by Sunday afternoon, and some ladies from St. Luke's Methodist Church bring food for us. Reverend Sommers offers up a prayer for us and for those men who desecrated the cross. Some of the men whisper about forming a group of vigilantes. Sheriff Macwain calms them down and tells them to go home. In a private talk with Daddy and Granddaddy, he asks them not to give any encouragement to organize vigilantes.

Daddy tells Chief Manners not to post a guard at our house.

"I want to show our neighbors and everybody in Laceola that we're not afraid."

Chief Manners agrees.

Sunday is a good night for radio. After *Archie Andrews*, *Our Miss Brooks*, and *The Shadow* go off, I listen to *The Jack Benny Show*. Daddy comes in and sits on the side of my bed.

"Sport, your mother and I've been talking about you and the situation we find ourselves in. How'd you like to spend the next few weeks with Uncle Luke and Aunt Minnie?"

"I can't do that. I'll get too far behind in school."

"We thought about that. We can get someone to help you catch up during the summer. You can still go into the eighth grade in September."

That sounds pretty good to me, but I'd have to leave my friends and my cedar tree. Before I agree, I ask Daddy, "Is that what you and Mama want me to do?"

"Yes. You'll be safer in Alabama. We can't watch you every minute of the day, and we're afraid the Thompsons or some of their friends will try to get to you."

"What if I don't wanna go?"

Daddy sighs. "We know how much school means to you, but you're in danger, and that cross is just a warning. Those scum play hardball, and they don't want the Thompson brothers to go to jail. So they'll try almost anything short of murder to keep you from testifying."

"I ain't changing my mind. Besides, if they can get me here, what's to stop them from going after me in Alabama? Wouldn't that put Uncle Luke and Aunt Minnie and my cousins in danger too?"

"Sport, you're right. But they won't know where you are."

"Daddy, the second I step outside the city limits, everybody in Laceola will know where I am. I don't wanna go because I know this town and feel safer here than any place. I'll stay here with you, Mama, my brother, Granddaddy, and Uncle Earl. I love staying with my cousins, and it's tempting, but this is my town. I belong here, not in Alabama. And I ain't going."

"You're a stubborn Scot just like all the Kirks. Just think about it for a while. You can always change your mind and don't go out unless you tell your mother or me. Always travel with a group and make sure you're in shouting distance of people. Your mother or granddaddy will take you and pick you up at school. And don't talk to strangers or anyone you're suspicious of. Tomorrow's a school day, so you'd better get some sleep. Your mother will come to tell you goodnight and turn the radio off."

"Daddy, I don't want anybody to take me or pick me up at school. That's sissy stuff."

21

SPORT

I keep my thoughts all bottled up, and sometimes it gets pretty hard to keep from screaming. For two days, nobody at school, except Jack, says anything about the cross burning. Even Eugene Laney keeps his mouth shut. I wish somebody would ask me something, but they act like it didn't happen.

Miss Langford, Principal Grant's secretary, knocks softly and enters Mr. Pritchard's classroom. She whispers something to him. "Ah . . . ah . . . Sport, your grandfather is waiting for you at the principal's office. He needs you to go with him. Gather your books . . . ah . . . ah . . . you may not be back today."

I get my books from my desk and walk down the hall to the office. I guess my parents decided to take me out of school after all. This is a double cross. Granddaddy stands at the office door talking to the principal.

Mr. Grant says to me, "Sport, if you don't make it back today, don't worry. We'll have your friend Jack bring your assignments to you." He turns to Granddaddy and says, "George, you take care of this boy."

"Ya know I will, Fred. Come on Sport. We've got things to do."

As we walk out to Granddaddy's old Roadmaster, he tells me that the colored people in Coosa County are up in arms. We're meeting with Sheriff Macwain and a group of citizens from Ducktown. The sheriff specifically requested my presence at the meeting.

It takes us five minutes to reach the sheriff's office at the courthouse. Waiting there are five men with Sheriff Macwain. Charles Jackson is there and gives me a big toothy grin, which makes me feel all right. Mr. Meeks, the undertaker, stands with Reverend Gibson and two others I don't recognize.

"Okay," Sheriff Macwain says. "Now that we're all here, let's get on with the meeting. Who wants to start?"

Mr. Meeks, a leader of the Democratic Party in Ducktown and a supporter of Sheriff Macwain, begins, "We've got some concerns. That's why we invited young Sport to be here because we want him to hear our concerns. We know the law's pursuing this Thompson brothers' case. We know y'all are doing the right thing, but our people aren't happy with the intimidating incident that happened last Easter Sunday. This is the first time a cross has been burned in front of a residence for at least forty years. What intimidates the Kirk family, intimidates us."

Charles Jackson grimaces. Reverend Gibson seems to be in deep thought or prayer. The other two men frown, but Sheriff Macwain shows no emotion.

"Sport and his family are in some danger," Mr. Meeks continues. "We want assurances that these good people will receive adequate protection by county authorities and Laceola police department. You have a good deal of influence with many elements of this county, and we want you to use that influence. Barring that, we expect you to furnish protection."

Granddaddy tells me on many occasions how the sheriff is the chief law enforcement officer in the county and how deep his authority runs. "If the sheriff is good, he knows everything that goes on in the county and can keep criminal elements in check. If he's bad, a county will rot from the inside out with corruption." Granddaddy has a lot of confidence in Sheriff Macwain.

Reverend Gibson looks up from his prayer and speaks, "We want the man who shot Dink Roberts to come to trial. Sheriff, you know Coosa County has had a long peaceful existence between races. Other than the Klan rally back in '45, there hasn't been extremism on either side. We want you to make sure there will be a trial, a fair trial, but there's gotta be a trial."

"There will be a trial," the sheriff says.

Reverend Gibson pauses and looks at the sheriff. "The Negro people in Coosa County are riled up, as you can imagine. I am united with other ministers in the county to keep a lid on this steaming cauldron. However, if the legitimate authorities cannot protect this boy and his family, we've got plenty of volunteers to see no harm comes to him."

"Sheriff Macwain, we know y'all can get word to certain elements," Mr. Meeks says. "We'd like for you to pass this message to that element. Guns and ammunition may be bought and used by all people."

"You've had yore say, now I'll have mine," Sheriff Macwain begins. "I woosh to God the Thompson trial was tomorrow. No one in Coosa County wants 'em to answer for this crime more'n I do, and y'all know it's true. They will be tried and found guilty. Tom Snow is a prosecutor on the move, and he wants to be a judge someday. He won't back off, so they's no need for people shooting at each other. I don't intend to have any kind of armed conflict in Coosa County. And that goes for all sides of this issue. Both Chief Manners and I have offered protection to Sport and his family."

The sheriff looks over at Granddaddy and me. "George'll confirm what I say's true, and they've refused our help. God knows why. I've sent a message to that element y'all refer to, but you know I cain't keep tabs on everybody every minute of the day. I cain't promise, even with a guard on Sport every hour of the day, that these people won't try something. They've made the Thompsons a cause, and I cain't do a damn thing 'bout that."

The men don't act satisfied, but they accept what the sheriff says. They spend another fifteen or twenty minutes talking politics with the sheriff and Granddaddy. Georgia is a one-party state, the Democratic Party, and all elections are decided in the primary. The general election just makes it legal. The men discuss about who may be running for local offices and who won't be running. Sheriff Macwain has the backing of the colored people because he opened up voter registration to them after the courts outlawed the poll tax. Granddaddy says that he will never be voted out of office as long as the colored community supports him.

The meeting breaks up, and Sheriff Macwain asks Granddaddy and me to stick around for a few minutes. After he escorts Mr. Meeks, Reverend Gibson, and the others out of his office, he tells Granddaddy, "George, you heard what I said about protection. Damn it, if y'all won't accept it, I can't force ya. What's the matter with you Kirks?"

"Billy," Granddaddy says. "Wheeler don't believe anybody'll hurt Sport or any of us. Even the cross didn't convince him. And frankly, I don't believe it either 'cause they ain't that stupid."

"But it's not the goddamned Thompsons. It's them agitators coming from outside our county. Y'all know who the leaders are, and they won't do nothing. But they'll agitate some crazy son of a bitch enough to start a race war. I just woosh I knew who that crazy will be," the sheriff says. "Listen. Y'all be careful and don't let Sport out of ya sight. Or maybe it would be better if Sport could disappear into parts unknown until we need him. We'll do whatever we can to keep things quiet 'til the trial."

"Sir, I ain't goin' nowhere."

"Okay, Sport. You're as hardheaded as your daddy and granddaddy."

"Yes, sir. I guess you're right."

Granddaddy cuts a piece of tobacco off a plug of Apple Sun Cured and pops it into his mouth as we walk to where the old Buick is parked on the street. Bert Appling, smoking a cigarette, leans against the front fender of the Buick.

"Howdy, George," he says to Granddaddy.

"Bert," Granddaddy acknowledges.

"I guess y'all been to see the sheriff and met with them niggers."

"Trouble with this county's everybody knows yore business 'bout as soon as you do," Granddaddy says.

"I just thought it was time I spoke with the boy. Might save a lot of trouble."

"Speak," Granddaddy says.

"Listen, boy. We don't wanna cause no trouble for ya, and that thar cross burnin' was a shameful act. I weren't involved, and them that was has had a good talkin' to. I tell 'em we kin reason with old George Kirk's grandson. That nigger boy didn't die, and nobody's got hurt yet. Hell, all's ya have to do's tell Macwain ya made a mistake. You could say ya just thought ya saw Frank Thompson shoot that nigger. Y'all kin do that, cain't you?"

"No, sir. I can't go back on my word. I know what I saw, and now everybody else does too."

"I'm truly sorry to hear ya say that, boy. I'd say yere just pissing into a strong wind 'cause no white jury's gonna convict the Thompson brothers no how. Now I stand opposed to any kind of violence, but they's some hotheads who don't care what they do. Why don't ya think about it? Ain't no skin off'n my nose if ya press this thang. I just thought I'd settle this without it agit'n outta hand."

Granddaddy spits a stream of tobacco juice at his feet and says, "Bert, you've delivered yore message. Now, I'll deliver mine. If any harm comes to this boy, I don't know if I can control Earl. He hasn't quite got killing out of his system, and he's just itching for action. And by god, I'll be right b'side 'em along with some people y'all don't wanna tangle with."

Granddaddy opens the passenger door for me, and I get in. The man's face takes on a pained expression as he flips his cigarette to the sidewalk and crushes it with his shoe. We leave him staring down at the crushed cigarette.

The meeting with the sheriff and the Negro community leaders surprised me. I feel better about my safety. But I'll be looking over my shoulder all the time and suspect everything and everyone. It'll be a cold day in Hades before anything surprises me, not the Thompsons, the KKK, or anything else.

22

JACK

I have my notebook open on the kitchen table and doing math homework when Mom gets home from the bank.

"Hi, Mom! Have a good day?"

"I had an excellent day." She smiled and sat down opposite me.

"Jack, I want to talk to you about something very important to both of us."

Oh, god. Here it comes. She found about what me and Sport did at the creek.

"I'll come right to the point. I'm going to marry Mr. Crocker. He called me this morning and proposed. I accepted because I love John Crocker. You need a father, and I need a husband."

I stare at her with my mouth open, and yet it was no surprise since I've been expecting something like this for a couple of months. Either by chance or will of the gods, Mom met Mr. Crocker at a bank conference last year. They've exchanged letters once a week, and he calls her long distance. He spent last Christmas with us, and we had a lot of fun, unlike some holidays when Mom moped around all sad and blue.

He has driven two hundred and fifty miles from Valdosta to Laceola about five times since Christmas. He takes a room at the Senator George Hotel and stays until Sunday afternoon. Mom cooks supper for him Saturday nights, and then they go out. Sometimes they invite me to go with them to a picture show in Palatine. But I say I have to study or have Sport come over to work on model airplanes. They never insist.

I really don't remember my dad, who died five years ago. Now my memory of him comes from photographs. Mama used to cry a lot. I could hear her at night. Mom's friends tell her to go out and have fun while she's still young. She did go out a few times with single men who came home from the war, but none ever interested her.

"No one can ever take your daddy's place," she told me, and I've had a tinge of guilt for keeping her from meeting someone. When she tells me about Mr. Crocker, I feel relief.

"That's great, Mom. Will he move to Laceola?"

"No, his job is in Valdosta, and we'll move there. John'll be in town tonight, and then we'll all sit down and discuss the details. We'll probably be married in Valdosta. I think it will be a June wedding."

Moving to Valdosta slams me in the gut. I'll have to leave Sport and my other friends, and I don't know what Sport will do without me because I keep him out of trouble. The truth is I don't know how I'll handle not having Sport around.

It's a long drive from south Georgia up to Laceola, so Mr. Crocker has to love Mom to drive hours and hours to get here. He seems like a nice enough man and tells me to call him John. He's never been married and doesn't have a family. When the two of them are together, they act real goofy. They giggle a lot and hold hands. It's pretty sickening to see two grownups act like that.

Jimmy Benefield says he saw them at the picture show in Palatine. "Mr. Crocker had his arm around your mother," he said. I guess that goes along with love, not that I know a lot about romance. What I know I learn from movies. But I'm not the only one who doesn't know much about romance. Sport doesn't either. He acts real goofy around Fiona Burns. I want to puke when he says, "She's awfully nice." Can you imagine him saying *awfully nice?* He's blind as a bat if he can't see how stuck-up she is.

It's time to read my dad's letter again. On my tenth birthday, three years ago, Mom gave me a letter my father wrote to me before the Germans shot him down.

"Jack, I have this letter your father wrote to you from England before he was killed," she said. "I have waited for the right occasion to give it to you. You turned ten today, and I think you're mature enough to understand and appreciate it now. I've read it, and it's a beautiful letter. I want you to read it alone."

Her hand trembled when she offered me the letter. I took it to my bedroom and read it.

November 21, 1944

Dear Jack:

I don't know how to start this letter, so I guess I'll plunge right in.

I hope you'll never have to read it, but I'm writing just in case. I cannot tell you that we are winning. But I don't see how the Germans can hold out much longer.

Now here's the "just in case." I volunteered for the Army Air Corps because I am an experienced pilot. I feel fortunate to have learned to fly at an early age. I have no misgivings about putting myself in danger since flying is a dangerous business anyway. Having been a little older than most of the men here, I thought I would be training pilots more than flying combat missions.

Nothing ever works out the way you plan it, so here I am. I have to fly just a few more missions before I complete my tour of duty. Believe me, I plan to be back there with you and your mother just as soon as I can. I miss your mother and you so very much.

I want you to support your mother with strength and honor. You have the God-given ability to distinguish between right and wrong. Use this ability. Always think before you act and do what you know is right. If you ever find yourself in a situation where you don't feel comfortable, then get out. You've started school. Study and learn.

Stay strong in mind and body. Prepare to cope with any situation in which you find yourself. Choose your friends carefully. Friends can either boost you or bring you down.

We hear that we are patriots and fighting for world freedom. I don't think much about patriotism or freedom. All I think about is getting the job done and coming home in one piece. I hope to see you soon, but if I don't, I'm always thinking of you and your mother.

Love forever,
Your Dad

Whenever I feel down or confused, I read Dad's letter. It is the only contact I have with the Copelands now. Dad's parents, my grandparents, died in a car crash in 1946, and Dad's brother, Les, settled in California after the war. Uncle Les sent me a birthday card and a Christmas present the year after my grandparents' death. But I've not heard from him for a long time. Uncle Les gave my grandparents' house to Mama and me. He said he didn't need to be tied down with anything in Georgia. That helped us out a lot, and someday I'll repay his kindness. When I get enough money, I'll surprise Uncle Les with a visit.

It doesn't make me sad to read the letter. I gain strength from his last words to me as I imagine him in his uniform, and I try to follow the things he told me to do. I'll bet Mom will put all of his pictures and things away now. But

I'll keep a picture of him and his letter with me wherever I go. I read Dad's letter again. I know it will be hard, but I'll prepare myself to face the marriage of Mom and Mr. Crocker.

"Jack, Sport is here," Mama calls from the kitchen.

"You want to eat supper with us?" I hear her ask Sport.

"No, ma'am. I can't stay but a few minutes. I have to go home for supper, but thanks just the same."

"Hey, old buddy," Sport says.

"Whatcha doing coming over here by yourself? Does your mama and daddy know where you are?"

"For some reason I felt a strong urge to come to see you. Hey, they'll never miss me. I'm like the Phantom, the Ghost Who Walks."

"Well, you could've called me. I planned to go over to your house after supper. But I'm glad you came because I got some news."

I tell him about Mom and Mr. Crocker and how I'll be moving to Valdosta. I watch his reaction. He forces a grin, but his gray eyes cloud up.

"Mr. Crocker seems like a nice guy, and I hear that Valdosta has sandy soil, not like this old hard clay up here. I bet y'all have a good time down there. Heck, you can play baseball year round."

Another reason why I like Sport is he does his best to make a bad situation into something better. I never chose Sport as a friend. It just happened. He has ways of getting us in and out of trouble, but it's times like now that I realize how much his friendship means to me.

"When you leave, I'll bet ol' Ulene MacFadden will fall into a deep sleep like Snow White and won't wake up until you come back and kiss her."

I throw a shoe at him.

"See ya later, lover," he says and slips out the door like the Phantom.

Sport makes me feel better. I don't know what time Mr. Crocker will be coming in, probably late, but I know Mom will want me to spend time with him tomorrow. I guess that means I can't hang out with my best friend.

23

SPORT

I never thought I could hate any Saturday, but this is absolutely the worse day of my life. I don't mind admitting that I'm on the verge of crying and that dang twitch of my eye bothers me. Jack Copeland and me have only four or five more Saturdays to run around together. So Jack's mama is marrying that banker she met at some meeting or something. My best friend is leaving, and I'll never see him again. I tell Jack I think it's great that he'll have a daddy, but I don't really feel that way. Neither school nor anything else will be fun anymore.

Granddaddy says that nothing is constant but change, and he's right. My plan with Jack to stay with Aunt Minnie and Uncle Luke this summer is shot down. And that dang trial is coming up, and I don't know how long it will last. Tom Snow says it will be over in two days, maybe less. I'm beginning to doubt anything adults tell me, all except Granddaddy. Max Mendeaux, the know-it-all turd, says a trial can last for weeks.

Granddaddy picks me and Jack up at school almost everyday now, and Mama and Daddy won't let me go anywhere alone. Yeah, you know I'll go along with that for about as long as it takes for me to get out of the house.

It's been two weeks since the cross burning, and nothing has happened. I've slipped out of the house a couple of times to be by myself or to go see Jack. The best place in this world to be alone is in my old cedar tree. Nothing bothers me there, but I can't do that too often for fear of being caught by my parents. The men, who burned the cross, wanted to just scare me and my family, and I know they won't do anything to me. Why should they? Everybody but my family says the Thompsons will never be convicted. But to be on the safe side, I shy away from strangers.

Yesterday, Max Mendeaux dropped by to cheer me up. Ha! He said I was paranoid because I suspect anybody I don't know. I didn't take his comment the wrong way after he explained what it meant. Ol' Max would be paranoid too if he ever looked Frank Thompson in the eye. I wish I had never seen the Thompsons shoot Dink. I wish I had never agreed to testify. Granddaddy said that maybe God put me at that place and time to save Dink's life. That sounds like predestination, and I don't think we're supposed to believe in it. Anyway I have to testify at a trial just because I wanted to get even with Max. Maybe God is punishing me for that.

Other than spending time with Jack, about the only things I do now is listen to the radio, read, and do homework. On the good side, I get As now. My last report card is pretty good. Granddaddy brought me *Betty Zane* by Zane Gray. He has read every book Zane Gray ever wrote. I'll have to read it, but I'm not really that interested in Westerns, except *The Cisco Kid*. I'm reading a collection of Jack London's short stories. "To Build a Fire" is my favorite. I like *The Call of the Wild* too. I saw the picture with Clark Gable and Loretta Young. The written story is a lot better than the picture show.

I look up to see Uncle Earl come into my room.

"Whatcha doing, Sport?"

"Reading."

This is the first time he has ever been in my bedroom. He's kind of perculiar.

"Want to go to the Maple Street Soda Shoppe for ice cream?

"Does a cat have a climbing gear?"

I jump out of my chair and head for the door. I'd go with the devil just to get out of the house.

Uncle Earl has a black 1946 Ford he bought when he came out of the hospital, and I think it may be faster than our Chevy. His car has a radio, but I don't turn it on when I get in like I do in our car. We drive down Main Street and turn left on Maple. Uncle Earl pulls into the parking lot at the side of the soda shop.

"Before we go in, do me a favor, Sport."

"Sure."

"Don't call me uncle. You make me feel like an old man. Just call me Earl."

"Okay, ah, Earl."

I say hello to Eugene Laney, Jimmy Bennefield, Ulene MacFadden, and Lucy Renfoe. Earl orders malt shakes for both of us and slides into a booth facing the door. I sit across from him. We don't have much to say to each other, and I watch Eugene Laney yapping at Ulene. I'll have to tell Jack that Eugene is trying to beat his time with her.

After Earl and I finish eating, he goes up to pay the ticket, and I walk out of the soda shop with Jimmy Bennefield. We're talking about a geography test coming up next week when a man says to me, "So yore that nigger-loving little bastard that's agonna to testify against Frank and Egg. Ya'd better have second thoughts if ya know what's good for ya, you little son of a bitch," the man says.

He pokes a fat finger in my chest and shoves me against the side of the soda shop. I try to get around him, but he holds me there. I hear my heart beating like the dickens.

"Hey, mister!" Jimmy Bennefield shouts.

A hand grabs the man's arm. It pulls the man around, bounces him off a parked car, and flips him over onto the ground. It's Earl. He winds up on top and has the man by the throat. The man outweighs my uncle by about fifty pounds, but Earl is choking him.

"You know I can kill you, you sorry piece of shit. If you come near that boy again, by god, I will."

Earl loosens his grip. The man gets an arm free and swings at him. Earl catches his hand and pulls it back across his arm, and I hear bones cracking. The man screams, gets up, and runs down the street. A crowd from the soda shop gathers around us, and Jimmy Bennefield tells them what happened. I hear Eugene Laney say that he always misses the excitement.

"Y'all want me to call the police, Earl?" Marshall Biggers asks.

Earl pulls out a Lucky Strike and lights up. "Naw, it's all over. We're going home."

I am stunned because I have never seen anything happen so fast in my life. It is all over in seconds. Uncle Earl is stronger than he looks. Back in the car I ask him, "Would you've killed that guy, Uncle . . . I mean, Earl?"

He thought for a second, then says, "If I'd had a knife, he would've been dead before he hit the ground. The army trained me to kill, an automatic reaction. I'm trying to get killin' out of my system, and I've been told it's a long process. But I'll tell ya this, don't dare repeat what I'm about to say. That felt damn good."

I'm glad he is with me. I don't think that man intended to hurt me, but it doesn't do a lot of good for my heart. I can't keep my eye from twitching like a leaf in a windstorm, and I have this empty feeling inside.

I make a serious error in judgment when we get home by telling Mama and Daddy about the fight. I may never get to leave my house again. Earl tells them it was nothing, but he agrees with them about keeping me close. They tell me I can get fresh air by helping Granddaddy in his garden after school and on weekends.

24

SPORT

I aced my geography test today, a flat 100. Tom Snow, the prosecutor, called Daddy to tell us the trial date is set for Monday, June thirteenth, just six weeks from now. It's just my luck for it to be on the thirteenth, but I'm glad it's not on a Friday. I'm not superstitious, just cautious. After school I go with Granddaddy to pull weeds in his garden.

"Come on, Prince," Granddaddy calls the puppy as he chases something at the side of the barn. Old Jen, Granddaddy's mule, watches as we pass.

"Why do you keep that old mule? She doesn't work anymore."

"Old Jen is like me. She's got some years on her, but she can still pull a good plow if called on. Jen was ya grandma's pet, and I just can't sell her or give her to strangers. Besides, you own the back half of her."

"I don't remember Grandma."

"She loved you. Thought you were the cat's meow."

Cal Slowman drives up in his old army jeep. I can't recall ever not knowing him He's Granddaddy's best friend, and I'm a lot closer to him than to Uncle Earl. Cal does't have a father, so I guess Granddaddy sorta adopted him. Granddaddy taught him to ride a horse and shoot. Since he was a little boy, Cal helped Granddaddy in his blacksmith shop. When Granddaddy stopped blacksmithing, he gave the shop to Cal.

Granddaddy says he is full of Creek Indian blood and can shoot the eye out of a moving squirrel at thirty paces from the back of a galloping horse, but I haven't seen him do it. Sometimes Cal disappears into the Alabama mountains for days at a time with nothing but a bedroll and a rifle. On those trips, he doesn't take his jeep or horse, preferring to walk twenty miles or more there and back. Folks say he knows the mountains better than any man alive.

Cal nods to me and says to Granddaddy, "How y'all doing, Top?"

"Strong as that old mule over there."

"I wanna talk to Sport," he says and sits down at the end of a row of string beans. "Ya know how to use a gun, Sport?"

"I'm pretty good with my Remington .22, .410 over and under."

Last Christmas Daddy gave me the Remington, which is a rifle fitted on top of a shotgun, and Granddaddy taught me how to shoot it. Of course, I can't take it out of the gun case unless there's an adult around.

"I'm speaking more of a handgun. A revolver."

"No. I can't hit the side of a barn with a handgun. Granddaddy let me shoot his Colt .45, and I can't even hold it steady."

"I have a .32 Smith & Wesson with a three-inch barrel. It's not heavy, but it's got enough power to tear through flesh and bone at close range. The pistol's yours if you want it. I can teach ya how to shoot."

"Cal, ya trying to arm this boy?"

"Yes. Yes, I am. I hear things around town I don't like."

His eyes flash an anger I have never seen.

"They shot a colored boy, and I might be next. Hell, any one of us might be next, and I think Sport should be ready."

"Now, Cal, I don't cotton to givin' a twelve-year-old a weapon. We appreciate the offer, and if you've a mind to, ya can teach Sport to shoot."

"Yeah, I'd like to learn to shoot a handgun."

I imagine carrying a .32 Smith & Wesson in a shoulder holster that makes a slight bulge beneath my sport coat. Naah, I could never get away with carrying a piece, that's what Granddaddy calls his gun. And I would look silly wearing a sport coat to school every day.

After Cal leaves, Granddaddy says, "He'll make a hell of a good soldier. He's as dependable as the sun, and he rides better than I did at his age. He knows weapons from *A* to *Z* and can track a wildcat over a rocky mountain. I wish I'd had him with me during my soldiering days, but I hope he don't ever have to fight them damn Communist."

"Granddaddy, how can I protect myself if I don't have a gun or something to fight back with?"

"Keep your eyes and ears open and think ahead of them. Don't put yourself in a dangerous position. The scum we're dealing with runs in a pack like coyotes, and they'll try to isolate you and scare you to death, so never be alone. They don't think the Thompsons will go to trial, but they want to make sure by getting to you."

"I'm scared."

"It's okay to be afraid. That can be a good thing because you'll be more aware of your surroundings. If you find yourself in trouble, scream as loud as you can. Someone will hear you. I can't give you any more than that."

25

JACK

"Hey, Sport. I'm going to the school library. Wanna come?" I ask as we leave Mr. Pritchard's class for recess.

"No, Jack. I'm gonna shag some flies. Pow-Pow says I can use his glove while he's hitting 'em to us. I'll meet you outside."

I go into the small library and check out a new book on mythology. You know, the one about Greek and Roman gods and goddesses. I take the book back to my desk in the classroom and go down the hall to the side door. I open the door and see Eugene Laney running and shouting, "Fight! Fight!"

"Who's fightin', Eugene?"

"It's Bobby Froman and Billy Buchanan. They're beating up Sport. Johnny Adkins too!"

Bobby Froman and Billy Buchanan are fifteen-year-olds in Miss Earnhart's seventh-grade class. Both are what you call social promotions. They'll never go any farther than the eighth grade, if they get that far. They're the ones who choose not to study or do homework, and they play hooky a lot. The teachers tolerate them until they are sixteen and can legally quit school. Both are bullies and mean for the sake of being mean. Most of the time at recess, they sneak off and smoke cigarettes. Sport, our friends, and I avoid them.

I follow Eugene out the side door and run around the side of the building. Bobby Froman kicks Sport as he lies on the ground. Billy Buchanan stands with his hand covering his face. Blood seeps through his fingers and runs down his chin.

"Take that, nigger-lover!" Bobby Froman shouts.

As fast as I can, I take a running jump onto his back and knock him down. Rolling over, he gets up the same time I do. Johnny Adkins urges him to get me. Froman squares off to take me on with the meanest look I have ever seen.

My heart is pounding so loud I can hear it, and I can't talk my way out of this. Sport struggles for breath on the ground.

"Copeland, ya jest screwed up," he mutters through clinched teeth.

"Get 'em, Bobby! The bastard broke ma nose," Buchanan spits out the words along with some blood.

Out of the corner of my eye, I see Pow-Pow Johnson coming with a baseball bat in his hand. Pow-Pow is big and powerful for his age, and right now he looks like one of those Roman gods from the book of mythology.

"Back off, Froman, unless you wantcha brains splattered all over the school yard," Pow-Pow shouts as he skids to a stop. Froman and Buchanan look at us and say nothing, a Mexican standoff. Ben Lloyd shows up.

"Ben, see if Sport is hurt," I tell him.

"I'll do it," Eugene Laney says. Ben and Eugene walk over to where Sport lies wheezing and help him up. Sport doesn't look so good.

"Okay, butt holes. What's it gonna be? You wanna fight or just stand there looking stupid?" Pow-Pow says as he taps the bat against his leg.

Sport's knees buckle. Ben and Eugene grab him and walk him around until he begins to breathe better.

"Boys! Boys! What's . . . ah . . . ah . . . going on here?" Mr. Pritchard asks as he trots up with Miss Earnhart not far behind him.

"Aw, we was just playin' around when Sport hits Billy and bloodies his nose," Bobby Froman says.

"Is that right, Sport?"

Sport is still breathing hard and can't answer Mr. Pritchard.

"I saw it all!" Eugene says. "I was comin' around the corner on my way to git a drink of water 'cause I was thirsty from runnin' after fly balls. Pow-Pow was hittin' 'em too far—"

"Ah . . . ah . . . get to the point, Eugene."

"Well, as I was sayin', I saw Bobby, Billy, and Johnny shovin' Sport back and forth and callin' him names."

"I didn't shove nobody," Johnny Adkins says.

"Shut up, Johnny!" Mr. Pritchard says.

"Well, anyways," Eugene continues, "Sport hits Billy in the nose. Blood spurts out all over his face and runs down on his shirt collar. Lots of blood. Then Bobby knocks Sport down and starts kickin' him. That's why Sport cain't hardly git his breath. I'll bet he'll puke any minute now. Ya always puke when ya git hit in the belly, so everybody better stand back unless he wants to git puke all over his shoes."

"Ronald, put that bat down," Mr. Pritchard says and turns to me. "What did you see, Jack?"

"About the same as Eugene. I don't know how it started, but when I got here, I saw Billy holding his nose. Sport was on the ground, and Bobby was kickin' him. I knocked Bobby down. That's when Pow-Pow and Ben showed up."

"They're lyin'," Billy says as he wipes blood off his nose with his shirtsleeve.

"Ah . . . ah . . . Johnny, what's your story?"

"Hey, I got here late. I didn't see nothing, and I didn't do no shovin' and like that. I didn't see nothing."

"Ah . . . ah . . . All of you go down to the office. We'll let Mr. Grant sort this out. I'll have Miss Kersey look at Billy and Sport to see if they're hurt."

Sport is breathing okay now. Boy, is he going to have some bruises. We go into the principal's outer office and sit in chairs along the wall. Mr. Grant comes out of his office and questions each of us while Miss Kersey looks at Billy's nose and Sport's ribs and belly. We tell our story again. I have never been in trouble at school before and hope Mr. Grant doesn't call my mom.

"Okay, boys. My judgment is Billy Buchanan and Bobby Froman deliberately picked a fight with Sport. Now you two will be suspended for a week. Sport, Jack, Ronald, and Johnny, for fighting, you all will stay in during recess for the remainder of the week. I'll not call your parents because you four have not been in any trouble prior to this. But let me warn you that I shall be more severe if it happens again. Do you all understand?" Mr. Grant settles the issue.

"Why da I hav' ta stay in? I din't do nothing," Johnny Adkins whines.

"Johnny, you're lying through your teeth. You take your punishment like the rest of these boys."

Either by chance or will of the gods, Mr. Grant won't call Mom. He is an "okay" principal in my book. Mom will have a nervous breakdown if she hears about this. By this time, recess is over. Sport, Ben, Pow-Pow, Eugene, and I go back to Mr. Pritchard's class. Everybody buzzes until Mr. Pritchard quiets 'em down.

After school Sport shows us the bruises on his ribs and stomach. He dusts his clothes off, but his shirt still has spots of dirt on the back. He'll have to tell his parents what happened.

"Boys, I thank y'all for coming in like that," Sport says. "I know it wasn't yore fight, and I'm sorry I got y'all in trouble. But I thought I was gonna die. Maybe I oughta start carryin' Pow-Pow's baseball bat with me."

Sport describes the fight to his granddaddy when he picks us up at school.

Sport's eye twitched. "I made a mistake by being alone, but I'll never do that again."

"But you have good friends nearby, and they showed a lot of backbone," he says with a hint of pride. "It reminds me of a time back at Fort Riley . . ."

26

SPORT

I'm all stove up, and my whole body aches. It hurts every time I breathe, and purple and yellow splotches have spread all over my belly. But I'm okay, and the battle scars will disappear in a few days. My one good punch broke Billy Buchanan's nose, and I hope he has to suck air through his mouth for the next month.

I tell Daddy and Mama about the fight. Boy, are they mad.

"That's it, Wheeler," Mama says. "We're taking him out of school tomorrow. He can go stay with Luke and Minnie."

My little brother, who looks on from his high chair, says, "Gago. Gagay, gore." He agrees with my mother.

"I guess we all had better move in with Luke and Minnie. Two builders cancelled their contracts today," Daddy tells us. "I'm makin' some sales calls in Palatine tomorrow. To hell with these people in Laceola."

"Wheeler! What are we gonna do about Sport?"

"Wait a minute," I say. "I can take care of myself. I ain't going to Alabama or anywhere else. Daddy, you said you'd back me up, and I'm holding you to that promise."

"Ilene, the boy's right. I made a pledge, and I'll keep it. Right now I'm ticked off enough to defy every man and boy in Coosa County. Sport, stay clear of those boys and always have a friend with you."

Mama looks at us and says, "All right. Sport stays here, but I don't like it. Not one little bit. With the next hint of trouble, he goes. Period."

I lie in bed and listen to WSB Radio in Atlanta. Vaughn Monroe sings, "My heart knows what the wild goose knows." I imagine a flock of geese flying north. This has to be what freedom is all about. I'd like to be able to rise up and fly away from all my troubles, but I made the decision to tell the truth. I got myself into this mess, and I'll have to get out on my own.

A couple of days ago, I overheard a couple of seventh graders at school. "Daddy says they'll never let him testify," one of them said.

"Yeah, I heard they'll run him and his whole family outta town."

"And even if he does testify, ain't no jury gonna convict the Thompsons. There won't be no niggers on that jury."

I don't care what the outcome is. Before the incident on Walnut Street, I thought people around here were great. Now I know better. Like Granddaddy says, "It takes all kinds to make a country," and I know where Bobby Froman, Billy Buchanan, and Johnny Adkins stand. Thank God for Jack Copeland, Ben Lloyd, Pow-Pow Johnson, and even Eugene Laney. They don't think I'm lower than a snake's belly.

I'll bet old Nathan Bedford Forrest would attack. That's what I want to do too if I knew who to attack. In war games me and my friends play, we always win against the Germans or the Japs. We know who we're fighting, but you can't fight an enemy you can't see. Now I understand the meaning of the "invisible empire." But the Thompsons ain't invisible, so I ought to go after them.

Old Vaughn Monroe finishes his song, and then Sammy Kaye starts up with "Lavender blue, dilly-dilly, lavender green."

I drift up over the treetops. I'm afraid of falling at first, but then I get the hang of this flying thing. I float slowly over Laceola and down Little Snake Creek. The creek overflows its banks into town. I look down to see the water rise high enough to flood some of the stores, and there were people paddling down the streets in boats. They don't see me.

Like a buzzard, I float over Little Snake Creek as it gently turns north, cutting through the western section of the town. I follow it through the valley, twisting and turning through great stands of cedar trees. I see the creek change direction once more, racing to the west as if it needed to hurry up and get to the Coosa River. When it hits the Coosa, the force is strong enough to create a deep mile-long channel on the south side of the river. I turn slowly to see the sand bar created by the creek. I float across dying, leafless trees and spot some men in a field on the other side of the creek. I dip my left arm and head in their direction. They spot me and point at me. I try to shout at them, but they don't understand me. They're dressed in German uniforms and are armed with rifles. "No," I scream. They aim their rifles at me, and I hear a bullet whiz past my head. They're trying to kill me. I try to fly faster to get away, but I float slowly over them. I can see their faces clearly now, and they're not Germans. It's Frank and Egg Thompson and other men. I dodge bullets. I'm losing control and altitude fast, but I think I can make it over the trees to the creek. I brush the top of a dead tree and fall. I scream as I splash into the cold water of Little Snake Creek.

My body jerks awake. Sweat soaks through my pajamas. Boy, another nightmare. The radio is still playing, and I turn it off. God, the Thompsons were real and shooting at me. Why were they dressed like German soldiers?

Today I find out Daddy lost some contracts for building projects in Coosa County, and he doesn't tell me that his losses are my fault. But I know it is, and I feel guilty. What can I do? Granddaddy said, "Do what's right and take the consequences." He didn't say what you should do if doing right hurts other people. Maybe it's time for me to holler calf rope and just give up.

I can't turn over; it hurts too much. I drift off to sleep hoping I can fly again in my dreams, but not in a nightmare.

27

SPORT

Today is May 1, a beautiful Sunday afternoon. I sit in my backyard reading the *Atlanta Constitution* while my friends are at the Maypole Pageant. The funny paper is the first section I pull out of the paper, and I read "Li'l Abner," "Dagwood and Blondie," "Buzz Sawyer," "Nancy," "Prince Valiant," and "The Phantom." Mama likes "Mary Worth" and "Little Orphan Annie." Daddy reads about everything.

There's nothing interesting in the sports section. The governor plans to improve education again. Every politician wants to improve education, and eventually they'll improve it out of existence. I read Ralph McGill, the editor of the *Atlanta Constitution*, whose column appears on the front page. Yeah, I know. I'm reading a newspaper while my friends are having fun.

Jack is at the pageant because he wants to see Ulene MacFadden prance around the Maypole. Ever since I got them together at the picture show, Ulene just happens to be everywhere Jack is. He doesn't mind her hanging around anymore. Jack says that she's just a danged ol' girl, but he can't hide the fact he likes her. Fiona Burns is there too. Seems like she's been avoiding me since the fight. Boy, am I sleepy.

Jack shakes me. "Hey! Wake up. You're sleeping your life away."

"What time is it?"

"Four thirty. Your mother told me to wake you."

"Yeah. Yeah. That's okay. Did you enjoy the Maypole Pageant?" But I know the answer before I asked.

"It was okay. Same ol' pageant as last year. Barbeque was about the only thing that was good."

"The Russians have a big May Day parade, and they march around Moscow showing off their army. I guess they honor Stalin or some Communist. By the way, who was there?"

"Just about everybody. Ben, Pow-Pow, Weasel, you know, the regular crowd."

I might as well ask him. "Was Fiona there?"

"Ha! Yeah, she was there. Like the other girls, she wore this white dress and had a crown of flowers on her head. You would of fainted in delight."

"Kiss my nasty foot! Did ya talk to her?"

"Not really. After the pageant, Ulene caught up with me, and Fiona was with her. They wanted me to go to the soda shop, but I said I had to visit a sick friend."

I don't show my disappointment. I had hoped Fiona would ask about me. Like Jack says about Ulene, maybe Fiona is just a danged ol' girl. So why should I care.

"You think American communists celebrate May Day?" I ask.

"Not on your life. The FBI would be on them before they hit the streets."

Spring is my favorite time of the year. It's better than summer. All coats and heavy shoes are abandoned, and the air is fresher with warm days and cool nights. I like the scent of green grass and weeds along Little Snake Creek. The minnows and sunfish are livelier as they prepare to nest in the creek gravel. Frogs go crazy after a spring shower.

Every year around the first of May, my family drives out to the country on Sunday afternoon to see wild azaleas and other wild flowers. Everybody in Laceola seems to know when wild flowers are in full bloom. It's an unplanned ritual. People just show up on dirt roads all over the county. Teenagers pick wild flowers and decorate their cars, and then they drive up and down Main Street to show off.

Mama and Daddy didn't want to go to the Maypole Pageant this year.

"Too many people will be there. We shouldn't put ourselves in harm's way," they said. I know they were talking about me.

I won't ever forget the spring of 1949 because I missed it.

28

SPORT

Daddy leaves at six o'clock this morning for some kind of meeting in Palatine. Granddaddy takes me and Jack to school in his Buick Roadmaster. As I get out of the car, I see a bunch of kids standing on the front steps of the schoolhouse. This is not unusual except the boy in the middle of the gang is Ace Coffey.

"Is that Ace Coffey?" Jack asks.

"Yeah. It is. I wonder what's going on."

"Maybe they're tellin' little moron jokes."

I've never heard Ace Coffey utter over two words at a time. Ace ain't his real name; it's Elmer. Back in fifth grade, some of the older kids started calling him "American Ace." That comes from a commercial announcement on the *Grand Ole Opry*, you know, the one where this woman screams, "Elmer, don't forget the American Ace Coffee!" His nickname was shortened to Ace by the end of sixth grade. Me and Jack walk up to the edge of the crowd and listen.

"Didcha know any of them?" Carl Lopes asks Ace.

"Nope."

"What happened, Ace?" Jack asks.

"Let me tell, let me tell!" Eugene Laney says. "Two big men grabbed Ace on his way home from school yesterday and throwed him in the back of a car, then blindfolded him and took him out in the country, but they didn't cut him up or shoot him or nothin'. And there wasn't no blood. Ol' Ace was scared to death. Didcha soil your pants, Ace?"

"No, I didn't, Eugene," Ace says louder and faster than he has ever spoken. "I was scaredt all right. I was more scaredt when they turned me loose on this old dirt road about fifty miles from nowhere. I didn't know where I was, and it started to get dark."

"What were they after? Did they rob you?" I ask.

"No. Didn't have but a dime in my pocket. They just drove out on a dirt road and met another man there."

"What did the other man do?" Jack asks.

"Oh, he didn't do nothing, but he got really pissed off at the two men who took me out there. He screamed and screamed at them. 'You got the wrong kid.' He had a cast on his arm and hit the side of his car with the cast. He just kept screamin' and hittin' the side of the car."

When Ace paused for breath, Eugene takes it. "I'll bet that hurt. Remember when I fell off my bike and broke my arm last year. Broke it clean in two places. My arm was so sore I couldn't of hit nothin' with my cast. And I nearly puked when the doctor set it. I betcha that hurt when he hit the side of that car."

The first bell breaks up Ace's story. We go quickly but orderly to our classrooms. We go into Mr. Pritchard's classroom, and Jack whispers to me, "They were after you."

"I had the same thought, but Ace don't look nothin' like me."

"Sure he does. Same height, same weight, similar hair color and haircut. Of course, he doesn't have gray eyes."

"Damn, I mean, dadgumit. You're right."

After the second bell, Mr. Pritchard says, "Ah . . . ah . . . settle down class. Eugene, stop talking and sit down."

Mr. Pritchard takes a deep breath and continues, "By now you all have heard about Elmer Coffey and the situation he was involved in yesterday. I want to assure you all that you are in no danger. This is an isolated incident. Ah . . . ah . . . our police chief has ordered extra patrol after school just to reassure you and your parents."

Mr. Pritchard is a good man. He doesn't keep anything from us but believes that knowledge helps us overcome fear. He tells us things our parents probably will never talk about.

"How'd Ace get home?" someone asks from the back of the room.

"Mr. Jim Bentley, who owns a farm out there, found Elmer wandering down the road and took him to Sheriff Macwain. The sheriff is investigating now."

"I'm glad he wasn't hurt," Lucy Renfoe says.

"Ah . . . ah . . . I think we have discussed Elmer Coffey enough. Let's get down to studying history. But if any of you are approached by a stranger, run directly to any adult and tell them. You may help the authorities find these culprits."

For the next two days, everybody in my seventh-grade class saw more strangers in town than had come through the county in the past twenty years. Carl Lopes reported a man with a cast on his arm. Ben Wills's investigation turns up Old Man Kraus, who got drunk, fell off his porch, and broke his arm.

This month, May, has a Friday the thirteenth. That's tomorrow. By now everyone believes the men who got Ace Coffey have left Coosa County. But I find myself looking over my shoulder every thirty seconds and walking closer to buildings. Besides that, I have other problems with the thirteenth. Jack says it's goofy to think unlucky things happen on the thirteenth. Still I avoid ladders and black cats anyway, and if a black cat crosses my path, I touch my finger to my tongue and make a cross in the air. I also stay away from crossroads 'cause witches usually appear there. That's what Granddaddy says. Maybe Jack is right, but I play it safe.

With his mother's permission, Jack comes over with the excuse of studying for an English grammar test. I say "excuse" because both of us know this stuff backward and forward, but Jack's mama will agree to anything if it involves studying. We bounce a few questions off each other until we get bored.

"Jack, I've been thinkin' about what happened to Ace Coffey. If those men were after me, what did they intend to do to me? They couldn't keep me locked up until after the trial. I just had a horrorible thought about being dumped in a well. Ya know, this whole situation is just plain stupid 'cause I didn't hurt nobody, yet I'm the one who's being punished. I'm carried to school; I'm picked up at school. I feel like somebody is always watching me, and I don't know who it is. I'm a prisoner, and I don't like it."

"Ah, nobody's watching you. It's your imagination. You could refuse to testify, and nobody'll fault you. Anyway you haven't been bothered since the guy got you at the soda shop."

"I can't believe you're suggestin' I give up! I'm tellin' you right now I'm fixin' to send the Thompsons a message to back off. I ain't waiting for any Klan member to clean my plow."

"You're dreaming, man. You can't do anything."

"I don't intend to sit around on my fist and wait for doomsday. I gotta plan in mind, but I don't have the details worked out yet. I need to talk to Cal Slowman. He'll help, and I trust him and you more'n anybody outside my family. But if I tell my family, even Granddaddy, I'll be locked in my room 'til my hair turns gray. Uncle Earl will be the only one for striking back, but he'll want to kill every dadgum one of 'em. I don't intend to hurt anybody, just scare the hell out of 'em. Hey, for god's sake, promise me you won't tell yore mama."

"I promise."

"Okay, I ain't doin' anything tomorrow. It's the thirteenth. But, if you will, catch Cal Slowman after school and ask him to come over to my house on Saturday. Tell him we'll talk in the yard where nobody can hear us."

"I don't think you should do anything. It doesn't sound right, but I'll tell Cal Slowman."

29

JACK

After school Sport, Ben Lloyd, Pow-Pow Johnson, and I walk out into the schoolyard. Sport looks at me and says, "Find Cal for me."

"Either by chance or will of the gods, I will."

We walk down to where Sport's granddaddy is waiting in his Buick. "You ridin' with us, Jack?"

"No, sir, Mr. Kirk. I gotta go to the library."

"Heck, boy. Hop in and we'll take you up there. It ain't that far."

Sport rides shotgun, and I get into the backseat. Mr. Kirk slips the Buick into low gear, slowly makes a U-turn and heads north on Academy Street toward the library.

"What you boys plotting?" Mr. Kirk asks.

Sport looks back at me, and I grimace. "Aw, Granddaddy, we ain't plottin' nothing. Why I can't even get out of my own backyard."

This old man has sixth sense. Now I know why he became such a good lawman. He knows, and Sport doesn't even have any plans yet. I better change the subject.

"How fast will this car run?"

"I can git it up to about eighty miles an hour goin' downhill. 'Course, it may take me ten or fifteen minutes."

He brakes to a stop in front of the library, and I get out.

"Thanks for the ride, Mr. Kirk. I'll talk to you later, Sport."

"See ya later, Jack."

Where in Laceola can I find Cal Slowman? I walk up the steps like I am going into the library and wait until the old Buick disappears down the street. Maybe he hasn't left high school yet. I move down Academy Street and take a shortcut across the backyard of the old Garnett mansion. When I come out on Troup Avenue, I am only a block away from the school. There are a few people around the schoolyard, and I quickly check the parking lot for Cal's jeep. It's not there, and then Bobby McKnight comes out of the gym.

"Hey, you seen Cal Slowman?"

"Whatcha want Cal for, kid?"

"Just want to talk to him, that's all."

"Well, he's done gone. Probably over at Devoe's Service Station working on that old jeep. Hey, ain't you the friend of that kid who saved that nigger boy's life?"

"Yeah. I'm his friend. So what?"

"Nothin'. I've seen you with him."

"Okay. Thanks."

I retrace my steps up Troup Avenue, passed Academy, and on to Main Street. I turn left and walk to the Devoe's Service Station on the corner of Cherokee and Main. Sweat soaks through my shirt, and I hate sweat. I should have left some of my books at school. Mr. Devoe stands in the doorway and watches his son wash down the grease pit. Weasel shuts off the water hose when I walk up.

"Hey, Weasel."

"How ya doin'?"

"I'm lookin' for Cal Slowman."

"I ain't seen him today. He may be at Blount's Drug Store. That's where the seniors hang out with their girls after school."

"Thanks, Weasel,"

I doubt I'll find Cal Slowman there since he's not the drugstore cowboy type. If I go down Main Street to Blount's, I have to pass Mom's bank, and if she sees me, I'll have some explaining to do. I skirt the bank by taking Cherokee to Academy Street and walk south past Troup Avenue and turn left on Maple toward Main. Dang it, I see Eugene Laney outside the Maple Street Soda Shoppe. I can't avoid him.

"Jack Copeland. Ol' Jack. Have I got a good 'un for you. You ain't heard this one," Eugene says.

"Not another one of your stupid little moron jokes."

"No, no. You gonna laugh your ass off. This third-grade teacher's callin' on kids to spell words out loud. She gets to this one boy and says, 'Johnny, spell *shirt.*' Johnny says, 'S-h-i . . . t.' 'Johnny, you know that's not right. Now spell *shirt,*' she shouts. 'S-h . . . i-t,' Johnny spells. 'I told you that's not the way to spell *shirt.* Now spell it right,' the teacher screams. 'S . . . h . . . r . . . t,' Johnny says. Another boy raises his hand and says, 'Teacher, Teacher, now you got 'im so confused, he can't spell *shit.*'"

Eugene lets out a horselaugh and snorts, "Ain't that funny?"

"Yeah, 'bout as funny as cat puke."

Actually ol' Eugene's joke is pretty funny, but I can't let him know. "Hey, I gotta get home."

I leave Eugene laughing at his own joke and go up Maple Street and turn south on Main. I spy Cal's jeep parked on the street two doors down from the drugstore. Good. I guess Cal is a drugstore cowboy after all. I look through the display window and see Cal with Kitty Downes in a booth near the back. I hesitate before going in because seventh graders don't invade territory staked out by seniors, and I don't know how Cal will take my barging in on him. Oh well, he can't kill me. I walk back to the booth with my eyes fixed on Cal. He and Kitty are in a serious conversation that I interrupt.

"Ah, hum," I clear my throat. "I need to talk to you."

Cal looks at me and then at Kitty. "Well, little brother, speak up."

"I mean in private."

"You're Jack Copeland, one of Sport's friends. Am I right?" His Creek Indian eyes bore into me as if he were searching for my soul.

"Yes. I need to talk to you."

"Okay, let's walk outside."

"He's cute," Kitty says.

"I'll be back directly," he tells her.

I follow Cal's lead outside to his jeep.

"I'm sorry I disturbed you. But Sport wants you to meet him at his house tomorrow if you can make it."

"Sure thing. What time?"

"Sport says anytime after noon. He says he ain't going anywhere since he can't get out."

"Tell him I'll be there."

Wow. What a relief. Cal Slowman killed a man, a bank robber two years ago, and he looks as if he could snap your neck and walk away without another thought. I always stayed as far away from him as I could get and never said over three words to him at one time. Sport has an odd collection of friends.

The gods have looked favorably on me. I completed my mission and head for home. I get a strange feeling as if somebody is sneaking up on me. Maybe Sport's superstitions are infecting me. Naw, he is wrong about Friday the thirteenth. I stop and look in both directions and start across the street. I hear tires screech, and out of the corner of my eye, I see a black car making a speed turn onto Lancer Street. I jump back but not fast enough to keep a fender bump me. I land hard and slide into the gutter on one elbow and both knees. My schoolbooks scatter in the street and on the sidewalk. The car speeds away with that crazy driver not even looking back.

A colored lady crosses the street and says, "Y'all lay right there while I see if'n you is hurt. Dat car looked lak it tried to run over you. We oughta call the police."

"No, don't call the police. I'm okay,"

The colored lady sets her bag down and checks me out.

"See if'n you can move yo' legs and arms."

My arms and legs are not broken, but the skin on my elbow and both knees is rolled up like little balls of red stuff, and it burns like Hades.

"I'm okay."

The knees of my pants are ripped to shreds. The pain brings tears to my eyes, and my heart beats like a mad snare drummer.

"Where y'all live? You wants me to walk you home?"

"No, ma'am, I don't live far from here. Thanks anyway."

I limp down Main Street to Walnut and look back. The colored lady still watches me. I knock on the door at Sport's house, and his mother answers.

"Come in, Jack. My Lord! What happened to you?"

"I fell down and skinned my elbow and knees."

"Sport! Jack is here! Now you sit down and let me wash those scrapes and put some Mercurochrome on them," she says and disappears down the hall.

Sport comes in and stares at me. "Jack, you look like you tangled with a wildcat."

"It was more like a car. You jinxed me, Sport. You and your Friday the thirteenth."

Sport picks up his little brother from the middle of the floor and says to him, "Jack just became a true believer in Friday the thirteenth."

Sport's mother comes back with a pan of water and a bottle of Mercurochrome. She gently washes my skinned elbow and knees. I grimace when she spreads red stuff on my cuts, but it soothes the burn. I like Mercurochrome better than iodine because it doesn't sting. But iodine heals better. Sport puts Cloverine salve on everything because he says he needs to use it up.

"Mama, I think Ted needs a change. No, I know Ted needs a change,"

Sport's mother takes Ted to his room. Boy, I will never have kids. They're almost as bad as dogs.

"Tell me what happened," Sport says.

"I tangled with a car, but I found Cal Slowman. Can you believe it? He hangs around Blount's Drug Store after school. He'll meet you here tomorrow afternoon."

"Jack, tell me about the car."

"It was an accident. The car came around the corner at Lancer, and I guess the driver didn't see me. The fender grazed me and knocked me down."

"Don't lie to me. That was no accident. It was deliberate. They're tryin' to get to you too, and I'm beginning to get really pissed off. Whoever is doin' this should know it's not yore fight. Jack, you lay low and watchcha back."

"I think you're crazy. It was an accident."

"I'm gonna get 'em. I'm gonna send them a message they'll not forget. That's what I'll do."

Sport's eye begins to twitch.

I go home and change clothes and make up a story about how I fell and got all skinned up so my mother won't worry. I don't want to lose my freedom like Sport has.

30

SPORT

Today is a great spring day, but not for me. Maybe the car that hit Jack was an accident, but I don't believe it. They are not going to use my friend to get at me, and I'm gonna do something about it, but I don't know what. What I know is Cal Slowman will help me.

"Hello, Sport," Cal says from out of nowhere.

"Cal! Dadgumit, don't sneak up on me like that!"

"Didn't sneak up on you. Ya should've heard me park the jeep out front. You need to be more alert."

"I'm glad you're here, Cal. I need a favor."

"You decided to accept the .32? I knew you'd come to your senses."

"No. I don't want no pistol. It's a different kind of favor. I'm tired of bein' locked up in my house, and I wanna strike back but not kill anybody. Ya can turn me down, and I won't hold it against you. But I want yore word you won't tell my parents what I got in mind."

We look at the kitchen window to see if Mama is watching. She's not.

"I won't tell your parents about anything that passes between us."

"Okay. Being watched and never bein' alone, except in my room, is getting old. Those jerks went too far when they tried to get Jack yesterday. Now, I'm more mad than afraid. I wanna scare the hell out of the Thompson brothers and anybody else that runs with them."

"What happened to Copeland?".

"Somebody tried to run him down after he left you. He banged up his knees and elbow. He said it was just an accident, but I know it wasn't.

Cal looks at me thoughtfully and says, "Sport, you're a man after my own heart, just like your old granddad. Sure, I'll help. Whatcha got in mind?"

"Can you get me down to the Thompson place without them seeing us? In the dark?"

"That's a piece of cake."

Mama comes to the back door and sees Cal.

"Hi, Cal. How you?"

"Just fine, ma'am. Just thought I'd drop by to see Sport since he's been kinda cooped up."

"Why, thank you. That's mighty nice of you to think of Sport. Would ya like to come in for a Coke or a glass of tea?"

"No, ma'am. I'd like to take Sport for a ride in my jeep. We'll be back in an hour or so. That's is, if you don't mind"

"Oh, I think he'll be safe with you. Sure, you two go ahead, but don't be gone too long."

I look at Cal, and he motions with a nod of his head to follow him. Without speaking, we walk around to his jeep. He jumps in and starts grinding on the starter before I settle into the passenger seat. The engine catches and explodes behind me. I almost jump out of my skin.

"It's just a backfire," he laughs.

"It ain't funny."

Cal lets out the clutch, and the jeep lurches forward with a bounce. He rigged his vehicle for warm weather by taking the canvas top off the first day the temperature topped sixty-five degrees. Cal bought this olive-drab piece of steel at an army surplus sale. Granddaddy says he gave $50 for it, and that is about what it is worth. Cal lets the engine slow the jeep before applying the brakes at the stop sign on Walnut and Main streets. He turns left toward town, pass Wright's Grocery Store, then turns again onto Highway 100.

"Where we going?"

"On a little scouting trip. I'm gonna git you so close to the Thompson place, you'll be able to pet their dogs."

"I said in the dark, and I didn't mean today."

"There's no time like the present."

Cal turns onto a dirt road. The jeep engine whines and complains on the rutted red clay road and slows to a crawl. After about twenty minutes, he points the jeep into the woods and up a mountain ridge covered with tall pines. Near the crest, Cal stops the jeep and switches the engine off.

"This is as far as we ride. We go the rest of the way on foot. It's not far, just over the ridge and down in that little valley. From now on, you stay behind me and talk in whispers. I suspect a normal voice'll carry and echo across the mountain to the other side."

Cal sets a fast pace through dense pine straw down the mountain. He silently glides along with feet hardly touching the ground while I slip, slide, and stumble behind him trying hard to keep up. I fall and grab a rotten hickory limb to keep from going down. The limb breaks and sounds like a shotgun going off. Cal stops and puts his finger to his lips.

"Sorry."

The tall pines thin out about halfway down the side of the mountain and are replaced by a thicket of small pines, scrub oaks, blackjacks, hickories, honeysuckle vines, and brambles. Cal halts and motions for me to come alongside him.

"Beyond those oaks is a clearing, and that's the Thompson place." He points down the hill. "From now on we keep low and quiet. Watch where ya step and follow close."

I can't see anything, but I guess Cal knows what he's doing. I follow him like a shadow. At the edge of the clearing, we drop to our bellies. I spy the roof of a clapboard house or a barn. Cal points to his right and indicates the direction we should go. We creep around the Thompson place, keeping a line of trees between the house and us. A dog barks, and we hug the ground behind an oak tree. Frank Thompson walks out onto the porch.

"Shaddup, you lousy, tick-carryin' dog," he shouts, then goes back into the house.

"Let's get outta here," I whisper

"Just wait. Be patient."

Minutes later Cal touches my shoulder and moves off to his right. Still skirting the clearing, we pick our way around the Thompson place where we find a large ditch created by erosion. Along the bottom, vines, brambles, blackjacks, and sassafras saplings grow through a thick thatch of pine straw and dead leaves. The dog barks three or four times.

"Let's go up the wash."

I follow Cal through the blackberry vines. Briars catch my pants' leg and try to hold me back. We crawl out of the wash under tall pines and stop to rest. The dog is still barking.

"Now you've seen the Thompson place. What do you think you're going to do?"

"My idea is to bomb their house with fireworks. Slip up there while they sleep and set off some of those big suckers that Cato sells at his store. You know, the mortars. There are three to a platform, and they go off one after another. I'll light them, then run like the devil. I see it ain't gonna be easy."

"Let me think about this. Maybe I can add a few angles of my own, that is, if ya don't mind my butting in."

"I don't mind, but all I'm asking for is transportation. I don't wanna get anybody in trouble."

"Listen, Sport, if I'm in for a pence, I'm in for a pound. I'll be a part of this whatever trouble we run into"

"Thanks."

All the way back to Laceola, we talk about how we can set this up. The only thing we decide is that we'll sneak down the wash, regardless of briars and bushes. Cal says he will take care of the dog or dogs.

He drops me off at my house, and I feel better than I've felt in weeks. Before Cal goes, we agree to meet next week. I'll have to let him know where because I need to figure out a way to keep my parents from becoming suspicious.

Mama goes on about what a nice boy Cal is and how thoughtful of him to take me for a ride. Mama doesn't suspect anything, but Daddy will. He'll question me about Cal's visit, and I have to be careful, so I'll tell him Cal came by before Mama does. The best place for our next meeting is Granddaddy's place if I can arrange it.

I haul out the small chest from under my bed. In it I store all my valuables like Indian arrowheads, buffalo nickels, five silver dollars, and a rock streaked with fool's gold. Ah ha! I find the Prince Albert tobacco can and take it out. I flip open the top and dump my emergency greenbacks on the bed. I count out twenty-two dollars in singles and one two-dollar bill. The two-dollar bill will bring me bad luck, so I put it in my pocket. I'll spend it as soon as I get to a store. I have enough money to buy plenty of fireworks.

Jack will be surprise with the plan I made today. I can't wait to tell him.

31

SPORT

Jack spent Saturday and Sunday getting to know Mr. Crocker, his daddy-to-be. I don't like to think about his move to Valdosta. It will be a great adventure for him, but I'll miss his stupid smile. I can't worry about that now because I have to take care of this Thompson business.

The first chance I get to talk to Jack alone is at lunch in the cafeteria. Fiona Burns sits two tables away from us, and I try to attract her attention without being too obvious. She ignores me. It's beef Stroganoff day, so I eat the beef and leave the thick tasteless noodles for the garbage can. I tell Jack how Cal and I went up to the Thompson house to see if we could get away with it.

"Cal agreed to help me with my project. We'll go up to the Thompson place around two in the morning, set up about five or six mortars around the house, and fire 'em off. It'll sound like the start of World War III. That'll scare them so bad they'll soil their pants, and my message will be real clear."

"It's too dangerous. Those people'll come after you with guns, and you'll get yoreself killed."

"Dadgumit, Jack. They won't be expecting anything or me, and I'll get away with it, especially with Cal on my side. You should've seen him moving through the woods like a ghost. Heck, we'll be in and out before they know what hit 'em."

"Sport, you'll never get out of your house without your parents knowing."

Fiona gets up with her empty tray and walks past me. I smile at her, but she turns away. I feel like a whipped dog and don't know what I did to make her act this way.

"I'll crawl out the window. They'll never know I'm gone."

"Says you. What if little Ted wakes up?"

"He's sleeping all night now. If Mama wakes up, she won't check on me, just my little brother."

"Well, if you can sneak out, so can I. But I still think it's a lousy idea."

"Whatcha saying? You ain't going with me, are ya?"

"Yes, I'm goin' with you, dumb ass. You're lost without me."

"Boy! If ya git caught, we'll be forbidden to ever be friends. Your mother'll blame me, and I can't let that happen."

"Listen. Number one, I'm leavin' this burg for Valdosta a few days after school is out for the summer. Number two, my Mom will never do anything to me. She's too happy about her upcoming marriage. Number three, we'll never get caught because I'm smart and you're lucky."

"Okay. But I gotta clear it with Cal."

After lunch we trudge back to Mr. Pritchard's class. English, Lord, have mercy—how boring. Almost everyone is nodding off. I imagine Jack, Cal, and me crawling through the woods like a squad of Confederate scouts creeping up on a Yankee artillery position. It's so dark we have to sense the man in front. Cal leads, Jack follows, and I am the rear guard. We go down the deep wash, packing everything we need, and wait until Cal takes care of the dogs. We plant the mortars around the house and set them off. If we run, we won't see the fun when the Thompsons swarm out of their house like yellow jackets. I have to work that out because I want to see the fear we create. Mr. Pritchard brings me out of my daydreams.

"Ah . . . ah . . . Sport! Does every young man's fancy turn to love in spring?"

"Huh?"

"I say 'Does every young man's fancy turn to love in spring?"

Pow-Pow Johnson laughs.

"Gee! Gosh! I dunno. Maybe. I never thought about it."

"Well, you've not been with us for the past fifteen minutes. I thought perhaps you've turned your fancy to love."

Everybody laughs.

"Oh no, sir. Maybe I dozed off a little. The sunlight sorta gits to me."

"Perhaps reading Lord Byron's 'She Walks in Beauty' will get your blood flowing. You'll find it on page 85, Sport."

Why me? I hate poetry. It's goofy and doesn't make any sense at all, except maybe "The Charge of the Light Brigade." I rise slowly from my desk and read, "She walks in beauty, like the night / Of cloudless climes and starry skies." My voice breaks on "And on that cheek, and o'er that brow." The class laughs, and I turn red. Dadgumit, I thought Mr. Pritchard was a straight arrow, but he just ambushed me. I finish and sit down.

"Thank you for an excellent reading, Sport. Ben Lloyd, don't slump down in your desk. You are . . . ah . . . ah . . . next. All of you will get your turn."

In Granddaddy's Buick on the way home from school, I ask, "Will it be okay with you if Cal, Jack, and I come out to your place Friday? Me and Jack will go home with you after school."

"Shore. I always like a bunch of young people around. Keeps my mind sharp. Hey, you two can work in my garden for a while. Them weeds are beginning to grow, but ya'd better ask yore Mama and Daddy."

Tuesday blooms like a giant magnolia tree. The sun is warm, and the air is sweet. I need somebody to take a message to Cal, and I don't want to put Jack in danger again. I'll ask Pow-Pow Johnson. No one will follow him. I find Pow-Pow at recess.

"Pow-Pow, I need a favor because I can't go out alone. Could you carry a message to Cal Slowman for me? He'll be at Blount's Drug Store after school."

"Sure."

"Tell him to meet me at Granddaddy's place on Friday after school. If you will, deliver it today or tomorrow."

"Why you meeting Cal at your Granddaddy's?"

"He's helping me with a project."

"Oh shit. We gotta a project that's due? I didn't know about it. Oh shit."

"No, no, we don't have a school project. Me and Cal are working on something you wouldn't be interested in. It's like an individual thing."

"What is it?"

"Look, it's secret. I can't tell you now, but I'll let you see it after it's finished."

"Okay, I'll go today.".

I just messed up. Pow-Pow is cat curious, and he'll keep on until he finds out what we're doing.

The weather couldn't have been better all week, and Friday is no different. Cal is waiting for us when we drive up.

While Cal talks to Granddaddy, Jack and I walk out to the barn where old Jen, the mule, waits for someone to pet her. Cal finishes talking with Granddaddy and walks to where we stand.

"Does Jack know what you're planning?"

"He's in."

"Okay, let's talk fast. Yore granddad expects you to do some weeding." He says and hands me a white sheet of paper. "Here's a layout of the Thompson house and outbuildings. If ya see anything I missed, tell me, Sport."

I take the paper. He has drawn out the Thompson place exactly as I remember, including the wash running up the side of the ridge. I like Cal more and more because he treats us like equals.

Cal explains his idea for an assault on the Thompsons.

"Ya see the layout I've drawn up. I like the mortars, a stroke of genius. I made some inquiries and found out the Thompsons play cards and drink all night on Wednesdays. They call it their prayer meeting. They recuperate on Thursday, and I figure that's the best time to hit 'em. I'll go in the night before and set up the mortars here, here, and here."

He points to the layout to show us where the mortars will be.

"What's on this line?" Jack asks.

"They're straw Klansmen. I'll get some sheets, stuff some straw into them to make heads, and tie them on a rope line every four feet. When the line is pulled taunt, the Klansmen will jump up to our screams. The light from the mortars will make them look like ghost. I'll need two people on these ropes."

"Who's gonna light the mortars?" I ask.

"Now that's a problem to be solved. The three of us will light the fireworks, but we need two more to handle the ropes."

I tell Cal about my encounter with Pow-Pow and that I know it was a breech of security. I love saying *breech of security*. I suggest we bring Pow-Pow and Ben into our plan since they'll find out anyway. I know Pow-Pow will be willing to go, and he'll drag Ben with him.

"Okay, fellows, you got anything to add?"

"I like it," I say.

"I think it's a little risky, but it looks good enough to work," Jack tells us.

"Okay, when do we go?" I ask.

"Thursday night, two weeks from now. If we hit between one thirty and two o'clock, the quarter moon'll be down behind the ridges. They'll never see us in the dark. The hard part will be how to get y'all out without your parents knowing." Cal looks at us with a serious expression.

"We need to leave around midnight in order to get there and make sure everything is ready. The vacant lot next to Wright's store will be our meeting spot. If any one of us doesn't make it, the project's off. We'll have one practice session this coming Thursday to see if y'all can slip out of yore house and back in without being caught. If anyone is discovered, the mission is scrubbed. There will be no argument. Is that clear?"

Me and Jack nod a yes.

"Okay. It's up to you two to recruit Pow-Pow and Ben. If they can't make it, we'll do away with the straw Klansmen. I just think it's a nice touch. Let's plan a meeting on Sunday afternoon. We'll meet at Sport's house around two and go in my jeep. For our cover, I'll bring a bow and some arrows to teach you all how to shoot. Meanwhile, memorize the layout."

The two of us snap to attention at the same time. Jack salutes sharply. I do my best imitation of David Niven's palm-facing-outward British salute.

Cal grins and reminds us this is serious business.

We answer with "Yes, sir!"

After he leaves, me and Jack do a fast job on the weeds in Granddaddy's garden. Pulling weeds ain't so bad if you have something to look forward to after you finish. My plan for the Thompsons is taking shape. What should I call it? A mission? An assault?

Granddaddy inspects our job.

"You boys do all right. Here, it's worth a couple of dollars to keep me out of the dirt."

"Hey, Granddaddy, I'll trade you a crisp, new two-dollar bill for two singles. I think it's bringing me bad luck."

Granddaddy looks at the two-dollar bill.

"Tear one corner off. That'll break the bad luck spell."

I do as he says and feel better.

32

JACK

The task of recruiting Pow-Pow and Ben falls to me since Sport hasn't been allowed to go downtown on Saturday for three or four weeks. I didn't want to get involved in this crazy scheme, but on an impulsive moment of absolute stupidity, I volunteered. I don't think we'll be able to pull it off. But Cal Slowman knows his business, and he seems to think of everything. I tell Mom I'm going to the Maple Street Soda Shoppe, and she says it's okay if I don't stay too long. When I hit Main Street, I hear someone running behind me. I remember Sport telling me to watch my back. I jump to the side and whirl to see Eugene Laney.

"Hey, Jack! You goin' to the soda shop?"

Of all times to meet Eugene Laney!

"Yeah, Eugene."

"Me too. Let's go. Is Sport meetin' up with you there?"

"No, Eugene. You know he can't be out in a public place without an adult. He could get into trouble."

"Yeah. Yeah. I heard some guys talking at school. They say some men gonna tie Sport up and throw him in the Coosa River if he tries to testify against them Thompson brothers. They'll probably cut his tongue out too. He could drown in his own blood."

"You're plain morbid. That's not gonna happen."

"I've heard the Ku Klux Klan will hang a man, then draw and quarter him. They did that to a man in Heard County last year."

"Dang it, Eugene. That's a myth. It's been goin' 'round ever since I can remember. Are you goin' to the picture show today?"

"Yeah, *Springtime in the Sierra's* showing. I never miss a Roy Rogers picture. Come on. Go with me."

"No, I saw it last year."

"I did too, twice. It's one of Roy Rogers's best movies. See, Roy Rogers's friend is killed by these outlaws and—"

"I know the story, Eugene."

We enter the Maple Street Soda Shoppe. As I expected, Pow-Pow Johnson and Ben Lloyd are there. Pow-Pow is having his favorite sundae while Ben watches. I slide into the booth beside Ben. Eugene sits by Pow-Pow.

"What are you guys up to?" I ask.

"Me and Jack are fixin' to see *Springtime in the Sierra*. Y'all want to come?"

Pow-Pow looks at Eugene without saying anything. Ben rolls his eyes toward the ceiling. I'm about to speak when the piercing sound of a siren rolls down Main Street. Either by chance or will of the gods, it's a fire truck followed closely by a police car. Eugene jumps up and runs to the window, but he can't see anything. The fire truck and police car continue down Main Street. A few seconds later, we hear the faint sound of an ambulance siren. It gets louder as it passes the corner of Main and Maple, then retreats down Main.

"Hey, that could be something big," Eugene says. "Could be a bad car wreck. I betcha a lot of people got hurt. Let's go see it."

"We're stayin' right here," Pow-Pow tells him.

"Well, I'm going. You guys don't know what you might be missing."

With that, Eugene bounds out the door and heads toward Main Street.

"Listen, guys. I want to ask a favor. It may be dangerous, and if you don't want to help, that's fine. Either way you've got to promise to keep it a secret. Okay?"

"I won't tell," Pow-Pow says.

"Me too," Ben agrees.

"Sport is working on a project along with Cal Slowman and me. He plans to scare the hell out of the Thompsons in their own backyard."

"I knew it. I knew it. Didn't I tell you, Ben? I knew something was up."

Holding nothing back, I outline the plan to them, and then say, "This is not a game. This is serious and could be very dangerous. Nobody'd think bad of you if you feel you don't wanna get involved."

"I can't speak for Ben, but I'm in. Sounds like fun," Pow-Pow says.

"If Johnson's in, I'm in too," Ben says.

"Okay, but remember, we're not doing this for fun. Do either of you think you'll have trouble sneaking out of your house in the middle of the night? We're having a rehearsal this coming Thursday night."

Both shake their heads, "No."

"Can you meet at Sport's house on Sunday afternoon around two? Cal will take us to his granddad's house where we can work on the project."

"I can make it," Ben says.

"I'm not doing anything Sunday afternoon. I'll be there," Pow-Pow tells us.

"Good. Now don't say anything to anybody. Do not talk about this with each other in front of anybody. Got that."

"Sure."

"Got it."

I leave the soda shop, and as chance would have it, I meet those danged ol' girls, Ulene MacFadden, Fiona Burns, and Lucy Renfoe. I try to ignore them.

"Hey, Jack," Ulene says.

"Oh, hi."

"Is Sport with you?" Ulene asks.

"No! Sport ain't with me. Why does everybody ask that? Sport ain't allowed downtown without an adult."

"Sport's always with you. We never see you without him, so you don't have to get so testy."

"He's not always with . . . ah, to heck with it. You people just don't understand. He's under a lot of pressure, and if you don't know what's going on, I can't explain it."

The girls glare at me.

"My father said Sport is a troublemaker who should have minded his own business," Fiona says. "He brought this mess on himself, and I'm not having anything to do with him."

Ulene and I stare at her.

"Yeah, you're not making it any easier for him," I say.

"I'm going to Washington, DC, this summer," Ulene changes the subject. "My whole family is going by train."

"Yeah. Well, I'm going to Valdosta, Georgia, this summer for good. My mother is marrying a banker, and we're moving right after school is out."

I immediately regret what I said because I've given away more stuff about me than I wanted any of them to know.

"Oh, Jack. I'm so sorry. Will I, we, ever see you again?" Ulene asks with a pained look on her face.

"Sure. I'll be back for a visit." Without any intelligent reason, I want to hug Ulene. "You know you'll always be my special friend."

Okay, I'm an idiot. I said too much, but frankly I don't care. I'm leaving, and nothing I do or say will follow me to Valdosta. Yes, I do like Ulene. So what? She's nice, a lot nicer than Fiona Burns who has her nose stuck up so far in the air she could drown in a heavy rainstorm. Sport is a fool to like her, but I'm not going to tell him. I refuse to do anything to make him feel worse than he does already.

"Hey, maybe we can take in a picture show one Saturday before school's out for the summer," I say to Ulene and ignore the other two girls.

"That's sounds super."

I wave goodbye to them and head for home to call Sport and report that my mission is accomplished.

33

SPORT

I tell Mama and Daddy that Cal is taking me, Jack, Ben, and Pow-Pow to Granddaddy's to teach us archery.

"That's okay," Mama says. "You'll be safe as long as you're in a group, and Cal is with y'all."

Around one o'clock, Cal drives up in his jeep with a big straw target in the back He shows Daddy the bow and arrows we'll use for target practice. Jack shows up next, followed by Pow-Pow and Ben a few minutes later.

"You boys be careful," Daddy warns. "Don't let your Granddaddy near the bow and arrows. He's dangerous."

We laugh.

The gang loads up in Cal's jeep, which is plenty crowded. Pow-Pow rides shotgun because he's the biggest, and we make a complaining Ben sit on the straw target. I'm glad to be out with friends on this Sunday afternoon lark and we talk over each other like a gaggle of girls.

"Did Eugene tell you his 'shit' joke?" Pow-Pow asks.

"Yeah!" Jack and Ben shout.

"He didn't tell me."

"It's about this boy in third grade. His teacher asks him to spell *shirt* . . ."

"Hey, I kicked the slates out of my crib the first time I heard that one," I say. "What's his best little moron joke?"

"What did the little moron say when he stuck his hand in the gas tank?" Ben asks.

"This feels just like ethyl," we shout and laugh. Even Cal gets a chuckle out of that one.

The jeep stops near the barn where Granddaddy is waiting.

"So yore gonna teach these boys how to shoot a bow and arrow. Ya can set the target up at the end of the pasture down there. Don't let 'em hit any of the animals or each other, ye hear. Keep Prince out of the way. He still squats to pee, so he ain't learned what's dangerous and what's not."

"Don't worry, Top," Cal says. "I'll make sure these archers don't get carried away with their lack of skill."

"Come on, Prince," I tell the puppy. He follows the five of us to the lower end of the pasture where we set up the target. Granddaddy goes in the house to listen to some radio show. Uncle Earl isn't home. I guess he's with his girlfriend at Piedmont.

"Did you bring the layout of the Thompson place?" Cal asks me.

"Here it is." I pull out the folded sheet of paper and hand it to him. He places it on the ground.

"Okay, guys. Gather 'round. First, our D-day's a week from this coming Thursday at 1:30 a.m. Now, let's go over what each of us will be doing."

The layout shows the Thompson house and four outbuildings. There is a block of cleared land about thirty-five yards wide that extends around the main house. The cleared strip narrows at the back to about twenty-five yards. Their outhouse is at the end of this strip. About forty yards to the left of the house is a storage shed and a small barn. A flock of chickens range around the barn and roost in trees nearby. A small pasture is located in the back of the barn. There is a garage used by Frank and Egg to repair cars to the right of the house. An unpaved drive turns off the county road and runs about a quarter mile to the house. Large hardwood and pine trees with some underbrush surround and isolate the house. Old Man Thompson, Frank, and Egg are the only ones who live there. Mrs. Thompson disappeared years ago. According to Granddaddy, Old Man Thompson said she went to Mississippi to visit relatives and never came back. Rumor has it they operate a groundhog whisky still somewhere in the woods. Cal and I didn't see any sign of a still, but we weren't looking for one.

Cal marked squares where the six mortars will be placed, three on each side of the house. When fired, the mortars will shoot up and explode over the house. A triangle on the right side of the house indicates a starburst. Cal says it will light up the whole area for about fifteen seconds. Across the yard in front of the house, he marked a line for the forty-five feet of rope tied with six sheets, spaced four feet apart. Each end of the rope will be looped around trunks of large oak trees.

"Each of you'll have a specific assignment," Cal says. "Sport and Jack'll take care of the mortars. Pow-Pow and Ben will man each end of the rope, and I'll set off the starburst. I got windproof cigarette lighters for each of you with a small box of wood matches as backup."

He pulls out a mortar from his arrow bag. "This is our fear machine. I bought eight of 'em. Sport, you and Jack inspect the mortars and get to know what you'll be working with. Does anyone have any questions?"

"It seems that cigarette lighters and matches are a little risky. A light might be seen by the Thompsons, and we'll have to light the mortar fuses at the same time for them to go off together. That'll be hard to do. Isn't there any other way we can light them?" I ask.

"Ya know, maybe we can do better than cigarette lighters and matches," Jack says. "Why can't we hook the fuses up to a battery and set them off electrically?"

"How we going to do somethin' like that?" Ben asks.

Cal just looks at me, and I shrug.

"Jack's got a good idea. But we don't know anybody who can rig electric switches."

"Yeah, I do. Max Mendeaux." Jack looks at me.

"That's a no. I wouldn't ask that turd to do anything like that. He'd spread it all over Laceola."

"You could ask your dad, Sport," Pow-Pow says.

"Yeah, in your dreams."

"You have something that Max doesn't want anybody to know," Jack says. "I can tell him you're thinking about going to the prosecutor to say that he witnessed the shooting too."

"He's a danged coward, and even if we put his head in a vice, he still wouldn't help us."

"Let me handle Max," Jack says.

"Okay. Y'all work it out. Take one of the mortars with you in case he does decide to help. If he can make a reliable electric system that can set off the fuses, I'll go along with it. But he'll have to work fast because we have less than two weeks before we go. That means testing any new system to perfection, and there'll be wires, so we need plenty of wire to set the mortars. We'll have to place them on the side of the house, close to the escape route. I can deal with that without too much trouble," Cal says.

"We'd better shoot some arrows before Granddaddy gets suspicious."

"This is our last bit of business. We'll have a dry run this Thursday night at one thirty. That's a.m., fellows. We meet at twelve thirty in the vacant lot next to Wright's store."

For the rest of the afternoon, the five of us try to hit the bull's eye at various distances. Jack and Ben are horrible. Pow-Pow and I are pretty good, but Cal shows us why Granddaddy sings his praises. It is bull's eye after bull's eye. He can't miss.

"A matter of a steady hand and practice," Cal tells us.

We finally give up and watch him do his magic. I believe he can hit a black gnat on a burnt post at a hundred yards, and his skill wins the respect of my three friends.

Me and Jack gather all the loose arrows, and Pow-Pow and Ben put the target in the jeep. Cal picks up Prince and takes him to the house. Granddaddy comes back with him to the jeep.

"I understand you boys did all right. Y'all oughta git out in the country more often. It'll do ya good."

"I gotta get these men home for supper. We'll see ya later, Top."

We sing badly all the way to my house. "Rag Mop" is our favorite, followed by "Your Red Scarf Matches Your Eyes."

34

JACK

I ask Max Mendeaux to my house after school to give me some advice on an electric project. Sport comes too although he's not keen on having anything to do with Max.

"Max, can you make an electric switch that will set off fireworks?" I ask. Sport stands silently with a sour look.

"Yes. That's a snap. All I need is a battery, some insulated copper wire, and a simple switch. I may have to figure out how to make a fuse hot enough to ignite the fireworks. What kind of fireworks?"

"Mortars. Three to a platform. You've seen them."

"Oh yeah. Those are powerful and loud. Why don't you light them with a match?"

"Because, moron, the mortars have to go off together, and we want to be as far away as we can. And we can't risk lighting a short fuse with a match," Sport says.

"That sounds like some hair-brained scheme you two are famous for. You can forget it because I won't get involved in something that'll get me in trouble. Just forget it."

Max emphasizes his decision with a sweep of his hands like he's calling someone safe at home plate.

I take a different approach. "Max, who knows more 'bout electricity than you? We are counting on yore expert technical knowledge, so don't disappoint us."

"No, sir. Not me."

I slam him with our trump card. "I think you should reconsider. Ol' Sport here is remembering more and more about what happened when Dink got shot. He's beginning to recall who witnessed this incident that got him into this trouble and may want a certain witness to back him up when he goes to court. I know the prosecutor would like an extra witness. Am I right, Sport?"

"Yeah. I'll tell Mr. Snow you saw the whole thing, got sick, and ran away. Why, that's a good story for the newspaper."

"Hey, that's blackmail. You can't do that. It's illegal."

"Dang it! Call it what you want, but if I don't tell what I know, wouldn't that be withholding evidence or something?"

"Okay. Okay. You got me. I'll try to make the electric fuses and switches for you but tell me what you're going to do. I want to be prepared for the worse when it comes."

"You let us worry about that, butt hole," Sport says.

"Wow! You guys are gonna get killed setting off fireworks. If you don't know what you're doing, you'll get into a lot of trouble."

"Max, I think you'll enjoy the Fourth of July celebration," I say.

"Here's a mortar for you to experiment with. We'll set off six of 'em," Sport hands Max a mortar. "We don't have a lot of time to wait. How fast do you think you can make the switches?"

Max looks down his nose at us.

"Give me three days to experiment. I'll have to discover what kind of battery to use and a way to hook up the electric wire. The electric fuses will take longer. But if you all get in trouble with the law, I'll deny everything. I don't even know you, do you understand? An Eagle Scout doesn't do anything illegal."

"Just make the fuses," I tell him.

Max is a good as his word. He calls me Wednesday afternoon to tell me he has something for us. Then I call Sport to tell him the news.

"Hey, man, I'm going over to Max's to see the contraption he's made. I'll call you when I get back."

"Be careful. The jerk could make a booby trap to blow ya hand off."

I take a shortcut through Mr. Waters backyard to the Mendeaux house. Max answers the door.

"My lab is in the basement."

What I see is unbelievable. A laboratory with all kinds of electric testing equipment and chemicals I have never heard of.

"What the heck do ya do here?"

"Oh, all kinds of experiments. I'm trying to get a good base before I enter Georgia Tech. I've already communicated with some Tech professors, and they're really encouraging."

I pick up a small thick glass bottle with silver stuff in it.

"What's this?"

"Don't touch anything! Set that down!"

"Okay. I didn't know it was an atom bomb," I say.

"It's mercury, and it's extremely poisonous. Here's what I want to show you."

Max holds up a metal box with three toggle switches on top and wires running out the side. He sets it down and picks up a strange looking piece of wire.

"This is a magnesium fuse. Watch this." Max lays the fuse on a board, attaches a wire to each end, and then throws a switch. It explodes in a blast of light, heat, and smoke.

"By the gods. It works"

"This metal box contains a twelve-volt battery. My magnesium fuse may be inserted directly into the mortar. But you have to pull the mortar fuse out first, and you may not do it right. I suggest you wrap the mortar fuse with my magnesium fuse so you won't have to tamper with the mortar."

"Max, you're truly a genius. This is one heck of a lab, and I'll bet it's better than the one at high school."

"Now there are three switches. Each switch will set off two mortars. There are six pairs of hot wires running from the box, and each pair has a metal clip soldered in place. Look, I'll show you. Wrap my magnesium fuse around the mortar fuse and clip the wire to each end like this."

He shows me what to do with the mortar fuse.

"I locked the switches on the box to off so you can't foul up and hook a hot wire to a fuse. Once everything is attached, unlock the switches like this." Max pulls the locking mechanism up and off the switches. "I'm sure you can remember all this, but just in case, I've written instructions for you. How many fuses do you need?"

"We got six mortars. Better make twelve in case one or two are lost," I tell him.

"You can pick the fuses up tomorrow afternoon. No, on second thought, I'll bring them over to your house. You can take the switchbox and battery now. The instructions are taped on the box."

"Look, this is a secret. We want to surprise everyone with our fireworks display. Don't tell, or you may find yourself in a courtroom."

"That's blackmail, and you know it."

I take the box home and hide it before I call Sport to report what Max had made.

35

SPORT

"I'm impressed, Jack," I say into the phone. "The turkey must have strained his brain to make the switchbox so quick."

"It's the dangedest thing I've ever seen," he says. "The box has three switches that hook up to a battery with all the wires we need to set off six mortars. Max says each switch'll set off two mortars, and the fuse is a masterpiece. Look, I wanna get this thing out from under my bed and to Cal as soon as I can. I'm afraid Mom will find it. Maybe we can take it to the practice session tomorrow night."

"No. That's too risky. If we get caught, we'd have a lot more explaining to do. It's better to have Cal pick it up at my house Friday afternoon."

The doorbell rings. "Someone's at the door, Jack. I gotta go. See ya later."

Miss Sally stands at the door. Her eyes are red and swollen from crying. "Spo't, Dink wants to say goodbye. Can y'all come with me?"

"Who's at the door?" Mama calls from the kitchen.

"It's Miss Sally."

Mama comes into the living room.

"Can I go with Miss Sally?"

"What's the matter?" Mama asks Miss Sally.

"Dink's daddy is taking him up no'th. They leaving tomorrow, and Dink want to tell Spo't goodbye. Buddy wait in da car to take us over to my house. He won't let Dink come over here. He say it too dangerous."

"You go on with Miss Sally, Sport."

Miss Sally and I walk to the street where Mr. Roberts is waiting in his black Oldsmobile. It's a beauty. It is bigger than Granddaddy's Buick and a lot newer. I open the passenger door for Miss Sally and close it when she settles in. Then I get in the backseat. The upholstery has that distinctive new smell.

Mr. Roberts says hello to me as he fires up the engine. I look at the gearshift on the steering column. It's an automatic. I have never seen an automatic. I feel the engine's power when Mr. Roberts pulls the shifter down and eases away from the curb. We go in silence all the way to Miss Sally's house where Dink stands on the porch. Not waiting for Miss Sally or Mr. Roberts, I get out of the car and run to Dink.

"Hey, my friend. You shore do look good. Is that a new shirt you're wearin'? It's a dandy," I say.

"Hee, hee. I'se goin' to Chicago, and I'se got all new clothes."

Miss Sally and Mr. Roberts walk onto the porch with heavy steps. I guess Dink's mother is inside with Aunt Nicey. I sit in the porch swing, and Dink sits down beside me.

"I'll bet you're gonna have a good time in Chicago. I ain't never been to a city that big. It's a lot bigger than Chattanooga or Atlanta, and you can go to Wrigley Field to watch the Cubs. Dink, you shore are lucky."

"Yeah, I guess so. But I'se gonna miss Laceola."

Miss Sally and Mr. Roberts go into the house and leave us alone.

"You'll be back for a visit now and then. Hey, when ya come back, we can go catch minnows in Little Snake Creek. And we can go down below Three Springs and fish for sun bream."

"I woosh we could go now."

"Me too. But I can't leave my house without an adult, and you'll be in Chicago before the week is out. I bet yore daddy will take you fishin' in that big lake up there. Why, fish in Chicago will be ten times bigger than what we catch. You can send me a picture, and I'll show everybody in Laceola."

"You wants ma Cap' Marble books? I done read 'em all."

"That's a mighty fine offer. If you don't wanna take them with you, I'll save them 'til you get back to Laceola."

"I wants you to have 'em."

Dink gets up and goes into the house.

Mr. Roberts comes out with Dink, who carries his collection of Captain Marvel comic books. Mr. Roberts holds a wrapped box.

Dink hands me the comic books. "Here dey is. Look. I writes my name on every one of 'em."

"Thanks, Dink. I'll keep them in good condition. If you ever want 'em back, you just ask."

"Sport, remember I promised you a gift from Chicago. Well, here it is." Mr. Roberts gives me the package. Dink grins at me.

"Can I open it now?"

"Please do."

I tear off the wrapping and carefully open the box. Inside is a Chicago Cubs baseball cap and a baseball. I take out the cap.

"Wow! This is great. A real Cubs cap."

"Come on. Look at the baseball," Mr. Roberts commands.

I take out the baseball and turn it in my hands. It's autographed.

"Phil Cavarretta," I read the name out loud. "Hey, he's a real hitter. Plays outfield. Right? How did you get his autograph?"

"I have a few connections."

"Thanks, Mr. Roberts." I put my Cubs cap on, and it's a perfect fit. "This is a real treat. Thanks a bunch!"

Mr. Roberts grins and turns to Dink.

"You'd better tell Sport bye. I have to get him home before his family sends out a search party."

I stick out my hand and say to Dink, "I'm gonna miss you, old friend."

Dink ignores my hand. He grabs me around the shoulders and hugs me. Dink is crying.

"Don't cry, Dink," I say and pat him on the back. "You gonna be all right. Chicago'll be a great big adventure."

Dink finally lets go and runs into the house past a crying Miss Sally. On the way home, Mr. Roberts and I talk about the Cubs and Chicago.

"I have season tickets to the Cubs, and we'll attend a lot of the games this summer. You ought to see Wrigley Field. It's something else."

"Dink doesn't have to show up for the trial?"

"No. The prosecutor says it won't be necessary, and it will be better for Dink if he doesn't have to go through a trial. Mama Sally will stand in for him. But just between you and me, I believe that means the Thompson brothers are going to get off scot-free with what we call white man's justice. Personally I think you should protect yourself by not testifying."

"I'll do what I have to do, and the Thompson's will go to jail."

Mr. Roberts stops in front of my house.

"Sport, I found out from Dink that you and your friends were the only ones, black or white, who treated him like a human being. I deeply and sincerely appreciate that. Now you take care of yourself."

"Thanks. Thanks, Mr. Roberts."

I wave to him as he drives away.

36

SPORT

I wait for Mama to put my little brother down for the night. I say good night to Daddy and Mama and go to my room. I decide no radio for tonight and lie in the dark under the quilt with my clothes on. It's ten forty-five. I'll sneak out of the house at twelve fifteen. I hope I don't go to sleep and miss the whole shebang. I watch my clock and wind it up again, just to make sure it doesn't stop. The worse thing a man can do is kill time. Did I leave my window unlocked? Yes, I did. Hey, it's time to go!

Dadgumit, I hit a stool. I forgot to move the stool. I'd better start concentrating. No sound comes from any other part of the house, so I guess the coast is clear. I raise the window very slowly and silently. Boy, it's darker than inside a coffin. I hope Jack, Ben, and Pow-Pow make it to the vacant lot without being caught.

I climb out the window and slip down the side of the house, stop in the shrubberies and count to a hundred. Mr. Boyd's stupid dog barks, and another answers somewhere down the street. The night is still. No breeze or wind at all. The streetlight casts shadows. My hands are trembling, and I tell myself, *I am the Phantom, the ghost who walks.* I dash from one shadow to another beneath trees that line the street, pause to listen, and hear nothing. I sneak to my old cedar tree and let its shadow hug me. I see movement down the street, one person. It's Jack. I stand in place and wait. Jack walks cautiously pass the cedar tree. I move out and match his stride perfectly.

"The Phantom strikes again," I say.

"Rat crap, Sport. Can't you give anybody a warning before you leap out at him?"

"I didn't leap out. I stepped out."

"You did too, leap out."

"Didn't. Come on. We'll be okay as long as there are no cop cars around."

We double-time it as we approach the footbridge and cross Little Snake Creek and then slow down to a walk as we approach the vacant lot.

"Ooooeeee," Cal Slowman signals.

We walk over to a clump of weeds where he waits for us. Ben and Pow-Pow ain't there. Cal checks his luminous WWII dial watch. It's twelve thirty. They'll come in together.

"I got the switchbox from Max Mendeaux," Jack whispers to Cal. "Max will deliver the fuses to Sport tomorrow. The switches are good, and the fuses work."

At ten minutes to one, Cal says, "They're late. We'll give 'em another fifteen minutes."

About five minutes later, we hear Ben and Pow-Pow come into the vacant lot.

"Ya stepped in dog shit, Johnson. I can smell it," Ben whispers.

"You're the one who stepped in dog shit. Let me walk in front so I don't have to put up with the stink."

"Clean your shoes off, Johnson."

"I can't see my shoes, birdbrain."

Cal stands up in the tall grass and calls the two boys over to where we wait.

"You're late. Five minutes could make a difference, so you gotta do better next week."

"Sorry, Cal. My bedroom window was stuck, and I had to go out pass my dad sleeping on the couch. I may have a problem gettin' back in," Pow-Pow says.

"Okay, but get your window fixed. My jeep is on the north side of the lot. Let's mount up."

Cal has put a canvas top on the jeep. Me, Jack, and Ben crawl in the back. Pow-Pow rides shotgun. The jeep whines into the night to Highway 100, and Cal turns toward his home.

"I mocked up a layout at my place. My mother knows we're comin' and will be listening for us. If she doesn't hear us with her good ears, we passed the test."

Cal and his mother live on a twenty-acre plot about three miles outside Laceola, just off Highway 100. His mother raises cut flowers and flowering shrubs. Florists from Laceola and Palatine buy all the flowers she grows. Cal's daddy disappeared before World War II. He was a gambler, and everyone figured he was killed on one of his gambling trips.

We pull into a clump of hardwood trees on the north side of Cal's house. Silently, we get out of the jeep and form a line behind him.

"Okay, if you remember your stations, you'll have to find them in the dark. We'll circle the house from the left and travel single file at arm's length. I'll lead. Pow-Pow, you bring up the rear. Let's see how quiet we can be. Do everything like it's real. We don't want any foul-ups next Thursday."

I follow Cal at arm's length and hear the others fall in behind me. We go over a little rise, and I see his house in the moonlight. Unlike the wash at the Thompson place, there is no undergrowth to stumble on. We move slowly down to the edge of the trees. Cal motions to Jack and me to go to our assigned posts. I leave Jack behind, circle the house, find a dummy mortar, and kneel beside it. I watch Pow-Pow and Ben go to some trees in front of the house and wait.

Cal taps me on the back, and I nearly jump out of my skin. I follow him as he walks like a panther to Ben and Pow-Pow, who fall in behind us. Jack sees us before we get to him but doesn't move. At ten feet, Cal motions for him to follow. We troop up the slope to the jeep. No one says anything until we are on Highway 100, then we burst into jubilant shouts, "We did it. Heck, yes. We did it."

Cal quiets us down, "Look, guys. It's gonna be harder at the Thompson place. We'll travel farther in rougher terrain. We did just fine, but don't get too cocky."

"Max Mendeaux's switchbox may change our plans," Jack says.

"How so?" asks Cal.

"It's set up to fire all six mortars from one place, and I just realized there's nothin' to hook onto the starburst. That means you'll have to lay wires to the mortars, but the starburst'll have to be fired off by a match."

Cal stops the jeep at the vacant lot.

"I need to see the switchbox, but I don't anticipate any problem, just a little inconvenience. Okay, fellows, go home. Travel in twos. Pow-Pow, Ben, you two go first. Jack and Sport will follow in five minutes. It's almost two o'clock, and our timing couldn't be better. Jack, I'll come by your house this afternoon to pick up the box. Pow-Pow! Ben!"

"Yeah," both answer.

"Don't step in any dog shit next Thursday."

Ben and Pow-Pow point at each other and say, "It was him."

37

SPORT

I hear a knock on the door and Mama answers.

"Sport, it's Max Mendeaux"

Ah, dadgumit. What does that jerk want? I go into the living room.

"Hey, Max"

"Jack's not home, so I brought these fuses to you," he says and hands me a wooden box.

"Shhh, I don't want Mama to know. Jack said you're a genius."

"I wouldn't go that far, but I probably rank pretty high."

What horse hockey! He's the most conceited guy in Georgia.

"I understand you're putting on an Independence Day show."

"Yeah. Me, Jack, Cal Slowman, and a couple more friends are planning it now."

"Cal Slowman? He's involved with you characters?"

"Well shore. We have to have somebody older to watch after us, or our parents wouldn't let us do it."

"I think it's a stupid idea. You don't know what you're doing, and you'll get your hands blown off."

"With your gizmos, we won't be near the mortars. I'll pay ya for the switchbox and fuses if you give me a cost."

"I'd like to see those mortars go off. That should be some show if you can pull it off."

"How much do I owe you?"

"Nothing. Not a thing. Consider it my contribution to the celebration."

"Thanks, but no thanks. I don't want to owe you anything. Here's ten dollars. Take it."

"Well, okay."

Max slips the money into his pocket.

"Max, if you had refused to help, I wouldn't have told Tom Snow about you. I was bluffing."

"Oh, I knew you were bluffing because you've got more honor and higher ethics than you realize. But don't blame me if you get into trouble."

"I won't ever tell who made the fuses and the switchbox. You just better not tell anybody about our celebration."

"Not a chance. You still hold the trump card."

I phone Jack after Max leaves.

"Hey, Max brought the fuses to me. He said you weren't home."

"He lied. I went out for about fifteen minutes."

I let it drop. "Has Cal picked up the switchbox?"

"Yeah. He just left and on his way to your house. Says he wants to test the box and fuses before next Thursday."

"Listen. If I can persuade my parents to drop me off at the picture show tomorrow afternoon, you wanna go with me. I don't care what's playing. I wanna get out of the house."

"Gee, Sport. I don't know. You see, I've sorta promised someone I'd go to the . . . ah . . . movies with them before I leave Laceola, and I'm keeping that promise tomorrow. I'd like for you to come, but you know how it is."

"Hey, don't worry, old buddy. I know three's a crowd. We'll do it next week after we've finished our project."

"Either by chance or will of the gods, we'll paint Laceola red next weekend, and that's a promise."

"I look forward to it."

My buddy is plenty sneaky. Did Jack ask Ulene, or did Ulene ask Jack? I'll bet Ulene wheedled him into taking her. Maybe I should walk right up to Fiona and say, "How about taking in a movie with me?" No. I don't have the nerve. After our assault on the Thompsons, I swear I'll get enough backbone. Meanwhile I'll be patient. Who knows, she might ask me.

"You are certainly popular lately," Mama says.

"Oh yes, ma'am. I really appreciate Max dropping over for a visit," I say without really meaning it. I stuff the wooden box in my back pocket.

"Looks like you have another visitor. Cal is comin' up the walk now."

"Great. Maybe I could get him to take me out for practice with the bow and arrow again."

Before Cal knocks, Mama says, "Come in. Sport's waiting for you."

"Thanks, ma'am. Hello, Sport."

"Would you like a glass of ice tea?" Mama asks and adds, "Why don't you boys sit on the porch. It's such a nice day."

"Why, yes, ma'am, I'd love a glass of tea. That's kind of you."

We move out to the porch, and I give the wooden box of fuses to Cal. He puts them in his pocket. Ignoring the porch swing and chairs, we sit on the steps.

"Ya having second thoughts about our project? You got that look in yore eye."

"It's not the project, but I got something else on my mind. Maybe you can help me."

Mama brings two glasses of tea to the door. Cal gets up and takes them from her.

"Thanks again, ma'am."

Cal hands me a glass and sits down.

"What can I do?" he asks.

"It's kinda personal. I don't exactly know how to ask."

"Is it girl problems? You too young for that."

"Yeah, it's sorta like a girl problem. How you get a girl to like you if she don't like you?"

"Does she hate you?"

"No. Maybe. I don't know. I thought we were friends at one time. But now she acts like I'm lower'n snail's trail. Won't give me a nod of her head."

"There's got to be a mutual attraction between a girl and boy. But sometimes a girl will treat you like that to keep you interested. Could be this girl's playing hard to get."

"If that's so, she's doing a dang good of a job."

"Only way you'll find out how she feels about you is ask her."

"Dadgumit, Cal, I can't do that 'cause I don't have enough brass. There's gotta be a better way."

"Then you'll never find out. Well, my advice mightn't be any good, but it's the best I got."

"Let me think about it."

"Meanwhile you concentrate on our mission this Thursday. Put the girl out of yore mind until we take care of business."

We finish our tea in silence. Cal goes into the house with our empty glasses and talks with Mama for a few minutes.

When he comes out of the house, he says, "I gotta go, little brother. I'll run a test on these fuses, and if they work, I'll change our plan accordingly. I'll let you and the others know before we jump off."

38

JACK

How did I get myself into this? Now I wish I had Sport with me. Maybe Ulene won't show up, or maybe she'll bring Lucy and Fiona. I asked her to meet me in front of the picture show, and that means I'll have to buy her ticket too. I'm not going to buy her a Coke because I'll have to buy her a sundae or milk shake at the soda shop after the movie. No sir. No Coke for Ulene in the theater. Why couldn't there be a good picture on today instead of that old World War II flick. Oh well, I promised Ulene, and I'll keep my promise.

The one good thing is my friends wouldn't be caught dead watching *Casablanca*. That means nobody will see us. I walk up Main Street, past where old Mose plays. He's not here today. I hope all the farmers are busy chopping weeds and milking cows or whatever they do instead of coming to town.

"Yere goin' ta HELL! Ye creature of sin and iniquity! Get down on yore knees now and repent before the fires of hell scorches yore eternal soul!" the preacher screams in my ear.

My god! I knew I should've invited Sport along. He would never have let me forget about this crazy man.

"Yore mind's full of evil thoughts. Only the blood of Jesus Christ can wash the devil out of yore brain. What profited a man to gain the world but lose his soul to everlasting damnation?"

I ain't running. He won't follow me too far down the street.

"Don't let the sun go down without givin' yore heart and soul to Jesus Christ."

Ha! He stops at the corner as he always does. Just see if I ever walk on this side of the street again. I wonder how many souls he's saved since he's been on that corner. Is Laceola the only place on earth where he can preach? I cross Main Street and pause in front of Burbach's Department Store, four stores down from the Princess Theatre. You see, I have to get my courage up because this is my first honest-to-goodness date with a real girl. I know Sport says I had my first date with Ulene the time we all met at the picture show, but that's not true. Okay, here goes nothing.

I walk to Ulene who waits under the Princess Theatre marquis.

"Hey, Ulene. Been waiting long?"

"I got here a few minutes ago."

"I hope you enjoy old World War II movies. Humphrey Bogart and Claude Rains are good actors, so it should be okay."

"I think I'll like it. Ingrid Bergman is beautiful and such a great actress."

I don't know who Ingrid Bergman is, but I don't let on.

"Look, I'll get our tickets."

I take a fast look to see if I anybody I know is around. Good. The coast is clear.

"Two, please."

"Adults or Children?" that butt hole Henry asks.

"Two students."

Henry, the turd, grins at me. Oh boy, I'm beginning to act like Sport with the name-calling.

Ulene and I walk in, and I give the tickets to Joyce. She doesn't take notice of Ulene or me. Good ol' Joyce. We wait until our eyes adjust to the dark and then walk together eight rows down on the right. I feel like a traitor for not having brought Sport. Ah, heck, he'll live. Ulene slides down to the middle of the row. I follow and sit beside her.

We have to go through a stupid Porky Pig cartoon, which is not funny. *Casablanca* comes on. Hey, I like this. Ulene and I concentrate on the story. Good lines. Dang it, it's a love story. Either by chance or will of the gods, I had to see this with Ulene. I can't understand why Ingrid Bergman could possibly choose old Paul Henreid over Humphrey Bogart. Thank God for small favors, Rick is finally going to get rid of that goofy Victor Laslo and his stupid wife. I glance at Ulene. Boy, she's crying. I'd better do something. Without thinking, I offer her my handkerchief. She takes it and my hand. She's holding my hand. Oh, well. What will it hurt if it makes her feel better? At last the credits are rolling. The lights come on.

"Jack, that's the most beautiful movie I've ever seen."

"Yeah. It's pretty good. But how could it miss with Humphrey Bogart, Claude Rains, and Peter Lorre. You wanna go to the soda shop for ice cream or Coke?"

"Oh, Jack. I'm really going to miss you."

We walk to the Maple Street Soda Shoppe without holding hands, but our shoulders touch. I could get used to this, but I'm not telling Sport. He would laugh his ass off if he knew how Ulene makes me feel. I glance through the window to check out the soda shop. Curses! Eugene Laney is there. I should have known. I hold the door for Ulene, and we walk in.

"Hey, Jack, Ulene. Where y'all been? Didn't go to the movies, did ya?"

"As a matter of fact, we did," I answer.

"You gotta be kidding. Y'all wenta see that old Casablanca *thing?"*

"It's a great picture. Humphrey Bogart, Claude Rains, and Roy Rogers. You should go, Eugene."

"Roy Rogers ain't in Casablanca.*"*

"Sure is. You just don't know your Roy Rogers's movies."

"I'll betcha a quarter he ain't in Casablanca,*" Eugene challenges.*

"Go see for yourself if you don't believe me."

"By golly, I will. Y'all wait right here. I'll be back in a minute."

With that Eugene bounds out the door and up the street.

Ulene and I sit in a booth in the back corner and order Cokes. She could win my heart because she doesn't care for expensive sundaes or milk shakes. A simple Coke suits her just fine.

"We'd better drink fast. Eugene won't be long," I say.

"Maybe he'll be distracted by something else. I'm glad we could get together before you left. I like you, Jack. I like you a lot because you're a gentleman."

"Thanks, Ulene. I like you too"

We finish our Cokes without more conversation.

"I guess I'd better go home," Ulene says.

"Come on. I'll walk you home."

God, I think she's going to cry. I rush her out of the soda shop, but we walk slowly to Academy and then to her house on Ross Street.

"I enjoyed the movie. Thanks for going with me," I tell her.

"This is the best Saturday afternoon of my life."

"Bye, now. I'll see you at school Monday."

"Bye, Jack."

I feel good about making someone happy. I wish I could tell Sport, but I think he would be jealous. Not of Ulene, but the feeling I have. I know, I'll tell him it was just okay. This is a perfect day in May.

39

SPORT

Me, Jack, Ben, and Pow-Pow walk home from school today. Mama is at a baby shower and won't be back until five thirty or six o'clock. Granddaddy is in Tallapoosa, so he couldn't come by to get me after school. Since nothing has happened for a while, my family thinks I'm safe with a group of friends, and I'll stay at Jack's house until Mama gets home. This is the first time an adult hasn't watched me like a hawk since Easter.

There's no way to explain how it feels to be watched all the time. I guess it's like having a prison guard outside your cell. I'm sorry for wild animals in a zoo and don't blame them for running away when they can. A man needs to be alone, and even when I'm with Jack, I want to run to freedom.

"I'm really keyed up for tomorrow night," Pow-Pow says.

"Me too," Jack says. "With the new plan, we can stay close together. Cal is the only one who may be exposed when he lights the starburst."

"I think it's a dadgum good plan," I say. "We'll be in and out before the Thompsons know what hit 'em."

"Yeah. I can't wait," Ben says.

"Cal told us to get lots of sleep tonight because we won't get any tomorrow night," Jack says.

"I know I won't be able to sleep tonight or tomorrow night," Pow-Pow says.

Ben and Pow-Pow peel off at Glenn's Lane to their houses. Me and Jack mosey on down Walnut Street past my house and on to Jack's. Before we get to his house, I have a strong urge to be alone, to run to freedom.

"Oops, I forgot. I should've stopped at my house to pick up a book. You go on. I'll be back in a few minutes."

"I'll go back with you," Jack says.

"Naw, that's okay. I'll only be a few minutes. What can happen? We didn't see anybody around, did we? I need to make sure George has water while I'm there. He drinks an awful lot of water."

"You won't do anything stupid, will you? I feel responsible, so I'll walk back with you."

"Look, Jack. I want to be alone for a few minutes. Can't you understand how much it means to me just to be alone? Don't worry. Today's not my stupid day."

"Okay, but for god's sake come right back as soon as you can."

Left, right. Left, right. I march to my house and leave my schoolbooks in my room. I check George's water bowl so I don't tell a lie. Then I'm out the door.

I walk fast to the end of Walnut Street, cross Main Street, and onto a well-worn path along the south side of Little Snake Creek. I climb up to the railroad bridge and onto the Seaboard Railroad tracks and pause to put my ear to one of the rails before I cross the bridge. Ah, no train is coming. Taking two crossties at a time, I quickly step down on the track that leads northwest to downtown Laceola. It won't take me longer than thirty minutes, maybe forty, to take a fast look-see and be back at Jack's house by four forty-five. Nobody will be the wiser except him, and he won't tell.

Man, it feels good to be alone, at least for a few minutes. In town I take the backstreets and alleys. Just as I thought, downtown is dead. I spot a man and two kids come out of Blount's Drug Store and stop to speak to a couple of teenage boys standing outside. I walk fast up Handy's Alley between Rose's Five and Dime and Handy's Shoe Shop. At the end of the alley, I turn right behind Rose's Five and Dime where the trash bins are. I stop and look over the old cattle auction yard and to the right toward Maple Street. That's when I see it, a green 1939 Hudson Terraplane. My heart tries to come out of my chest, and I run across the cattle auction yard to Academy Street, which parallels Main and heads south. I glance back to see the Hudson Terraplane coming after me. My eye twitches, and my heart pumps hard enough to make my ribs vibrate. I run. It is the Thompsons, but they won't catch me. I cut into Mr. Beasley's backyard and race flat out behind six or eight houses and then onto Lancer Street. I'm only a hundred yards from Main Street and safety. I slow down and look for the green car. Good. Good. I lost it.

I trot down to the vacant lot next to Mr. Wright's store to take a shortcut to the footbridge. The tall weeds in the vacant lot haven't been cut since last year and make a perfect cover. When I cross the footbridge, I'll be home free. I slow my pace through the weeds and hear my heart still pounding in my ears. My clothes are wet with sweat, and green weed things stick to my shirt and pants.

Coming out on the far side of the vacant lot near the footbridge, I stop. Oh Lord! Egg Tompson blocks my way. I freeze for a second, and my arms shake. My legs turn to rubber when I try to dart around him toward the footbridge. I'm not fast enough. He grabs me and pulls me to the ground. I try to scream, but he clamps his hand over my mouth. I smell axle grease. The sour taste of puke rises in my throat.

"Don't 'cream, 'port. I ain't donna hurt you," Egg says in my ear. "I'm donna let you up. I'm not donna hurt you. I dust want to talk."

He loosens his hands from my mouth but keeps his massive arms around my waist. I try to pull away but don't have the strength.

"Don't run, and I won't hold on ta ya."

I relax, and he releases me. We both sit up and face each other. I stare at Egg without saying anything.

Egg looks real serious.

"I wanna tell you I didn't hurt that nidder boy. It wa Frank. He dust took out that dun and 'hot that boy. I didn't know wha Frank wa adoin'."

"You were driving," I managed to say.

Up close, Egg is not as scary as he was in jail.

"Frank tell me 'low down, and I did. He be mean, real mean. Frank don't care wha he do. He beat me up fur nothin' and make fun of the way I talk. He even call me he ba'tard brother."

Egg can't talk plain and acts goofy.

"'Port, I don't like wha they doin' to you. It ain't right to 'care a little boy, and I wanna warn you about Frank and 'em. They dot 'omethin' planned fur you 'fore the trial. I don't know wha. Dust you watch out."

Egg looks at me with a crooked smile. "I ain't donna be here 'cause I'm leavin' in my dreen Hudson and doeing to California. I work keepin' 'em motor running at the 'aw mill for 'ix month to buy ma car. I kin work my way out. We't by fixin' motor. Frank and nobody can find me."

"Ya can't do that," I say. I look at Egg and feel sorry for him. I think he's telling the truth. "The law'll hunt you down like a mad dog. You'll never be free."

"I done made up ma mind. I'm doein'."

"Is Egg your real name?" I try to keep him talking until I can think of something to tell him.

"My real name be Melvin."

I almost laugh but say, "My real name's Bedford. You can call me that if you wanna."

"Okay, Bedford. That kinda funny name."

It's not as funny as Melvin, I think. "Yeah, I know Melvin. If ya didn't know what was happening when Frank shot Dink, why don't ya tell Tom Snow, the prosecutor? He'd let you go."

"Oh, no. I can't do that 'cause Frank'll kill me. Ya don't know him. He robbed a 'tore in Alabama and turned me in for it. I work on the chain dane for 'ix month becau' of 'im."

"Let me talk to my Granddaddy. He'll know what to do. If you don't go to jail, you can go out West without being afraid of the law or Frank. If you're innocent, you won't go to jail."

"Okay. But don't tell nobody I leaving."

"Melvin, I gotta go or someone will come looking for me. After I ask my Granddaddy what to do. How can I get in touch with you?"

"I find you. How that little white and tan puppy of your'n, Bedford? Tee. Hee-hee."

"How'd ya know about the puppy? You, you were the man who pulled me out of the creek."

"Yeah, I did. I had a fishnet in my car trunk, and I watch out for you long time now."

Again I promise to talk to Granddaddy, and we part. I walk to the footbridge and Egg, that is, Melvin, walks to the other side of the vacant lot to his car. How stupid of me. It could've been Frank. Granddaddy tells me to always take the high ground. I should have avoided the vacant lot by following the path along the levee on the north side of Little Snake Creek. I would've seen Melvin before he waylaid me. But, on the other hand, going that way means a shortcut through Laceola City Cemetery. Hey, I chose the best way.

Jack sits on his front steps when I get to his house.

"Where the hell have you been? You're beginning to piss me off, and you're wetter than an old dog."

"I went for a little walk. See, I made it all safe and sound. Piece of cake, old boy."

"Dang."

40

SPORT

I rush through school today trying not to be jumpy. At home I act casual, but I feel guilty. Not that we've done anything. That comes later tonight, so I do everything exactly as I always have. It's a great night, and there's no rain in sight. I say good night to Mama and Daddy and go to bed at ten o'clock. I read Rudyard Kipling for about thirty minutes and then turn out the light. I check my clock. In my mind's eye, I go over the route we'll take down the ridge to the Thompsons' place. Me and Cal are the only ones who've been there, and I try to think what can go wrong. What do we do if we're discovered? Will one of us tell somebody about the mission if we pull it off? There may be a lot of things we haven't planned for, but I can't think of any. Maybe we should call it off and be done with it.

I check the clock again at midnight and wait fifteen minutes before slipping out of bed. I still have my clothes on, and this time I don't stumble over the stool. I raise my window and lower myself to the ground, pause, and listen for any sound from inside my house. Nothing. I move through the shadows to the street.

"Hello, Phantom," whispers Jack.

"Hey, you're early, and I didn't see you."

"Let's go."

We move from tree to tree and didn't disturb the dogs. The only sound comes from frogs. We walk past my old cedar tree and pause to listen. Hearing nothing, we continue on to the footbridge and cross the creek. Pow-Pow and Ben are waiting for us.

"Hello, guys," I say.

"Hey," they respond.

"Ready to go?" Jack asks.

"Let's wait for Cal on the other side of the lot," Pow-Pow says.

We walk through the weeds to the north side of the vacant lot. We're early, so the four of us sit down a few feet from the street. We hear the buzz of Cal's jeep coming, but no backfires. I guess he tuned the engine to keep it from making noise. About the same time, Jack spots someone coming down the sidewalk on Lancer. He catches our attention and points to the man who walks toward our hiding place. Cal's jeep whines down the street behind him. He moves to within five yards from us and stops.

"Hey, you guys. Sport, Jack, Ben, Pow-Pow, are y'all there?"

"Max Mendeaux, what the hell are you doin' out here?" Jack asks.

"I'm looking for you. I want to find out what y'all are doing. I know it's not Fourth of July fireworks."

"How'd you find us?" I ask.

"I knew you were planning something before school is out, so I kept my ears open. I overheard Pow-Pow and Ben talking about something you were going to do tonight and the time you planned to meet. I don't want to get into trouble if anybody finds any of my stuff."

"I'm sorry, Sport," Pow-Pow says.

"Dang you, Max. It ain't none of your business. Why don't you go home like a good little boy?"

"I'm not going anywhere 'til you tell me what you're doing."

"What are WE gonna do?" Jack asks.

"You'd better get out of sight, or Cal will drive pass us," I say.

Max steps off the sidewalk into the weeds. Cal stops the jeep near enough for us to get to it in one big jump.

"Saddle up," he commands.

"Wait, Cal. I think we gotta small problem. There're too many of us," I say.

"One, two, three, four, five. Okay, who's the extra?"

"Max Mendeaux. He followed us," Jack says.

"Damn it, we can't take the whole city of Laceola."

"Let's tie him up until we get back," Ben Lloyd says.

"I don't want to get into trouble for making fuses, and I'm not going anywhere with y'all." Max says.

"You're in trouble now with us," I say.

"Whether you like it or not, you're going," Cal tells him.

"We can scrunch up in the back," Ben says.

"It's now past twelve thirty. Let's get to work," Cal says.

Pow-Pow rides in front, and the rest of us scrunch up in the back of the jeep. It was uncomfortable before Max joined, and now it feels like twenty fat men in a phone booth. Cal drives down Highway 100 almost to Lawson Hill Community. He turns off on a dirt road and then turns again on a trail that leads up the ridge to a stand of large pine trees. The jeep's engine strains under the load as it creeps up the ridge. About three quarters of the way up, Cal stops the jeep. So far, so good.

"Okay, guys. Dismount. We walk the rest of the way."

A sliver of moon shines through the tall pines. Within thirty minutes, it will disappear and leave nothing but darkness. Cal calls us to attention.

"I had to change our plans slightly because of Mendeaux's switchbox. Last night, I went in and set up six mortars north of the house. The switchbox is ten yards inside the underbrush, on the right side of the house. Everything's connected and ready to fire. For some reason, the dogs are gone, so we don't have to worry about their barking. Follow my lead and don't walk in front of the switchbox, or you'll get tangled in the wires strung out to the mortars." Cal pauses. "Max, you're a fifth wheel, so you stay with the jeep. We'll keep to our plan. Sport, you have the honor of pulling the switches. Jack stay with Sport as our lookout. Ben and Pow-Pow will man the rope lines. The starburst is the signal for everything to start. Stay at your posts until I come and lead you to a safe spot where we can watch the fun. Are there any questions?"

We mumble, "No."

"Okay, let's go to work. I lead. Sport follows me, Jack, and Ben. Pow-Pow brings up the rear. We go single file, and each man keeps an arm's length from the man in front. We don't know what's down there so maintain absolute silence. Ready! Go!"

He moves out slow enough for us to keep up. We climb up to the crest of the ridge and down through the tall pines on the other side. The moon has disappeared, and I have to silhouette Cal against the sky in order to see him. Cal finds the wash and slides down the bank to the bottom. Each of us follows, fighting brush and scrub trees that slow us down.

Cal stops short and whispers, "I see an owl. It's a bad sign. We'll go on a little farther, but I don't like it."

I don't see anything and can't judge time in the dark. We've been traveling for at least thirty minutes, maybe. I spot the clearing and then the outline of Thompson's barn. Still walking in single file, we skirt the clearing. Cal pauses and motions for us to sit.

"The owl follows us. I see him in the top of that oak tree," he says. "It's a bad sign, Sport, and I don't think we should tempt fate. Let's get outta here before anything happens."

"What does the owl mean, Cal?" I ask.

"Death."

I shiver. Someone just stepped over my grave.

"Are you trying to scare us?" Jack asks.

"No. Never. It is true. The owl means death."

"Is that some Creek Indian superstition?" Pow-Pow asks.

"Yeah, but it's not a superstition. It's real, and I believe it."

I have never seen Cal afraid, but I can tell by his voice that the owl scares him.
"Where's the switchbox?" I ask.
"In front of you. Stick yore hand out and feel."
I find the switchbox. "Okay, let's fire off the mortars."
"Shhh, listen," Cal cautions. "I hear cars. More than one, coming here."
We look across the clearing through the trees and see lights moving fast toward the Thompson place. Three cars and a truck roll to a stop in front of the house. Twelve or thirteen men, shouting profanities and making noise, get out of the cars. All of them are carrying guns, and one man lets two dogs out of the back of the truck. They start barking and raising hell. I recognize Frank when he walks in front of the car headlights.
"Hey, ya tongue-tied son of a bitch, wake up in there," Frank screams. "Ya gonna fix us some sausage and eggs and biscuits. Wake up, ya bastard brother of mine, before I drag ya out and beatcha half ta death."
Frank laughs and shoots his rifle in the air.
The five of us freeze. I don't know what to do now, but I'm thinking fast. Cal touches each of us.
"Get goin'. We're pulling out. Pow-Pow, keep low and lead the way. Everybody follow Pow-Pow. I'll bring up the rear."
Pow-Pow duckwalks around the clearing toward the wash. Ben and Jack follow. I sit still and grit my teeth. I make a decision the others won't like.
"Hey, dang it, who is there?" Pow-Pow asks.
"It's me, Max."
"Get your ass up the wash. We're leaving."
"Sport, let's go," Cal says.
"No. You go on. I'm finishing what I started. I'll be right behind you."
"What the hell are you gonna do? It's too dangerous to stay around here. The plan is off."
"No, we've come too far to turn back now. I'll wait 'til they get in the house and then throw the switches."
I lift the safety up and off the switchbox.
"If it's gotta be done, I'll do it. Now go with the others," Cal says.
"It's my fight, not yours. You go."
"You stubborn Scot, we can't waste any more time. I'll light the starburst. As soon as you see it streak up, hit the switches for the mortars. Don't wait for me, run to the wash."
Two or three of the men set up a howl with Frank leading.
"Get yore sorry tongue-tied ass up, ya egg-headed son of a bitch, and get out here. Hahahaha."
"Okay," I agree.
Cal disappears toward the starburst. No more than a minute later, I hear a hissing sound and a small pop. A small white light arcs gracefully into the

black sky, and I click the switches that send an electric current to the mortars. A loud bang and a shower of blinding light bursts over the house. Almost at the same time, Cal and I slide into the erosion ditch and turn to watch. We wait for the mortars.

"They're not gonna work," I say.

"Be patient."

We see a red glow from six locations along the tree line.

Wahop! Kaboom! Wahop! Kaboom! Wahop! Kaboom!

It sounds like World War III. One by one, the six mortars explode.

By the light of exploding fireworks, we watch Frank Thompson and his friends run around in confusion and flop on the ground. They hold their hands over their ears and crawl under cars and truck. The dogs whimper and run under the house.

The noise from the last mortar echos up and down the mountains, then silence. The men crawl out of their hiding places.

"The bastards who did this is out there somewhere. Let's git 'em," Frank shouts. With that, he starts shooting with an automatic shotgun in every direction.

"Goddamn it, Frank. You shot me," a man screams.

"Over there! They're over there," another shouts and shoots a rifle in our direction.

"Get that flashlight out of my truck."

"Time to go," Cal whispers

"Look at that."

Egg stands on the porch with a flashlight dancing and laughing at Frank and the others tripping over each other.

Something hits a tree with a splat not more than two feet away. They're shooting at us. Lead shot from shotguns sounds like a handful of gravel thrown against the tree leaves. My eye begins to twitch, and I can't move.

Cal sees what is happening, grabs my arms, and pulls me down behind a log.

A beam from a flashlight sweeps over us. Frank and the men stomp toward us.

"Sport, they've got us pinned down, and if we stay here, they'll find us. Can you move?"

"No, my legs won't go. You run for it."

One of the men fires three rapid rifle shots. Two bullets slam into the log where we're hiding.

"I'm gonna surrender. Lay low until you can crawl out," Cal says.

"You do, and you're a dead man."

"Hey, stop shooting. I'm coming out," Cal shouts.

41

SPORT

I grab Cal's arm to pull myself up because I'm not going to let him face these outlaws alone.

The flashlight in the man's hand explodes, and the sound of a rifle shot echos from the opposite side of the mountain. Frank and the men stand frozen in their tracks. Bullets from the unknown rifle began to hit the ground around them.

"Some sumbitch is shooting at us from over there. Git down! Git down!" Frank shouts. Their gunfire stops.

"Somebody is giving us cover fire. Let's go," Cal says.

Cal pulls me toward the ditch until I finally get my legs to work.

We catch up with the others about halfway up the wash where they watched the show. Led by Pow-Pow, Cal herds us up through the brambles and vines to the top of the ridge where we rest.

My eye stops twitching, and I lean against a pine tree to keep my legs from shaking. Frank curses at everybody and everything below us, but the men don't follow us.

"There's one more thing I gotta do," I say.

"What's that, Sport," Jack asks.

"The loudest, longest rebel yell that's been heard since 1865. Yeeeeeeeeeehaaaaaaaaaa," I scream as loud and as long as I can. The other guys join in. Our voices echo across the mountains and up and down the ridges then die out somewhere at the edge of Alabama.

We jam into the jeep, and Cal drives as quiet as he can down the ridge to Highway 100.

Jack keeps checking behind us to make sure no one is following, and we ride silently into Laceola. Cal slows the jeep and brings it to a stop at the vacant lot.

"Listen up, boys. Sport and I came real close to being shot by those crazy bastards. The shotgun pellets hit around us like hornets, and then someone began to shoot at Frank and his gang. Whoever it was covered us until we could get away."

"Who knew our plans?" Pow-Pow asks.

"I don't know, and right now I don't care," I say

"But why? Why would anyone do that?" Jack asks.

"Let's just be grateful we weren't hit," Cal says.

Cal lets us out at the vacant lot. Pow-Pow and Ben leave for home first. Max, Jack, and I wait a few minutes and then walk across the footbridge and up Walnut Street together.

In my mind, I keep going over what we had done and how I froze up. Maybe Jack and Max were thinking the same thing because they didn't talk or nothing.

As we split up to go home, I say, "Max, you were a danged ol' fool to spy on us tonight."

Max walks away without saying anything.

I sneak into my bedroom through the window, fall into bed, and go to sleep. I dream. Boy, do I dream.

42

SPORT

I dress carefully. My shirt and pants match, and my shoes are clean. Why am I doing this? I don't know, except I have the feeling that I will have to recite something in front of our class. Naw, our schoolwork has pretty much wound down with only three and a half more days to go.

"You're up early this morning, son," Daddy says when I sit down for breakfast at 6 a.m. All through the night, I see and hear the mortars going off and the men running around like confused rats. This sight will never fade from my memory.

"Yes, sir. I got up to see the sunrise. Next Wednesday's the last day of school, and it's sneaking up on me."

I want to tell Daddy about our successful attack on the Thompsons last night. But I can't risk it. That's the trouble with good secret stuff. You can't let anybody know what you've done. Someday I'll tell Granddaddy.

Mama makes bacon and eggs and sits down with Daddy and me. I keep thinking about how things seem to speed up and crash in on a person without him even knowing until it happens.

"Jack leaves for Valdosta on Thursday or Friday next week, and I need to talk to him" I say and go to the phone.

The operator rings Jack's number.

"Hello," answers Mrs. Copeland.

"Oh, good morning, Mrs. Copeland. Will you please wake Jack up."

"Jack is up already. What kind of scheme are you two boys cooking up? You never get up this early."

"No scheme, Mrs. Copeland. I wanna spend as much time with Jack as I can before y'all move to Valdosta, that's all."

"Okay. Here's Jack."

"Hey, Sport, how you feeling this morning?"

"Maybe a little like Nathan Bedford Forrest. Winning a battle, but not the war."

"Yeah, I know what you mean."

"I decided to walk to school today, Jack. I gotta clear it with my parents and call Granddaddy. Come on over as soon as ya can, so we can get to school early."

"Okay."

When I come back to the breakfast table, I look at Mama and Daddy and say, "I'm walking to school with Jack today. I'll call Granddaddy and tell him not to come."

My parents look at me in a strange way.

"Okay," Daddy says, just like that. No argument or nothing.

I get Granddaddy on the phone. "You don't have to take me to school today. I'm walkin'."

"So you're declaring yore independence. We oughta set off some fireworks."

"Wh . . . what did you say?"

"I said, 'We oughta set off some fireworks.'"

He knows. Dadgumit, he knows what we did.

"I wouldn't go that far. Fireworks are for the Fourth of July or Christmas and New Years."

"You want me to pick ya up at school this afternoon?"

"Yes, sir. I need to ask you something real personal."

"Okay. I'll see ya this afternoon."

Daddy answers a knock on the front door.

"Come in, Billy."

It's Sheriff Macwain.

"You're out early this morning."

"Yeah, Wheeler. There was a little ruckus down at the Thompson place last night. Ol' man Thompson almost had a heart attack, and two old boys got nicked up a little with buckshot. We found some electrical wire used to set off some firework bombs, and the wire could've come from yore place. Frank Thompson thinks it's yore boy's doin'. Says he's gonna bring charges."

"Well, it wasn't me, and it couldn't have been Sport. Hey, Sport, come in here."

I walk into the living room where Daddy and Sheriff Macwain stand and try to look innocent.

"I'm leaving for school as soon as Jack gets here."

"You have anything to do with bombing the Thompson place last night?"

"Bombing. I don't know nothin' about bombing. I slept all night last night."

"Look, Billy. How in the world could Sport have gotten down there and back? He certainly didn't walk."

"The Thompsons think he's involved. Said they saw a couple of boys runnin' 'round their place."

"Well, he's not involved. And that's that."

Jack knocks on the door, and I let him in. I signal to him with my eyes and shake my head.

"Hey, Jack. You ready for school?"

"Yeah, Sport. Let's go."

"Wait a minute, Copeland," Sheriff Macwain says. "You know anything about what happened at the Thompson place last night?"

Oh, no. Jack can't lie very well and always looks guilty.

"What happen? I went to bed early last night."

"Do you know who bombed the Thompson place?"

"I don't know anything about the Thompson place, but I'm not surprised. Somebody was bound to get to them."

Sheriff Macwain looks hard at Jack. "I believe you boys know somethin' about this little shenanigan. But if ya say you don't, then ya ain't gonna talk. I don't cotton to any vigilante action in my county, and that includes cross burnings or bombings. When I find the ones responsible, I'll be coming down hard on them. Do y'all understand me?"

Sheriff Macwain turns and leaves without hearing our answer. Daddy says nothing as he looks at the two of us.

On the way to school, Jack and I catch up with Pow-Pow and Ben.

"Listen. The sheriff came to Sport's house and asked about the fireworks. He suspects us, but he doesn't know anything about you two. You guys gotta keep quiet. I know Cal Slowman'll die before he tells, and nobody'll ever suspect Max Mendeaux. So it's up to you guys to keep our secret."

"We'll never tell," Ben says.

"I won't even talk about it with Ben," Pow-Pow swears.

I don't tell them I suspect Granddaddy knows.

The four of us march up to the school entrance. Pow-Pow and Ben stop to talk to a gang of boys who hang out there until the first bell rings.

"Come on, Jack. Let's go to the classroom."

We go into our homeroom. Fiona Burns, Lucy Renfoe, Ulene MacFadden, and a couple of other girls are talking at the back of the room. I walk back to where the girls are and say, "Fiona, can I speak to you?"

The other girls stop talking. Fiona fixes her beautiful eyes on me and says, "No, you can't. My parents said you're a troublemaker and run around with colored people. They told me not to have anything to do with you. So just leave me alone! I don't want to speak to you now or ever."

I freeze with shock, and I feel my eye twitch and my face turn red. I go to my desk and flop down. Mr. Prichard watches at the front of the room. Jack and Ulene follow me.

"Sport, we gonna paint the town tomorrow. Remember?" Jack says.

"Yeah. The three of us can go to the picture show and then to the soda shop," Ulene says.

"Let me think about it. Let me think about it."

Mr. Pritchard is especially kind to me in class. He doesn't call on me for anything. Jack, Pow-Pow, Ben, and Ulene surround me at lunch and tell stupid stories and jokes. To forget how Fiona embarrassed me in front of my friends, I hide out in the school library at recess. I try to forget the Fiona thing and think about what I'll tell Granddaddy about Egg.

I make myself as small as possible at my desk until the last bell rings. Granddaddy waits for me in front of the school, and I get into the old Buick.

"Ya look down, Sport. Seems to me after last night's doin's you'd be sitting on top of the world."

"Ya know, don't you?"

"Hell, boy. I'm old but not stupid. I knowed y'all were plannin' somethin' two weeks ago. I figured y'all might need some backup, so I followed you."

"So you were the one shooting at the Thompsons."

"Not at them, just around them, and I enjoyed the show. Couldn't have happened to a nicer bunch of polecats."

"The sheriff suspects us, or me. He came by this morning and asked some questions. Said he's investigating and will come down hard on whoever did it."

"Don't worry none about Macwain. He ain't gonna look too hard."

I looked Granddaddy in the eye.

"Egg Thompson caught me at the vacant lot Wednesday afternoon."

"What! Did he threaten you?"

"No. He said he didn't have anything to do with shooting Dink. Egg drove the car but didn't know Frank intended to shoot. He hates his brother and is leaving Coosa County before the trial." I let that sink in.

"Can Egg testify against his brother? I promised him if he stays for the trial, I'd get you to talk to Tom Snow about his situation. I think Egg'll testify against his brother."

"Ya trust him?"

"Yes, sir. He saved my life on Little Snake Creek when I went after yore puppy, but I'm not sure he trusts us."

Granddaddy makes a turn on Lancer and another on Main.

"Listen. Let's see if Tom Snow's in this afternoon," he says and points the Buick toward the courthouse.

A clerk shows us into the prosecutor's office, and Tom Snow rises from behind his big mahogany desk and greets us.

"Afternoon, George, Sport. To what do I owe the pleasure of this visit? I hope it's not about what happened last night."

"Tell him, Sport," Granddaddy commands.

"Sir, I think Egg Thompson will testify against his brother."

I explain how Egg had saved my life and what Egg told me about how Frank shot Dink and how Frank framed Egg for the robbery in Alabama.

"Egg don't want to spend any more time in jail on Frank's account. He says he's leaving Coosa County to go out west before the trial. My question is, If Egg testifies against Frank, you can do anything for Egg?"

"Why didn't you bring Egg with you?"

"He's afraid of Frank, and he won't talk to nobody but me."

"It sounds like a reasonable idea, but I can't give you a yes or no before I talk with Egg. Can you get him in?"

"I think Egg's afraid to be seen with any law officer. Can we meet at yore house instead of the courthouse?"

"That'll be fine. Let me know when he wants to talk."

On our way home, I tell Granddaddy I'll have to be seen in a public place. It's the only way Egg will contact me, and that means going downtown tomorrow.

"Heck, Jack'll be with me. Pow-Pow and Ben too if I ask them, and I don't think I'll be bothered by any Thompson or their friends after last night."

"I'll square it with yore Mama and Daddy."

I phone Jack as soon as I get the word that I can have Saturday downtown.

"What time do you wanna go?" Jack asks.

"How about eleven o'clock? We can sleep late and then eat lunch downtown."

"I'll see you tomorrow at eleven."

Jack is right on time as usual. I say goodbye to Mama and Ted. As we walk down Walnut pass my cedar tree to the footbridge, Jack says, "How many times have we made this Saturday trip together?"

"Too many to count. This'll be the last unless ya come back for a visit. You will come back, won't you?"

"Sure. I won't forget my best friend, and I'll be back after I settle in Valdosta."

I glance at him. "Remember the frogs at the baptizing. And the time we got caught watching the hoochy-koochy show through a tent hole. What was the name of that hoochy-koochy girl? Jack, we had some danged good adventures."

"I still like the time you fooled Old Man Howard into thinking you were God. Hey, let's not get sentimental. We got more adventures coming."

"Listen. We're gonna wander around until Egg Thompson sees me."

"Have you lost your mind? You trying to get yourself killed?"

"Egg sorta contacted me on Wednesday afternoon when I slipped away from you."

I explained to Jack about how Egg grabbed me in the vacant lot and what we talked about.

"I need to get him to the prosecutor so we can convince him to testify against Frank. He'll contract me if he sees me."

"Why didn't you tell me before now?"

"Ahh, you'd get all bent out of shape, that's why."

We cross Main Street to avoid the street preacher condemning someone to hell. At Handy's Shoe Shop, I turn into Handy's Alley and walk to the old cattle auction yard.

"You know, Egg's name is Melvin. Ain't that funny? And he's not a bad sort, just dumber than a fence post."

"Max's not a bad sort either, but he's smart," Jack says.

"Max is a turd, and you know it."

We cut across the cattle yard and come out on Maple Street.

"Let's check out the soda shop," Jack says.

"Aw, it's too early for any of our friends to be there. But I betcha a dime Eugene Laney's there."

"That's a sucker bet, and I'm not anxious to lose a dime. Let's go by anyway."

We look in the soda shop window and see Eugene talking the ear off a sixth grader. Max Mendeaux reads a book in his favorite booth. Jack and I look at each other.

"Want to harass Max?" Jack asks.

"Now you're talking."

We go into the soda shop and sneak up on Max. He's concentrating so hard on his book that he's not aware anyone is around. Jack and I slide in across from Max, and I say softly, "Jeb Stuart was a lily-livered, yellow-streaked Confederate coward."

Max puts his book down and looks at me with a flash of anger. Jack and I burst out laughing.

"You troublemakers are at it again."

"Max, we could've given you a hot foot," Jack tells him.

"You'd better be more aware of things around you," I say.

"You sound like my mother, Sport."

"If I were, I'd put you up for adoption."

"Get back to studying atomic energy, Max."

We leave the soda shop and move up Maple Street to Blount's Drug Store. As we pass the store's service alley, I spot a green car parked at the back of Rose's Five and Dime.

"Stay here, Jack. That's Egg's car."

I walk where Egg sits watching me. He waves, and I wave back.

"How ya doin', Melvin?"

"I liked them firework."

"You knew it was us, didn't you? They didn't scare you, did they?"

"No, but it 'care Frank. He doo-dooed in he pant," Eggs says and laughs with a snort.

"Are you ready to talk to the prosecutor? Granddaddy says we can meet at Mr. Snow's house."

"I'll 'peak to Mr. 'now if you think it okay."

"It's okay, Melvin. Meet me and Granddaddy at Mr. Snow's house Monday afternoon at four o'clock. Do you know where he lives?"

Egg nods a yes.

"We'll tell him you're coming. Drive around to the back of the house so no one can see your car."

"I be there."

I walk back to where Jack waits.

"What happened?"

"He's gonna talk to the prosecutor. I'm hungry. Let's eat and then go see *The Yearling*."

"You think he'll testify?"

"I don't know. We'll find out on Monday."

After the picture show, me and Jack walk down the Seaboard Railroad track. At the railroad bridge, we take the trail along Little Snake Creek and explore the banks like we always do. We part at my house, and Jack goes home to have supper with his mama and Mr.Crocker.

I phone Granddaddy and tell him Egg agreed to meet with Tom Snow Monday afternoon.

We get out of school for the summer on Wednesday, just two and a half more days. I try not to think about Jack leaving town. I just want to be out of school and to get through the trial.

Granddaddy picks me up after school and drives directly to Tom Snow's house. Cindy, his wormy daughter, meets us at the door and shows us into the living room. The prosecutor arrives a short time later.

Tom Snow says, "Sport, we'll have the jury selected and run through preliminaries on Monday afternoon, June 13. We won't need you at the trial until Tuesday morning at nine o'clock. At that time, we'll call you to testify."

"Great! I'm glad I won't have to be in court on the thirteenth."

About four o'clock, Egg drives around the house and parks his car. He knocks at the front door.

"I'll let him in," I say and open the door. "Come in, Melvin. We're waiting for ya."

Egg follows me to the living room and nods hello to Granddaddy and Tom Snow.

"Sit down, Melvin," the prosecutor says and points to a straight-back chair. I sit with Granddaddy on the sofa while Tom Snow stands.

"Melvin, I understand you're willing to testify against your brother in the Dink Roberts trial."

"Ye', dir."

"Start from the beginning and tell me what happened."

Egg tells his story almost word for word the way he told me. When he finishes, Egg asks, "Can I det out of doein' to pri'on? I jet wanna leave Coo'a County."

"If you testify, this is what I'll do. I'll drop the attempted murder charge against you and charge you with reckless driving. Then drop that charge as soon as you testify. You can leave immediately after the trial, but you'll have to face Frank in court."

Face Frank. Where have I heard that before? I know how Egg feels 'cause Frank is mean enough to do anything.

"I won't do it unle' I have 'ome kind of protection from Frank."

"I'll arrange for you to sleep in the city jail before the trial. Report to Chief Manners this Sunday afternoon, and then the Chief will bring you to the courthouse for the trial on Tuesday morning. Is that good enough?"

Egg looks at me. I can't tell him what to do. He'll have to decide for himself.

"Okay."

43

JACK

Leaving Laceola won't be so bad. Heck, as Sport says, Valdosta could be fun. If I joined the air force, I'd have to leave everything and everybody behind anyway. I hate packing. Sport says he'll help me pack my books tomorrow since we only have half day of school. I'll finish tonight so we can kick around town one last time. Of course, all the stores will be closed, but that's okay. We can just walk around. Oops!

"Jack!" Mama calls. "Some of your friends are here."

I walk into the living room and see Sport, Ben Lloyd, and Pow-Pow Johnson grinning at me.

"Hey, guys," I say.

"We figured you need some company," Pow-Pow says.

"Yeah. We'll scatter to the four winds tomorrow," Sport chimes in, "and we thought you'd like to have a keepsake from us."

"As usual, Max Mendeaux is late. He's got your gift," Ben says. There's a knock on the door. "Here he is now."

I open the door to see Max with a gift-wrapped box. "I believe this is yours."

The four stare at me with silly grins on their faces.

"Well, go on. Open it up," Sport says.

I tear the wrapping off the package.

"By the gods, where did you get this?"

"You'll never believe this. Egg Thompson brought it to me," Sport says.

It is the original, the one and only, switchbox we used in the assault.

"Thanks, friends. I'll keep this box to remember our little adventure, and it will occupy a place of honor under my bed."

They laugh and make goofy noises.

"Let's walk up to the soda shop for an orange smash," Sport says.

"Gee, I'd like to, but I have to eat supper pretty soon."

"Mrs. Copeland!"

"Yes, Sport?"

"Does Jack have to eat supper right away?"

"I don't think he'll starve to death. Jack, go to the soda shop."

The five of us walk the familiar path down Walnut Street.

"Why don't we take a shortcut through the Laceola City Cemetery?" I suggest.

"Not me. That ain't no shortcut," Sport says.

We laugh at his superstition. This is a happy feeling, and just what I need. We invade the Maple Street Soda Shoppe where Ulene MacFadden sits in a booth near the window. Sport leads us to her booth. My four friends sit down but leave a space next to Ulene.

"Hey, Jack," Ulene says as I slide into the booth next to her.

"Hey, Ulene. Are you part of this, this, whatever it is, too?"

"Mr. Biggers!" Sport shouts. "Jack Copeland'll be leaving day after tomorrow for the wilderness. Give him whatever he wants. As long as it don't cost over a quarter, it's on us."

We talk about this past school year and about old times together until we finish our sodas and run out of anything else to say. Ulene goes home. The five of us walk in silence to Main and then down to the vacant lot. The tall weeds are gone, leaving it ready for summer softball games. We cross Little Snake Creek on the footbridge and turn west on Walnut Street then stop to look up into Sport's old cedar tree. These guys have been my friends since first grade, and after I move, I may never see them again. A lump comes in my throat, and I can't say anything. I salute as each one slowly peels off to go home.

Sport doesn't say "I'll see you" or nothing. He doesn't even look at me when he waves "so long."

44

SPORT

By eleven fifteen, Mr. Pritchard gives in to Eugene Laney. "Ah . . . ah . . . Eugene, if you insist on making noise, talking and disrupting the class, come up front and tell your stories."

"Ya mean I can really tell ma story, and you ain't gonna mind. Oh, boy!" Eugene rushes to the front of the class and settles in.

"First, let me tell a mystery. Last Saturday night, 'bout midnight, there was this huge explosion over in the western section of Coosa County next to the Alabama line. A hundred acres of trees were blowed flat down and charred black as coal. Wild animals like squirrels and rabbits were burnt to a crisp, and birds died on their roost. Three men from Alabama disappeared without a trace." Eugene pauses and looks around. "A man who have seen it said it was somethin' from outer space. He said a white ball came in right out of the sky, streaked right down, and busted into blinding light before it hit the ground. Another man said he heard engines, airplane engines high in the sky, so high he couldn't see a plane just before the bomb went off. He said it was a military accident. But if it was a military accident, why wouldn't soldiers be investigatin' now like they did when that plane crashed back in 1945? I believe it was a meteor from outer space."

Someone in the back of the room says, "Where do ya get these stupid stories? It's the most ridiculous thing I've ever heard."

Eugene defends his story. "No, it's true. I swear I didn't make it up. If you go out there, ya kin see for yoreself."

"I believe him," Jack says.

"Yeah. It could've happened. I think Eugene's telling the truth," I say.

Pow-Pow Johnson agrees, "I do too."

"Me too," Ben Lloyd says.

"That story is . . . ah . . . ah . . . a little farfetched," Mr. Pritchard tells the class. "I haven't heard of an explosion anywhere in the county. But Eugene seems to have news sources far superior to mine."

The bell rings, the last of the school year. A new batch of eighth graders get up to leave as fast as they can.

"Stay at your desks, class! Ah . . . ah . . . I haven't dismissed you yet. Listen up. You've been most responsive this entire year. I appreciate your participation and your earnest effort to learn. Now, go and have a good summer and excel in high school."

Me and Jack start out of the room to join Pow-Pow and Ben waiting outside. Mr. Pritchard calls me back. "Sport!"

"Yes, sir."

"Ah . . . ah . . . Here's a little volume I'd like you to read this summer. It's a gift. I think you'll find it interesting and perhaps even helpful."

He hands me a thin little book.

"Thanks, Mr. Pritchard. You're a great teacher."

I glance at the book as I follow Jack out the door. Hummm. *A Shropshire Lad* by A. E. Housman. I tuck it under my arm and join my friends.

Jack and his mother are leaving tomorrow morning, and I help Jack pack his books and other things in boxes. Most of his books are about airplanes and flying and such. Before long we finish, and Jack is ready to travel to Valdosta. The movers pack all the boxes in their truck except two chairs and two beds. Me and Jack leave and walk up and down Little Snake Creek until the streetlights come on, and the sun disappears behind the Alabama mountains.

"I'll see ya off in the morning, Jack."

"You don't have to do that. We're leaving early, seven or eight o'clock."

"I'll be there."

I get to Jack's house at six thirty. The movers pack the remaining furniture in a van and close the big doors. I wait outside while Jack and his mother go through their house one last time.

"Everything is packed, and we're ready to go," Jack says.

Mrs. Copeland slides under the steering wheel of their 1948 Ford and says, "It's time to go, Jack. Say goodbye to Sport."

Jack Copeland and I look at each other. I stick my hand out, and he grabs and squeezes it.

"I wish I could be with you at the trial on Monday. I feel bad about running out on a friend," he says.

"Oh, I forgot to tell you. I won't have to testify until Tuesday morning. I don't have to worry about the thirteenth."

"Hey, that's great. What time does the trial start?"

"Nine o'clock. Listen, I'm gonna miss you. You're a danged fine friend, and I'll write ya as soon as the trial's over."

"So long, Sport."

"So long, Jack."

He opens the car door and then turns to face me. I click my heels smartly and bring my right hand up, palm facing outward, and stop it just above my right eye in a perfect imitation of a British salute. Jack snaps to attention, slowly moves a stiff right hand up to his forehead, and stops it above the right eye, the perfect American salute. Then he gets in the car and shuts the door.

I watch until their car disappears down Walnut Street. Dadgumit, if it wasn't for that old trial, I could have gone with Jack to Valdosta and help him unpack. Ah, heck. I still have Pow-Pow Johnson and Ben Lloyd, even old jerky Max. Did I just say that? I don't think Max can get close enough to anyone to be a friend.

I walk down Walnut Street humming the "Garry Owen." Time stands still as I move past my house and head for my old cedar tree. I jump and grab the lowest limb of the old tree and pull myself up. Dew gathers in droplets that slide off the outside limbs onto the ground. I climb into the thick, fresh-scented green needles and find a large limb to sit on. I look over at the footbridge and then down Little Snake Creek and cry.

George, my cat, greets me at my front door. He runs and hides when Mama and Ted come out of the kitchen.

"Did Jack and Mrs. Copeland get off okay?" Mama asks.

"Yes, ma'am. They left awhile ago."

"It's sad to see you two split up, but Jack can come for a visit anytime."

I walk back to my room and see the book Mr. Pritchard gave me on the floor where I dropped it when I came home from school yesterday. This is as good a time as any to start my summer reading. I open *A Shropshire Lad*. Hey, Mr. Pritchard put a paper marker on this page. He wrote something on it:

Dear Sport:

I think this little poem was written for you and millions of young men like you. You'll find the road of life takes many twists and turns, but in the final analysis, life takes care of itself.

Yours truly,
D. L. Pritchard

I silently read the poem.

When I was one and twenty
I heard a wise man say,
'Give crowns and pounds and guineas
But not your heart away;

Give pearls away and rubies
But keep your fancy free.'
But I was one and twenty
No use to talk to me.

When I was one and twenty
I heard him say again,
'The heart out of the bosom
Was never given in vain;

'Tis paid with sighs a plenty
And sold for endless rue.'
And I am two and twenty,
And oh, 'tis true, 'tis true.

It only takes a second before my dense brain knows why Mr. Pritchard gave me this book. He saw Fiona Burns tell me how bad I am. He has a dadgum good heart, and I feel better when I realize I'm not the only man who has been tossed aside by a danged ol' girl. And I don't care because she's turned ugly, and I don't want to be around her. I think I'm a lot better person than she will ever be.

45

JACK

It's a day's drive from Laceola to Valdosta. Mom and I stayed in a motor court last night and, this morning, began moving into the house that Mr. Crocker bought. It's just outside town, unlike our house in Laceola, but it's newer and not too far from downtown. Sport is right about the sandy soil here. It's a lot different from the red clay of northwest Georgia. Mom and Mr. Crocker will marry Saturday, June 25. I miss Sport. I shouldn't have left Laceola until after the trial, and I feel real guilty.

Mr. Crocker and Mom are unwrapping dishes from one of the packing boxes.

I say, "Is there any way I can get back for the trial in Laceola? I can catch a bus tomorrow, and I can stay with Sport until the trial is over."

"Jack, honey, you know you can't do that. It's too far for you to travel alone. Sport will be okay. He has his family with him," Mom says.

"I've run out on my best friend. He'd stick with me no matter what."

I try to hold back the tears forming in my eyes, but I can't.

"Don't cry, Jack. You're too big to cry, and there's nothing you can do," she says.

"Is this the kid who saved the colored boy?" Mr. Crocker asks.

"Yes, sir. Sport has been my best friend since I can remember. You met him once."

"Sport shouldn't have gotten mixed up in this mess and should've refused to testify against those men. They'll never be convicted."

"He sounds like a pretty good kid. Tell me about him, Jack," Mr. Crocker says.

"Well, he's a straight arrow and real loyal. He kept Dink Roberts from bleeding to death, and he saved a puppy from drowning in Little Snake Creek.

He's tough and won't let anybody push him around. I want to be at the trial to back him up because he'd do the same for me. Anywhere. Anytime."

Mr. Crocker says to Mom, "Sounds like he's describing a couple of buddies in my old outfit."

"Well, you just can't go back to Laceola, and that's that," Mom says.

We spend the rest of Saturday and all day Sunday unpacking, and as I work, a plan begins to form. There has to be a bus that runs daily from Valdosta to Columbus. From there I can catch a bus straight up U.S. 27 to Laceola. I have never gone against my mother's decisions, but this time she's wrong. My friend needs me more than my mother.

I wake up at five o'clock on Monday morning and quietly stuff a change of clothes in a bag. I pull eight dollars out of my savings bank and put it in my pocket.

"I'm going to Laceola. I'll be back on Thursday," I write on a page of notebook paper, sign it, and leave it on the kitchen table. I take a deep breath and let it out as I sneak out the front door. The sun has risen through puffy clouds by the time I walk a mile to the bus station. I go into the bus station to the ticket counter.

"Can I catch a bus from here to Laceola?" I ask.

"Sure, kid. Bus leaves at eight fifteen."

"How much is a ticket?"

"Let's see. It'll cost you four fifty."

I buy the ticket and sit down on a bench outside to wait for the bus. I think what a stupid thing to do, but it's right, and I don't care what happens as long as I can be with Sport at the trial. Oh, rat crap. I forgot to pack my toothbrush. Oh well. I'll get some chewing gum or something. A car makes a U-turn and pulls into the bus station parking lot. It's Mr. Crocker and my mom. I can't run or hide, so I just sit.

Mr. Crocker gets out of his car and walks over to the bench.

"Hey, Jack," he sits down beside me.

I don't say anything.

"I've talked it over with your mother. She's pretty upset, but I calmed her down enough for a little rational thinking. I'm taking you back to Laceola, and we'll make it to that trial or bust a gut trying. Come on, let's go back home and see if you've packed everything you need for a trip."

"I forgot my toothbrush."

My admiration for Mr. Crocker goes up 100 percent. I realize he has explained my actions to Mom a lot better than I ever could. He's going to make a good dad, and I don't think he'll mind if I start calling him Dad.

We leave at eleven o'clock after Mr. Crocker opens the bank. "We'll drive as far as we can today and stop for the night. An early start in the morning will get us to Laceola before the trial begins," he tells me.

After we stop for a hamburger and french fries at Tifton, we go over to Albany and then pick up Highway 27 at Cuthbert. The miles roll by slowly behind farm tractors and big lumber trucks. Outside Albany low clouds gather over the flat farm country, and the sky darkens. Flashes of lightning, the booming of thunder, and driving rain slow us even more.

"I don't think we'll ever make it to Laceola by tomorrow morning."

"Don't worry, Jack. We'll make it."

I lay my head against the car door window and try to sleep, but I can't. We turn north on U.S. Highway 27 at the little town of Cuthbert. The thunderstorm stops, and the small amount of daylight left sinks into twilight. As we pass through Columbus, I recognize a street.

"My great-aunt lives down that street."

"That must be Miss Thelma Brannon your mother talks about."

"That's right. We spent Easter with her this year, and that's when somebody burned a cross in front of Sport's house. Sport said it almost scared him to death. Everybody knew the Thompsons did it, but they just couldn't prove it."

"That's a pretty drastic measure. I haven't heard of a cross burning at a house since I got out of the army. Your mother tells me Sport is under a lot of pressure not to testify."

"You don't know the half of it. But Sport decided to let them know he wasn't gonna roll over and play dead, so he bombed the Thompson place with fireworks, mortars. I got involved too, but he will never admit I took part. He protects me and his other friends too."

Mr. Crocker laughs when I explain how we planned and carried out the assault.

"You boys are a resourceful lot. Look. This is LaGrange. Let's get a barbecue and find a tourist court for the night. We'll leave by six in the morning which should give us plenty of time to get to Laceola by nine o'clock."

We leave LaGrange behind as the sun rises over the rolling hills of west Georgia. I know we will get to Laceola on time when we turn off Highway 27 and on to Georgia Highway 100. In my mind, I urge Mr. Crocker's Buick on.

When we cross Little Snake Creek, he says, "It's eight o'clock. You can see Sport before he goes into court."

Mr. Crocker parks his Buick at the end of Jasper Street, just down from the courthouse.

"You run on ahead and catch Sport. I'll follow you in."

"Yes, sir."

I jump out of the Buick, dash down the street, and run up the courthouse steps. I enter the front door and pause to let my eyes shed the bright sun and adjust to the darker interior. I see Sport in his blue Sunday suit standing in the hall near his mama, daddy, and granddaddy. Egg Thompson and Chief Manners sit on a bench near the courtroom door.

"Hey, Sport!" I yell.

I have to laugh at the shock on Sport's face when he sees me. Mr. Crocker walks up beside me. Sport hurries over to where we are.

46

SPORT

I'm wearing my only Sunday suit with a white shirt and a red and blue tie. Mama straightens my tie for the fifth time.

"It looks fine, Mama."

I'm always uncomfortable in this getup, but everybody tells me I have to look presentable in court. I don't care; I just want to get this over with.

"You look cool and collected," Daddy says.

"I don't feel cool, just nervous and scared."

"It'll be okay. Judge Blalock is a fair man, and he'll be patient. But when you're on the witness stand, look into the eyes of whoever is asking questions. Don't look down or away," Daddy says.

Judge Blalock. God, he knows me. Me and Jack raked leaves in his yard last fall. Mrs. Blalock was the nice lady who paid us, but as well as I remember, he just said hello to us.

Mrs. Lacy settles in with my little brother to look after him while we are at the trial. Granddaddy will meet us at the courthouse. Uncle Earl is working on a summer job in Atlanta, so he won't be here. Cal Slowman has been lying low since our visit to the Thompson place, so I don't expect him to show up.

Tom Snow says that my part won't take long, and then I can stay to hear the rest of the trial. I'll stay for sure. I want to see Frank Thompson found guilty and out of my life for good. And I want to make sure Egg, I mean Melvin, gets out of Coosa County.

Granddaddy says Melvin is waiting in the city jail. There are only four cells, reserved for the Saturday night drunks, in Chief Manners's jail. Unlike the county jail, no real criminals are kept there.

Daddy makes it a point to be early for everything, and according to the courthouse clock, we got there a few minutes past eight. A small crowd has already gathered on the courthouse steps, and Daddy leads Mama and me through the door into a large hall. I don't look at anybody, but I feel stares stabbing the back of my head.

The courthouse is old. Dark wood panels cover the lower part of granite walls on both sides of a wide hall. The entrance to the courtroom is directly in front of us. I guess everybody waited until we arrived because people begin to move into the courtroom. Thank God, there are a few friendly faces. Miss Sally greets us first and then, in turn, Reverend Gibson, Mr. Meeks, Charles Jackson, and Deputy Miller. Tom Snow comes out of the courtroom and tells us to have a seat on the benches provided for witnesses. Granddaddy comes in from a side door.

"Hey, Granddaddy!"

"Howdy, Sport. Wheeler. Ilene," he says and sits down beside me.

Small groups of people talk in whispers like it's a funeral instead of a trial. I take Daddy's arm and turn it so I can see his watch. It's 8:35.

Ben Lloyd and Pow-Pow Johnson come in and walk over to where we sit.

"Hey, Sport. Man, you're dressed to kill," Pow-Pow says.

A shiver goes up my spine. Somebody stepped over my grave.

"He's gonna impress the girls," Ben says.

"There ain't no girls at this trial, birdbrain. Except maybe Cindy Snow, and Sport don't have to impress her."

"I'm glad y'all are here. Just don't make me laugh when I'm testifying."

I wish Jack Copeland were here, but I know he can't come all the way from Valdosta.

"We'd better go in and get a good seat. Later, Sport," Pow-Pow says.

"Yeah. Later," Ben says.

Several family friends including Mr. Grant, my principal, say hello to us as they go into the courtroom. Old Man Howard, who never misses a trial, comes in and goes directly to the courtroom without looking at us. He's always looking down anyway. I'm too jittery to stay still. I get up and walk over to where two portraits hang on the wall. I read the nameplates. Judge James Ahern Carter, chief justice of the Georgia Supreme Court, 1878-1944. The next one is of Judge Ezekiel Jeremiah Smith, superior court judge, Coosa County, 1848-1865.

I'll ask Granddaddy what these judges did to get their pictures in the courthouse. Another two pictures hang on the other side of the courtroom door. I start to walk over to them when I see Frank Thompson.

"Where the hell's ma goddamn worthless brother," Frank Thompson says loudly when he walks in, followed by his old daddy, his lawyer, and three other men. Unlike the time I saw him in jail, Frank wears a white shirt, dress pants, and a sport coat. He's not wearing a tie.

"Quiet down, Frank. There are ladies present," Mr. Ambrose Geist, his lawyer, tells him.

Frank looks around and, in a quieter voice, says, "Goddamn it, they got 'im locked up where I cain't talk to 'im. The bastards're tryin' to turn 'im against me. Why in the hell don'tcha do som'in'?"

"There's nothing I can do, Frank. Just have respect for the court," Mr. Geist says.

"There's nothin' I kin do, Frank! There's nothin' I kin do, Frank," he mocks his lawyer. "Pa is payin' ya good money to do som'in'. Now why don't ya get yere sorry lawyer ass busy. I shouldn't even be goin' to trial 'cause it wuza accident."

Mr. Geist puts a hand on Frank's shoulder.

"Why don't you just calm down? You know you won't be convicted on the testimony of a kid. And if Egg has agreed to testify, it won't matter because he was driving the car. The jury will know he's just working a deal for a lesser sentence."

Frank slaps the lawyer's hand off his shoulder and turns around.

"I dunno any sucha goddamn thing. Egg's a low-life bastard. He's only ma haf brother 'cause Pa ain't his daddy. Ain't that right, Pa?"

Frank whispers to one of the men with him. They look directly at me as the lawyer leads Frank into the courtroom. His daddy and three men follow. My stomach does a flip-flop when Frank walks pass me.

Mr. Snow comes out of the courtroom and says to me, "Court will be called to session in about twenty minutes, and you'll take the stand first. Chief Manners is bringing Melvin Thompson around now to wait out here until we call him. Don't be nervous, Sport. Just tell exactly what you saw and answer questions truthfully."

"Yes, sir."

I detect a strong scent of paper and wood, and I smell something I can't identify. It could be leather, and it's not unpleasant. Maybe the scent comes from the leather bags lawyers always carry around.

I hear footsteps and voices behind me, and I turn to see Chief Manners and Egg Thompson coming down the hall. Great. Now we can get this over with.

"Hey, Melvin."

"Hey, Bedford."

"Sit here, Melvin." Chief Manners points to one of the benches, and someone says, "Hey, Sport!"

Jack Copeland's familiar voice calls to me. I do a double take when I see Jack and Mr. Crocker standing at the courthouse door.

"Hey, Jack! You son of a gun. You made it back"

I want to squeal like a goofy girl, but I don't. I hurry over and shake Jack's hand. Mama, Daddy, and Granddaddy follow me.

"This is my dad. He brought me back just for the trial."

Mama hugs Jack, and Granddaddy pats him on the back. Daddy shakes Mr. Crocker's hand and says, "Thanks. Having Jack here means a lot to Sport."

"It means a lot to Jack too," Mr. Crocker says.

"When did y'all leave Valdosta?" I ask.

"Yesterday at noon. We stayed in LaGrange last night, and I had to get up at some ungodly hour this morning."

Deputy Miller opens the courtroom door and announces, "Judge Blalock's comin' in."

"I guess we'd better go in," Mr. Crocker says.

"Can I stay out here with Sport?"

"Sport's probably nervous enough, and it may be a while before he's called. I think it's best for us to find a good seat."

"You gotta tell me about yore trip. After I testify, I can watch the rest of the trial from the courtroom, so save me a seat," I tell Jack.

"Okay."

"I'll go with y'all," Granddaddy says.

Jack, Mr. Crocker, and Granddaddy disappear into the courtroom, and Mama, Daddy, and I sit down on a bench. Egg and Chief Manners are sitting across from me. I wave at Egg. He smiles and waves back.

We all sit without talking, and I silently recite what I can remember of "The Charge of the Light Brigade." "Half a league, half a league, / Half a league onward, / All into the valley of Death." That's not a good poem to remember right now. Let's see. Edgar Allen Poe's "The Raven" is pretty good. "Once upon a midnight dreary, while I ponder weak and weary." Why are all those danged old poems about death? I wish I had paid more attention in class. Forget about poetry. I'd like to know what they're doing in the courtroom. I thought I would go right in and testify and get it over with. I heard that justice is swift and speedy. Maybe Judge Blalock has to read a wad of papers or something, and he's a slow reader. I look at Daddy's watch for the third time. It's already been an hour and a half, and I'm hungry. I hope my stomach doesn't growl when I'm on the stand. I check my fly just to make sure it's zipped. Deputy Miller opens the courtroom door, sees me, and laughs. I feel the blood rush to my face, and I pretend to pick a piece of lint off the front of my pants

"Okay, Sport. They're ready for you," he says.

Mama, Daddy, and I get up and walk through the courtroom door the deputy holds open. Why do I feel like I'm going to my own hanging? Everybody turns and looks at me as I walk down the aisle to where the prosecutor waits. I tell myself, *Remember to speak loud and clear. It'll be a piece of cake.*

"Sport, take the stand and be sworn in," Mr. Snow says.

"Feets don't fail me now." I think of that bit from a picture show as I move to the witness stand. Judge Blalock, dressed in a black robe, looks down at me. Hey, it's just like in a picture show, except he's not wearing a white wig. Oh yeah, I forgot. This is America, not England.

"Raise your right hand and place your left hand on the Bible," orders the bailiff. I do as he says. "Do you swear to tell the truth, the whole truth and nothing but the truth, so help you God?"

"Huh?"

"Say, 'I do'," he whispers.

"I do."

"Are you one of the boys that raked my leaves last fall?" Judge Blalock asks.

"Yes, sir."

I look up straight into the judge's eyes.

"Y'all did a mighty fine job. Mrs. Blalock and I were pleased with your work, and we'll be expecting you to come back in October."

"Yes, sir."

The courtroom is not as crowded as I thought it would be. Miss Sally is at the table with the prosecutor. Reverend Gibson and Charles Jackson sit on the back pew, and Mama, Daddy, Granddaddy, Mr. Crocker, and Jack are together in a row of seats about halfway down the middle aisle. Cindy Snow sits on the front row behind her daddy. I'll bet she'll be a lawyer like him. Nah, she ain't that smart.

"Now, Mr. Snow, you may proceed with this witness," Judge Blalock tells the prosecutor.

"Sport, please tell us what you witnessed on the afternoon of Thursday, March 24 of this year."

The muscle in my left cheek and eye twitches. I cover it with my hand until it calms down.

"I was playing in an old cedar tree on Walnut Street close to the footbridge when I saw Dink Roberts coming down the sidewalk." *Slow down. You're talking to fast,* I say to myself. "Then I saw a green 1939 Hudson Terraplane coming down the street. Just as it got near Dink, it slowed down almost to a stop. I saw Frank Thompson aim a pistol out the window and fire at Dink. Dink fell down, then I saw the car drive off real fast."

"Can you point out the man who fired the shot?"

"Yes, sir. It was Frank Thompson." I point to him.

"How can you be sure it was Frank Thompson?"

"I saw the snake tattoo on his arm, and I recognized his face."

"Thank you, Sport," he says and then turns to Mr. Geist. "Your witness."

Mr. Geist walks up to me with a friendly smile.

"Now, Sport, I'm going to ask you some questions, and I want you to answer truthfully."

"Yes, sir."

"What were you doing up in that cedar tree?"

Oh, god. Why did he ask me that? I can't tell him that I was waiting to put a dart in Max Mendeaux's butt.

"Playing."

"Isn't a thirteen-year-old kinda big to be playing in a tree?"

He looks over at the jury.

"I'm twelve, and I like to climb, and I like cedar trees."

"How can you be sure whose green 1939 Hudson Terraplane came down the street that day?"

"I ain't never seen but one green 1939 Hudson Terraplane in Coosa County, and that one belongs to Egg Thompson."

Someone laughs.

"Did this look like an accident? Could the gun have fired accidentally?"

"No, sir. Frank Thompson deliberately fired the gun at Dink Roberts."

"Well, how do you know this for sure?" Mr. Geist asks.

"My granddaddy says that you don't point a gun at somebody unless you're gonna use it."

"But you don't know that it was deliberate. You don't know for sure that Frank's gun didn't discharge for no reason. It certainly could have been an accident."

"Objection, Your Honor. Mr. Geist is testifying."

"Objection sustained. Ask questions, Mr. Geist," Judge Blalock says. "Ask questions."

Mr. Geist raises his voice.

"Are you absolutely sure Frank Thompson's gun didn't accidentally discharge?"

"I saw Frank Thompson stick the pistol out of the window and fire. The gun was pointed directly at Dink Roberts."

I glance at the prosecutor, and he looks relieved.

"No more questions, Your Honor," Mr. Geist says.

Judge Blalock looks at me and says, "The witness is excused."

I hesitate.

"That means you can go down and sit with your family, Sport."

"Thank you, sir."

"You may call your next witness, Mr. Snow," Judge Blalock says.

I walk down the middle aisle and slide into the pew next to Jack. He gives me a soft punch on the arm, and Granddaddy whispers, "Good job, Sport."

"I call Melvin Thompson as my next witness," Tom Snow announces.

Deputy Miller opens the courtroom door and says, "They're ready for you, Egg."

As Egg walks down to the witness stand, Frank Thompson says, "Damned bastard."

Everybody in the courtroom hears his comment.

Egg is sworn in, and Mr. Snow says, "Melvin, tell us about the event that happened on the afternoon of March twenty-fourth of this year."

"Me and Frank wa' ridin' 'round, and we turn off Main 'treet on Walnut. We rode down Walnut pa't the footbridge acro' Little 'nake Creek. We 'ee Dink Robert walking down the 'idewalk. Frank 'aid 'low down. I did what he 'aid. He took the gun and 'tuck it out the winder and 'hot that nidder boy."

"Did you try to stop him?"

"I din't know what he wa' gonna do. I din't have time ta do nothin' but 'ay, 'Don't do that Frank.' Frank 'ay, 'I havin' a little fun with that nidder.'"

Egg pauses, and the prosecutor tells him to go on.

"I got 'cared, an' I 'tep on the petal and got outta thar. That all."

"Thank you, Melvin. Your witness, Mr. Geist."

Mr. Geist walks up to the witness box and asks, "Did the prosecutor make a deal with you for your testimony?"

"Yeah, he did."

"What is that deal?"

"Attempt'd murder charge dropped."

"So you're testifying against your own brother just to get out from under an attempted murder charge?"

"No, Frank 'hot da nidder boy. I din't have nothin' to do with it."

"Now, Melvin. Wasn't this an accident? Didn't Frank wave his gun, and it went off accidentally?"

Egg pauses and then says, "Frank din't wave he gun. He 'tuck it out da winder and fired."

"Did he tell you he was going to shoot at the boy?"

"No."

"Do you know what was in his mind?"

"No."

"Then you don't know if Frank deliberately shot or not? No more questions for this so-called witness, Your Honor."

"You may step down now, Mr. Thompson," Judge Blalock says. Egg walks down the middle aisle and sits down next to Chief Manners on the back bench.

"Do you have any other witnesses, Mr. Snow?"

"No, Your Honor."

"Your Honor," Mr. Geist says, "may I have a short time to confer with my client?"

"It's getting along toward noon. I declare this court in recess for lunch. Mr. Geist, you can do your conferring now."

Judge Blalock looks at the jury and says, "Do not talk to anyone outside this courtroom about this case and do not discuss it amongst yourselves. Be back in your seats at one thirty sharp. Bailiff, please escort the jurors over to the bus station cafeteria."

"Let's get outta here," I say.

Egg still sits with Chief Manners on the back bench, and when I pass by, I nod at him. He smiles back.

Me, Jack, Mr. Crocker, and my family gather in the hall outside the courtroom.

"You did a good job on the stand," Daddy tells me.

"You sure did," Mr. Crocker agrees.

"Boy, I'm glad that's over. Can me and Jack go to Kelly's Diner for gravy burgers?"

Before anyone can answer, Frank Thompson comes out of the courtroom with his lawyer. Frank stops and looks at me.

"Damn it! I ain't gonna go to no chain gang," he shouts.

Chief Manners and Egg walk out the courtroom door and turn to go down the hall in the opposite direct from where Frank stands.

"Ya rotten dirty little nigger-loving bastard. You to blame for all this. I'm agonna send ya straight to hell," Frank screams.

He reaches behind his back and pulls a pistol from beneath his sport coat. I see Chief Manners reach for a gun. He has a surprised scowl on his face because he didn't bring it to court. Frank points his gun at me, and I freeze. Boom! Boom! I hear two shots before I'm slammed to the floor. My left arm hurts like hell, and something heavy lies on top of me. I hear another shot and then another.

I hear people running, and I see a light. But it gets smaller, and I float down and down. Then the light disappears as I fall backward into a deep, dark pit.

Jack is running fast, and I'm chasing him, but I don't know why. I can run faster than he can. I realize we're moving along the top of the levee on Little Snake Creek. Jack looks back with fear in his face. What is he afraid of? I don't see anything. A big bird swoops down past my head and flies toward Jack. It's an owl, an old barn owl. I run faster and faster. I have to catch it because I can't let it get to him. I leap for the owl but miss, and I tumble down the levee toward the creek.

47

JACK

We follow Sport into the hall outside the courtroom. "Boy, I'm glad that's over," Sport says. "Can me and Jack go to Kelly's Diner for gravy burgers?"

Yuck! I don't like gravy burgers, but I don't say anything to Sport. I'm sure I can get something else to eat. Frank Thompson comes out of the courtroom with his lawyer.

"Damn it, I ain't gonna go to no chain gang," Frank says. "Ya rotten dirty little nigger-loving bastard. You to blame for all of this. I'm agonna send ya straight to hell!"

As if by magic, a gun appears in Frank's hand, and he points it at Sport. I see Egg moving fast toward us before Mr.Crocker grabs me by my shoulders and pulls me away. Two shots echo through the courthouse hallway.

"Sport!"

I turn to see Egg lying on Sport. Blood gushes from Egg's back and pools on the floor.

Spectators scream and scramble out of the way. Deputy Miller pulls his gun and points it at Frank, but the small crowd running past him blocks his aim.

Frank swings his gun toward the deputy and shoots. The deputy goes down but fires from the floor. Frank drops his gun and grabs his throat. He staggers and falls.

My god, no. I feel my face go tight, and my heart tries to pound its way out of my chest. I run over to where Sport and Egg are lying on the floor. His granddaddy pulls Egg off, and his mama and daddy are bending over him. I don't see any blood. Maybe the bullet missed him. Sport shakes but doesn't move. Mr. Crocker puts a hand on my shoulder.

"Come on, Jack. Give them room."

"Jim Styles is upstairs at the jail. Go git 'im," Chief Manners shouts at one of his police officers.

I glance over at Deputy Miller. A dark spot spreads on his uniform above his knee.

It wasn't more than three or four minutes before the doctor comes in with his bag, but it felt like an hour.

"Okay, everybody, move back," orders the doctor. He looks at Deputy Miller first.

"I'm okay. See to that boy over there."

The doctor pulls Sport's coat up and cuts his shirt away so he can see the wound.

"It's not bad," he announces to no one in particular. "Took a hit in the shoulder. He'll have to go to Palatine Hospital. Chief, get me some bandages and call an ambulance.

The doctor looks at Egg. "This man here is dead."

I can't see what the doctor is doing because people crowd around to look at Sport and Egg.

About the same time as a nurse runs in with bandages, two men pull a stretcher into the courthouse.

After bandaging Sport's side, Dr. Styles supervises the two men as they carefully set him on a stretcher.

"Where's Jack?" Sport asks.

Someone pushes me through the crowd up to the stretcher.

"I'm here, Sport."

"Ya got away. The owl didn't get ya. I'm tired, Jack."

"Nothing got me, and nothing's gonna get you."

He closes his eyes, and the men push and carry the stretcher out the courthouse door and down the steps to a waiting ambulance.

"Can we go to the hospital in Palatine?" I ask Mr. Crocker.

"Sure thing, Jack. Let's go."

Pow-Pow Johnson, Ben Lloyd, and Eugene Laney watch as they load Sport into the ambulance.

"Is Sport all right?" Pow-Pow asks.

"Yeah. They're taking him to Palatine."

"Why don't I ever getta see the excitement? I chased the ambulance down the street, but I didn't get ta see Sport's blood or nothing. And they done covered them two bodies up before I got here. I'm just unlucky, I guess," Eugene Laney says.

I look into Eugene's eyes and say, "For one time in your life, Eugene, shut up."

Forty minutes later, Mr. Crocker and I walk into Palatine General Hospital where Sport's family and Miss Sally wait for a report on his condition.

Almost in tears, Mrs. Kirk tells us, "Sport's gonna be okay. I know he is."

Miss Sally keeps reassuring Sport's mother. I walk back and forth between the entrance to the hospital hall and a window overlooking a small park outside the hospital. I don't know what I would do if Sport died. I thought I lost him in Little Snake Creek, but he came out okay. He leads a charmed life, and I don't care what he says about Friday the thirteenth or black cats or crossroads. Either by fate or will of the gods, we'll have more adventures together. After a long time, a doctor pushes through the swinging doors.

"Who does Sport Kirk belong to?"

"Us," Sport's parents and grandparent answer.

"Well, I have good news. He's fine. A slug busted his arm, and he's lost some blood, but there's no other damage. He'll have to recover here for a couple of days, and then he can go home. He's in Room 107. He's awake now, and the family may see him. The rest of you will have to wait outside."

"Thanks, Doctor," Sport's dad says.

The Kirks and Miss Sally follow the doctor through a door.

"I want to stay to talk to Sport," I tell Mr. Crocker.

"We've got all night and all day to get back to Valdosta."

I pace up and down the hallway for a long time before Sport's daddy, granddaddy, and Miss Sally come through the swinging doors.

"Y'all can go in now. Sport is asking for Jack," his dad says.

"Come with me," I say to Mr. Crocker.

Sport's mother sits next to his bed, and he looks at us with groggy eyes when we walk in. He doesn't have any color.

"Hey, Jack," he says weakly.

"I thought you would sleep all day, ol' buddy."

"Egg saved me, didn't he?"

"Yeah. He didn't make it."

"I'm so sorry," Sport says and begins to cry. His mother wipes his eyes.

"Jack, I didn't mean to get you mixed up in this mess. Thanks for coming."

I try to get him not to think about what happened. "Look, I don't think I'll ever have an adventure like this in Valdosta, but I guess just about anything can happen in Laceola with you around. You know, you're an adventure unto yourself."

Sport looks at Mr. Crocker and says, "Thanks for bringing Jack."

"We have to go back to Valdosta this afternoon, but maybe I'll come back sometime this summer."

"I don't think I'll be going to Uncle Luke and Aunt Minnie's farm after all."

"Hey, boys, I have an idea," Mr. Crocker says. "Jack's mother and I are going to Florida on our honeymoon on June twenty-fifth. I'll bet I can find a way to have Jack come stay with you for a week or so while we're away. How does that sound?"

"Would you really do that?" I ask.

"That sounds great," Sport says.

"Then it's settled."

"Hey, thanks a lot," Sport and I say together.

"We have to leave now. But I'll be back in a couple of weeks, ol' friend."

"So long, Jack," Sport says and moves his good hand in an attempt to give me a goodbye salute.

I snap to attention and give him my best salute. Mr. Crocker and I leave Sport with a big grin on his face.

We leave through the front door of the hospital and meet Tom Snow and Cindy, his wormy daughter, followed by Cal Slowman.

EPILOGUE

SPORT

A man of my age often looks back at events and asks, "What if?" Had I not saved Dink Roberts's life fifty-seven years ago, would I have chosen a career in the U.S. Cavalry instead of becoming a federal judge? I disappointed Granddaddy. I know it's a useless exercise to speculate because one plays the cards fate deals.

It still haunts me a jury never rendered a verdict in the Thompson brothers' trial. I want to believe an all-white jury would have rendered a guilty decision. Prosecutor Tom Snow, my father-in-law, thought so. I never saw Dink after his parents took him to Chicago for safekeeping. About two years later, a black Chicago street gang robbed him of five dollars and proceeded to beat him to death. In the final analysis, Frank Thompson accomplished what he set out to do.

After the night when my four friends and I raided the Thompson place, I decided being shot at was not a priority in my life, but it didn't bother Jack Copeland. Either by chance or will of the gods, Jack joined the air force after college and became a fighter pilot. In September 23, 1970, a surface-to-air missile hit his F-4 Phantom, and it went down in the jungles of Vietnam. They never found his body.

Jack never left me. Even today I'll see something funny or ridiculous and say to myself, *I have to tell Jack about that.*

He left a wife and two sons. One, Bedford, is my godson. When young Bedford visits me, I always apologize for the name his parents saddled him with. Like Jack, he tells me it's not such a bad name.

Our group of conspirators grew older, and we decided to meet at least once a year. Today is our annual get-together. I drop Cindy off at the nursing home to visit Tom Snow and head down Main Street to Lucinda's Coffee and Tea Shoppe. The Maple Street Soda Shoppe is a memory, gone like all the other small shops on Main. Laceola's shopping district moved out to a large shopping center anchored by Wal-Mart on the edge of town.

I park at the curb three doors down from Lucinda's and look up the street to the corner of Cobb and Main. I can almost hear the street preacher screaming at the sinners going about their Saturday shopping. He would have made a great television minister.

Ben Lloyd, Pow-Pow Johnson, and Ulene MacFadden Simmons sit around a wrought iron table in Lucinda's. We invited Ulene into our group because she knew our secrets, and she never got over her first love, Jack Copeland. They grin like a mule eating briars when I walk in.

"How ya doing, Sport, I mean, Judge?" Ben asks.

"Hey, Lucinda, we got another customer for ya. Get him a latte," Pow-Pow shouts.

"You Laceola misfits don't look a day older than when we last met," I say.

"I try to keep my girlish charm," Ulene purred.

"Yeah, me too," Ben says.

"Ben, you never had girlish charm or any other charm." Pow-Pow frogs him on the arm.

Lucinda sets the latte in front of me along with a book. "I think this guy went to school with you," she says.

I pick up the book and look at the title: *The Definitive Biography of Roy Rodgers* by Eugene Laney. "Son of a gun, I didn't know Eugene published a book."

"Yeah, what a shame. He didn't live long enough to enjoy the infamy," Ben says.

"You mean he's dead?"

"A Palatine police car hit him when he ran out into the street to watch a fire engine go by," Ben tells us.

"He wasn't a bad sort," Pow-Pow says.

We agree.

I turn to Pow-Pow. "Speaking of being run over by a truck, is your baseball team going to the finals this year?"

Pow-Pow Johnson stands straight and carries a solid 255 pounds very well for a sixty-seven-year-old man. He became McIntosh University's head baseball coach thirty years ago and compiled a decent win/lose record that included two national championships. On the other hand, Ben Lloyd looks much older with white hair and a large paunch that came from years sitting behind a desk at his Chevrolet dealership in Laceola.

"Hell, I'm getting too old to coach baseball. My freshmen have played baseball from the time they're five years old, and they know more than I do. I plan to hang up my spikes after this season."

"That's what you said last year," Ben says. "By the way, Sport, your old buddy, Max Mendeaux, gave a talk to the high school assembly last month. I heard the students couldn't understand a damn thing he said about his work with NASA."

"He was always spacey and stuck-up. Listen, my friends, I want you to be the first to know. I'm hanging up my robes and leaving the bench next month."

"You're too young to resign." Eulene frowns. Her eyes still sparkle, and there's just a light streak of gray in her thick blonde hair.

"There's no challenge for me anymore. I feel as if I've heard it all, and my mind wanders during arguments."

The three nodded with understanding.

"Are you and Cindy gonna retire to some lakeside mansion in North Georgia?" Ben asks.

"No. We'll stay in Atlanta, but I have a mission I want to complete next year. Y'all have heard of MIA groups looking for lost service men in Vietnam? I'm going to find Jack's plane and maybe his dog tag or something that I can bring back. The Vietnamese government will furnish us with all the information they have."

My friends are stunned at this announcement.

"You always were a crazy SOB," Ben says.

"Yeah, you're in no shape to traipse around in jungles. If you're bound and determined to go off half-cocked, I'll get you in shape," Pow-Pow says.

Ulene's eyes fill with tears. She never got over Jack Copeland.

"Thanks, Pow-Pow. I'll take you up on that."

"You'll get yourself killed or catch some horrible disease, but I'll help pay some of the expenses," Ben tells me. "Just don't blame me if you come back with leprosy."

"Is Cindy going with you?" Ulene asks.

"No. She's not up to it."

"Would she care if I went along?"

This time I'm surprised.

"I don't think so. Are you sure? What would Frank say?"

"He knows how close we all were. And as long as he can play golf, he won't care."

"Think about it before you make a decision. Meanwhile I'll square it with Cindy."

"Y'all going back to Atlanta this afternoon?" Ben asks.

"No, first I'll visit my cedar tree, and then Cindy and I are going down to Fort Benning to visit General Cal Slowman, retired. He agreed to help me with my mission in Vietnam."

Before we leave Lucinda's Coffee and Tea Shoppe, we agree to meet again in six weeks to plan a strategy for our search for Jack Copeland.

The End

CPSIA information can be obtained at www.ICGtesting.com
Printed in the USA
LVOW12s0729080316

478162LV00001B/88/P